Dear Reader,

When I met Lauren, I was in the middle of a classic episode of mid-life crisis. *Passages* is another popular term for one of these times in a person's life. I think of them as growth spurts, and I've had more than one.

What I've learned is that these times pass and so do the pain and confusion they bring, but if a man is smart, he keeps the lessons learned.

And if a man is very lucky, he finds a woman like Lauren to show him himself and love him for what he is. This is what I hope for our children and why I make sure I tell them our story.

Sincerely,

Jason Kenyon

P.S. Oh, yes, we have three children now— Jason, Jr., Jeannine and Jesselee.

MEN MADE IN AMERICA

CURTISS ANN MATLOCK

A Time to Keep

Kansas

Silhouette® Books

Published by Silhouette Books New York

America's Publisher of Contemporary Romance

SILHOUETTE BOOKS
300 East 42nd St., New York, N.Y. 10017

A TIME TO KEEP

Copyright © 1987 by Curtiss Ann Matlock

ISBN: 0-373-45166-0

Published Silhouette Books 1987, 1993

Printed in the U.S.A.

Chapter One

Kansas City. Someone, some poetic dreamer no doubt, once called it the most beautiful city in the world, and it was said to have more miles of boulevards than Paris. Lauren wondered now just who'd located and counted all those miles of boulevards in either city. And what odd need had possessed this mad counter? She smiled slowly. To her the city, the place of her birth, was the most beautiful in all the world—and she'd seen Paris.

She stood staring out at a small park, winter stark now in late January. Giant wooden seesaws sat idle, deserted, and bare tree branches moved in the winter wind. Even so, she found the park lovely, tidy in its bareness, holding the promise of summer days to come.

She'd always loved Kansas City, had come home often after her career had taken her far away. Even with an apartment in San Francisco, she'd manage a few days here, a week or so there, to come home to visit. And every time she'd had the opportunity to work in the city, she'd taken it.

But not so Scott, she thought sadly, the memory of her brother coming suddenly and unbidden, as it always did. And the guilt came, as well.

She and her brother had been as different as summer from winter. Though quiet, he'd been ambitious and driven. By the young age of thirty, Scott had become a highly successful attorney. He'd seemed happy. But then, Lauren knew so little about him. Even their parents didn't seem to know him. He'd made and kept it that way for some time.

The stark image of her brother as she'd last seen him filled Lauren's mind. And the horrible guilt and sorrow rose in her throat. It often happened this way. She'd go for days, even weeks, without remembering him, and then there he was. Probably because she didn't want to think of him, she reflected ruefully. The memory she held of his face was still terribly painful. And so was all that had come after: the endless pain, the questions, the conjecturing, the nagging thought that if only she'd been more careful, if only she'd done something.

Lauren pushed the memories aside. One thing she'd learned was that "if onlys" never helped anyone, least of all herself. Someday it wouldn't hurt so much, she knew. Today was better than yesterday, and yesterday better than last year. It was behind her now.

She glanced at her watch. After examining her, Dr. Susan Walter had wanted to talk, so Lauren had been escorted into her private office to wait. A dubious privilege because it was given only to those patients of long-standing, people whose severe illnesses had brought them close to the doctor. Lauren looked to the office door, expecting the doctor to appear any minute. That was usually what happened just when one was thinking dark thoughts about being kept waiting.

But this time it didn't work that way. After a few seconds she moved to sit in one of the two leather chairs near the desk. She deliberately relaxed her body, feeling the dull ache in her hips ease. She should have known better than to stand so long in one place. Lifting her skirt, she stretched her legs and gave them a thoughtful survey. It was a reminder to herself of how fortunate she was to have them, to be able to walk. And they were still damn good-looking legs she thought pertly, even if she was about fifteen pounds underweight.

"You've still got those dancer's legs" came a voice from behind her, and Lauren glanced around to see Dr. Walter entering. She was a tall, handsome woman of middle age, who spoke and moved slowly and quietly. It was no surprise that Lauren hadn't heard the door.

"But not the strength," Lauren said, smoothing down her skirt.

"No, not the strength," Susan Walter agreed, seating herself smoothly behind the desk. She eyed Lauren sharply. "You'll never have the strength. We both know that, but you've sure beaten the odds, Lauren. I have to admit I never would have believed eighteen months ago that I'd be seeing what I do now—you walking, without an aid of any kind." She raised an eyebrow. "And I venture to say you attempt a bit more strenuous movement at times. Your mother told me about the practice room in your apartment."

"Don't you start on me, too," Lauren said. "It's just a place to keep in shape—and the exercises are how I got here in the first place."

Dr. Walter smiled. "I think it's a fine idea. Within reason. Don't try to push."

"I know what I can and can't do."

"Good." The doctor closed the file in front of her with a snap. "I've just finished examining your latest X rays. You've healed well. Not perfect, but good. And I believe your body will go on healing, Lauren—as long as you stick to your regimen. You know the routine: don't lift anything over ten pounds—five's plenty—don't stand too long, don't sit too long, lie down whenever possible. And, yes, keep exercising. Mildly!" She smiled softly. "I'm formally releasing you. No more visits. I can't do anything more for you."

Lauren sat there, took a deep breath and looked at the doctor. Somehow she'd guessed it would be today. After all, it'd been a full month since her last checkup. But strangely, after all the months, it'd seemed part of her life to come to this center, these offices, to be examined, poked and prodded. It was odd to think of it ending now.

Then the joy of realization leaped into her heart. It was another milestone for her. Perhaps the biggest, most complete.

"Thank you, Susan," she said sincerely as Dr. Walter rose. She felt like hugging the doctor, like hugging the whole world. She settled for a warm handshake and a wide smile.

"You're more than welcome, Lauren." Dr. Walter held Lauren's hand, her voice softening. "But more than we doctors, I believe it's due to that bit of iron beneath your porcelain exterior." She winked. "Take care, and don't hesitate to call for any reason."

Slipping into her white wool coat, Lauren thought she had to be the luckiest human being alive, certainly the happiest at that moment. It was all such a miracle, beginning first with simply surviving, let alone being able to walk away from these offices for good.

It had been an automobile crash. They'd had to cut her from the wreckage; it'd taken two hours. Her brother Scott had lain beside her, dead. That she'd been the one driving was the hardest thing to take, to live with, never mind that for months they'd wondered if she would ever walk unaided. The accident had taken Scott's life and much from Lauren—her freedom of movement, her ability to dance, her entire way of life.

Closing her eyes, she mentally forced the stiff fingers of her right hand to fasten the buttons of her coat snugly at the neck. *There, they did it.* Such a feat sometimes. Though anyone observing would rarely notice. She made sure they wouldn't.

She looked down and rubbed the small scars at her right wrist. She was lucky, she repeated to herself. The hand still worked. There was a time when she'd wondered if it would.

A soft quietness touched her spirit. Yes, the accident had taken much, so very much. And the scars to her heart were much deeper than those on her wrist and back.

But the accident had also given back, a thousandfold. Because of it, because of her determined struggle to become whole again, she'd found a person and a life within herself she hadn't known existed. A rich, vibrant life. A life she wouldn't trade for all the tea in China, she thought saucily, snugging a white tam atop her head.

The "if onlys" tried to creep in, but she firmly pushed them aside with thoughts of the day, and the night ahead.

The sky was gray with pending snow; the cold January air nipped her nose. But the day was beautiful for Lauren. It was another first day of the rest of her life. Just like the day she took that first step months and months after the accident. Not only had Dr. Walter formally released her, but this evening she was having her first date in well over a year and a half.

In celebration, she splurged and took a taxi to work. She usually took a bus, but a cool, damp bus was not good on her bones in the wintry weather—and she wanted to get to the office before her boss. She didn't want him making special concessions to her, at least not any more than he already had. She didn't drive. She'd not worked up the courage. It was hard enough just to ride in an automobile, and driving would still be too painful for her back and legs. But not forever, she promised herself. No, not forever.

She made it in about twenty minutes before Ian Walsh. He rarely arrived before ten o'clock on any morning. And from then on Lauren's day was kept very busy. It probably would have been a breeze for a trained secretary, but she was far from that. The only reason she could manage the job at all was because Ian used one of the firm's trained secretaries for anything more complicated than rough typing.

The skills he required from Lauren were basic, requiring plain common sense. She filed, kept his appointments straight, did light typing, greeted his clients and other businessmen, ran errands—or rather walked them—and brought him coffee, something professional secretaries were giving up these days.

This day Ian kept her quite busy with more typing than usual and mounds of filing. She hardly had time to let her mind flit to the evening ahead. Almost no time anyway. Tony Kenyon's handsome features did manage to insert their way into her thoughts while she struggled to peck words out on the typewriter.

She'd met Tony her first day at the office when he'd come for a business meeting with Ian. He was the head of the brokerage division of the Stockman's Bank across the street which Lauren knew of from childhood. While probably not the biggest or the most prosperous bank of the city, it definitely was the oldest and most respected, a veritable institution dating from the city's cattle heyday. Begun and still run today by Kenyons.

Right from the moment she'd seen his handsome face and laughing eyes, she'd pegged him for a flirt and a charmer. He was somewhere around thirty-five and unmarried. Lauren got the idea he was a confirmed bachelor. He'd even readily admitted the fact when on his third visit he'd asked her out. She'd accepted his invitation because of that admission; he'd be a fun, easy date and nothing serious. That was all she was looking for at the moment.

At four-thirty she looked up with a great deal of pride. Her typing was improving. She'd managed to type an entire eight pages of notes for Ian. Arranging them into a neat pile, she rose to take them to him. But the next instant, she stared at the papers as they fluttered to the plush carpet, dropped there by her right hand, a hand that periodically decided totally of its own accord not to work.

She should have been more careful, she scolded herself. She knew she had to concentrate. Why had she forgotten? What about tonight? What if her hand did this and embarrassed her? Maybe she shouldn't even have considered going.

Then firmly Lauren fought the melancholy that tried to overcome her. It served no useful purpose. Bending slowly to kneel, she gathered the papers, concentrating on making the fingers of her right hand come together, but using mostly her left hand. In the kneeling position there was only a bit of ache in her hips. She never would have been able to squat. Ian Walsh's cane thudding on the carpet preceded his voice. She worked faster to pick up the papers, not wanting him to find her. He already knew how inept she was.

But she wasn't quick enough. "What's this?" Ian asked, stopping in the doorway.

Lauren picked up the last of the papers and looked up. "Oh, just a bit of clumsiness." She shot him a smile.

His sharp pale eyes upon her, he didn't smile back. Ian Walsh didn't smile often; in fact, his lips seemed permanently turned downward from a lifetime of frowning. He was a hard, irascible old man. Or so everyone thought, especially the five secretaries he'd gone through in the last year. Nonetheless, Lauren found herself liking him.

"Why haven't you left?" Ian barked sharply. "Don't you have a date for some fancy shindig with that young Tony What's-his-name?" Ian Walsh was a poor Kansas boy who'd grown up to become a successful lawyer and powerful state senator. The man even smoked five-dollar cigars, yet he'd deliberately retained his backwoods style of talking. Reveled in it, Lauren had decided.

Stiffly she rose to her feet, conscious of Ian's eyes upon her and hating the pathetic picture she knew she made. When he moved quickly and nearly as stiffly to grab her arm and help her stand, she was surprised. She'd been working for him for three weeks and this was the first time he'd shown the slightest concern toward her. Catching his pale gaze, she smiled again.

"Quit that smiling," Ian ordered gruffly. "Do you always have to smile so much? Damn stupid nuisance," he muttered. "Now, why haven't you left? Thought I told you to leave a half hour ago."

"I'm going," Lauren said, forcing the smile from her lips, though not her heart. She slipped the stack of papers into a file cover and handed them to him. "Here're those notes you wanted on Abilene Jack, all typed. Now you can look them over this weekend."

Raising a bushy white eyebrow, he grunted. "Fine. Now, get out of here," he said; then he and his cane thumped back into his office.

Again Lauren smiled. She guessed simply putting up with the old man's rude and crabby ways was a full job in itself.

She covered the typewriter and straightened her desk, then checked the potted plants for moisture. Her office was comfortable and refined, with gleaming cherry wood furniture, bookcases, paneled walls and two traditional wing chairs; hers matched Ian's more elegant office, as well as those of the other attorneys of his firm.

She slipped into her coat, and as she was adjusting the tam over her hair, Ian poked his head from his office.

"I've ordered my driver to take you home," he stated. "He'll be waiting downstairs."

She regarded him a brief second. "Thank you," she said quietly, being very careful not to smile again.

His eyes narrowed as he observed her. "Uh," he grunted, and disappeared into his office.

"Good night, Ian," she called as she left. There was no response, but that didn't keep the soft smile from her lips now. Briefly she recalled an episode that had happened the end of the first day she'd worked for him. Just as she'd been leaving she'd said, "Good night, Ian."

"Don't you think you ought to call me Mr. Walsh?" he'd demanded.

"Would you prefer to call me Miss Howard?" she'd asked in return.

"Uh" was all she'd gotten from him that time, too. And they'd continued to call each other by first names. Anything else seemed foolish; Lauren had known Ian Walsh since her birth.

"Regardless of what Felice has said, Senator, I haven't made any firm decision about running." Jason frowned as he spoke into the telephone receiver. "This was an idea that just cropped up a month ago. It'd never even entered my mind until then."

"Ah hell, Kenyon, what's there to think about? You'd have it in the bag—and be doing the state and many other people a good deed."

"I'm thinking on it," Jason said in a deliberately bland voice. He wouldn't be pushed.

"Well," Senator Collins replied in a slow drawl, "I understand your caution, believe me. But I want you to take my place. We'll find time to discuss it next week—lunch together. I'm sorry I can't be at the dinner party tonight. Please give Felice my regrets again."

"Yes, I will. Good night." Jason returned the receiver, feeling nagging exasperation. From one small comment, things sure could get out of hand. At a charity luncheon he'd attended during the holidays some mention was made of his running for the U.S. Senate, and now people seemed to be watching him like a hawk. Good grief, the rumors were ripe, and he'd yet to say a public word—or few private ones—on the matter.

He buzzed his secretary, then tried to return his attention to a dividend report on his desk. Minutes later, realizing Beth hadn't answered, he buzzed her again, wondering in irritation where she was. A half second later his office door opened, but instead of his secretary, it was his brother Tony. With a characteristically charming grin, Tony sauntered across the room.

"You may be buzzing for Beth a long time," Tony said. "Her desk is closed up for the night."

Jason grunted in answer, sheepishly remembering that he'd told her to go on home more than half an hour ago. It was Friday, and the weather was sour.

Moving some papers aside and propping himself on a corner, Tony gave Jason's desk a disapproving look. He waved his hand, indicating the stack of files. "Our lovely *sister-in-law* suspected all this." There was a humorous, knowing gleam in his eyes as if he, too, recognized Felice's maneuvering nature and found it amusing. "She called me with explicit instructions to come by here and remind you of the party and to make sure you left at five o'clock. Promptly."

"I hadn't forgotten," Jason said, checking figures even as he spoke. "I was just finishing. You want to have a drink and wait? We can walk down together." He glanced up to see Tony give a shake of his head.

"Nope," he said, and gave a wink. "I, big brother, have a beautiful date for tonight. I'm heading home pronto and getting spruced up."

Jason chuckled. "You always have a beautiful date. Is this one any different than the rest? And how can you manage to leave the telephone long enough?"

"Stock markets are closed for the weekend. And this one is the most beautiful of them all. You'll see tonight," Tony vowed, hopping from his perch. "Don't get busy now and forget. Felice will have my hide if you do." As he left, he cast Jason a warning glance.

Jason gave the pages before him a disgruntled look, pushed his chair away from the desk and stretched his legs, wiggling his toes within his boots. His one real vanity, he thought, looking at the gleaming, custom-made Western boots. Maybe it was the one thing in life he really appreciated, the one trait he'd managed to hold on to and could truly call his own.

Rising, he moved to the window. It had begun snowing, the flakes large, their falling creating a shadowy curtain in the evening's growing dimness. Lights shone from other office windows, and the city traffic inched along below. Leaning against the polished oak window frame, hands stuffed into his pockets, he watched the scene.

Rush hour. Everyone wanting to get home. To families, to wives. The thought was bleak. He had neither. Not really, anyway.

Forty-eight. The number popped big and bold within his mind. He was forty-eight years old—two years away from fifty. It didn't seem possible. It sounded so... so old. The fact sat heavily.

But he still felt like thirty-five. The thought came almost as an angry protest against the injustice of aging. Physically he could pass for that or younger, he thought with a twinge of male pride. Youthfulness was characteristic of his family. He could still play a half hour of racquetball and end up barely puffing, could still ski the high slopes all day, could still ride a tough old bronc if he had to. The only thing that gave his age away was the cast of silver to his hair, the near pure white growing at his temples. But then, that was another family trait: early graying. He'd found white hairs in his head before he'd turned twenty.

With the nudge of some inner remembrance, he glanced to his watch. It was five o'clock. Instinctively his gaze skimmed the sidewalk three floors below. *Would she appear today?*

Three days this week and two the week before, at this same time, Jason had been looking out the window and had chanced to observe a young woman appear from the office building across the street. Actually the first time had been chance, the others pure deliberation on his part. It had been the sheen of her dark hair and her white coat that had caught his attention. And maybe the way she walked as well, graceful and slow, not the usual rush of everyone else who was hurrying home. Certainly something had set her apart. He wondered if she would be there again today.

With a shake of his head, he laughed at himself. What did he care if she was there? Well, he answered the mocking inner voice, he liked looking at her. He was a man after all. And it was just some game to relax his mind, he thought as he strained to see. The flakes had thinned, but it was rapidly growing darker. People streamed from the old and august building across the street and up and down the wide sidewalk. How could he possibly see her in that mass of humanity?

Yet, he continued to stare.

Seconds later he was rewarded by the sight of a white coat that stood out clearly against all the others in dark winter colors as his mystery woman stepped from the ornate doorway of the elegant old building. This time her dark hair was covered by white, as well, but he was sure it was her. There was no mistaking the gracefulness of her movements or the way she refused to hurry. She stepped to the side of the doorway and looked around—for someone, perhaps, but almost as if she was observing the world around her.

Jason wished he could see her face clearly. Would she be as beautiful as her movements indicated, as beautiful as he'd imagined?

The next instant he turned from the window and grabbed his coat as he sprinted from his office, not even pausing long enough to turn out the lights. His only thought was to catch her, to see her.

He ran down the hall, tugging on his overcoat as he went, only vaguely aware of several people about and their curious glances. He smacked the elevator button, then pivoted impatiently and ran on to the stairway.

He burst through the door, coming face-to-face with a young woman, her arms full of boxes, almost upsetting her.

"I'm...sorry..." Jason apologized, righting the top box for her. She stared at him with wide eyes, no doubt thinking him crazy. And he felt a little crazy, exhilarated, hopeful, alive, he thought, as he leaped down the stairs, two and three at a time, his topcoat billowing out in his wake.

Bursting from the door out into the bank lobby on the first floor, Jason didn't stop running. Even when he heard the guard call to him. He darted around a young girl, nearly collided with two old men and fairly pushed an elderly woman out the door ahead of him. Then he seemed to be pushing his way upriver through the people on the sidewalk. Weaving his way to the curb, he stopped and peered across the street to the doorway, his gaze searching for a white coat, his pulse sounding in his ears.

But there was no one there. No one at all.

Still his gaze searched hopefully up and down the sidewalk in front of the opposite building. She had to be there. Had to be . . .

But she wasn't. And at last Jason sucked in a long breath. *He'd missed her.*

Disappointment swamped him. A feeling of extreme foolishness came after that. What in the hell had he been thinking? Running down here like some idiot for a look at a woman he'd seen only from a distance, *didn't even know.*

He was a grown man, damn it! He was Jason Kenyon, of *the* Kenyons. The thought came with not a little sarcasm. Nearing fifty and the president of one of the oldest banks west of the Mississippi. What in the hell kind of thing was it to chase down three flights after a woman he'd never seen closer than several hundred feet?

Slowly he began to fasten his coat and equally as slowly turned to walk toward the parking garage, the weight of family heritage and years of responsibility pressing down on him. He remembered the briefcase left in his office. It could stay, he thought, almost angrily. He became aware of cold, slick concrete beneath his soles and of snowflakes falling cold upon his hair. The air drawn into his lungs was cold, too.

What if he had seen her? he asked himself. What then? Would he have spoken to her? Good Lord, what could he have said?

What was happening to him? he wondered, and not for the first time. Lately he'd been doing the screwiest things, like nearly crying over an old Cary Grant romantic comedy and driving out to the old family ranch before he'd even realized where he was going. And last week he'd popped into a car dealer for a casual look around, and when he'd come out he'd held the keys to a bright red Corvette.

He couldn't seem to keep his mind on anything. Thoughts and questions assaulted him as he tried to read reports and discuss business. Thoughts that had nothing whatever to do with financial matters. And the face that stared out at him from the mirror each morning seemed that of a stranger—a vaguely accusing stranger.

"Don't get out," Lauren said with a soft smile to the driver of the long black limousine. "I can manage fine." Opening the door, she slowly slid her legs out and stood, pulling up her coat collar against the growing cold and damp.

Bending her head against fine snowflakes, she crossed the sidewalk and mounted the brick stairs to her apartment building. It was a dignified, brown brick structure dating from the mid-thirties, comfortable and roomy, housing only two apartments. At the moment, it looked inviting in the glow of the streetlamp, with the porch light shining out in welcome and lights on behind the curtains of the apartment above hers. Two sisters in their sixties inhabited that apartment. They were casually friendly when Lauren met them in the small hallway, which was seldom. She'd gathered that one sister worked nights, the other days, and both appeared to travel often, as well.

Fifteen minutes later, Lauren slipped her aching body into a deep hot tub of water and relaxed. The ache seemed to ease almost immediately, helped on by mild pain medication.

Her mind dwelled on what to wear for the evening and failed to come to a firm decision. She quaked nervously with rising apprehension. She probably shouldn't have accepted Tony's invitation, she chided. *What if her hand dropped her glass or her muscles locked up?* Her mind conjured up a mortifying picture of herself sitting down, then trying to stand, only not being able to straighten. She would somewhat resemble a female Hunchback of Notre Dame.

Firmly she pushed the picture away. *She wanted to go.* She couldn't stay in a cocoon forever and had resolved to begin entering the world again. She'd begun that with her job with Ian Walsh and her own apartment. Now was not the time to stop. She had to press on with LIFE. She saw the word in big, bold letters.

At last she was recovered enough to have a date with a man. There was a large bit of triumph in the thought. A year and a half ago the doctors had said she would definitely never professionally dance again, and there was question of her even walking.

Humph! Lauren thought smugly as she rubbed a wet cloth down her arm.

Instinct telling her the dinner party that evening was bound to be quite formal, she decided in favor of a glistening, long-sleeved white gown with loose lines from her neck to her toes. Having lost weight to the point of being painfully thin, this gown was the best. It was supposed to look as if she didn't have a shape anyway. Falling straight to the floor, it had a slit on one side nearly to her thigh. Thin legs looked good, she decided, and the rest wouldn't show.

She felt much better after the bath, medication and a few limbering exercises. But again doubts nipped at her as she slipped into low-heeled dress shoes. Because of her back, she no longer wore high heels.

She couldn't risk any more pain medication, she thought uncertainly, catching her bottom lip between her teeth. How would it look if she fell face-first into the hors d'oeuvres? But what if her hand...what if her legs...what if her back...

Regarding her reflection in the long mirror on the closet door, Lauren pulled a funny face and told herself she hadn't gotten this far by dwelling on "what ifs."

She was pleased with herself, she decided, finding in her reflection a woman of grace and poise, perhaps even of loveliness. She would hold any glasses and pass any dishes with her left hand, would not stand or sit in one place for very long and, if she began to feel achy, she'd ask Tony to bring her home. No one would ever guess her physical condition. No one would feel sorry for her.

"Well, hell-ooo," Tony said appreciatively when she opened the door to his ring. He was quite handsome himself, with dark, almost black hair, classical good looks and a black suit fitting his slim frame perfectly. She'd been right about the scheme of the evening, she saw as her gaze skimmed over Tony's formal black-tie attire.

Casually leaning against the doorjamb, he ran a deliberate gaze from Lauren's head to her toes.

"Thank you," she said with a throaty chuckle. And even though she felt shy, it was good to have a man look at her in such a way again. "Would you like a drink before we go?"

"Oh, I'd like it all right, but I promised Felice I'd return as soon as possible to help with things. Though I doubt if she'll need any help. This is her forte, so to speak."

Lauren nodded. "I'll just get my coat." Reaching into the closet, she pulled out a silver fox cape, a remnant of better times. Tony assisted in settling it on her shoulders.

"You're quite beautiful, Lauren," he said, bending close enough for his breath to brush her temple.

Lauren moved away. "Thank you," she replied quietly, letting the fact that she wanted to remain casual show plainly in her eyes.

Tony nodded, understanding written in his eyes, as well, though they twinkled flirtatiously. "I'm glad you accepted my invitation tonight, Lauren," he said on their way out the door. "You'll be the bright spot in an evening of interminable conversation, behind-the-scenes flirting, business deals and politics. I hope you don't find it too boring." He was playfully apologetic.

"If you find this event so odious, why are we going?" she asked in wonder as Tony opened the outer door of the building. It was cold and crisp outside. A thin white film covered the holly bushes, the steps and the sidewalk. The road glistened.

"Watch your step." Tony took her arm as they descended the brick stairs. "Felice," he said, answering her question, "my sister-in-law. She enjoys putting together these elaborate dinner parties." His tone had softened. "I pretend to enjoy them because it makes her happy. It's the least I can do. She's been keeping house for Jason and me for years now." He led her toward a dark Porsche.

"Jason?" Lauren asked, puzzling at just who was who.

Tony opened the car door. "My brother, Jason Kenyon. I live with him in the family home." He grinned. "Guess I've never grown up," he teased. "Felice spends most of the year there with us—has ever since Jason's wife died ten years ago. Felice was her sister."

"Oh," Lauren said as she slipped into the low-slung car, concentrating on keeping her movements smooth. She silently thanked her body for a good performance.

"It's sort of confusing all thrown at you at once," Tony said just before slamming her door. "But not nearly as confusing as it will be when you're introduced to everyone at the party tonight," he said as he slipped into the seat behind the steering wheel.

Lauren looked at him and smiled. She was glad to be with him, glad to be going, but a bit frightened, as well. What would she have in common with these people? The social world she knew of before, while quite wide, had been a bit avant-garde, mostly dancers and other show people, artists, writers and such. She tended to gather with very good friends. And that had been so long ago. It seemed very far away. How would she relate to people in this type of world— financial and political? In an instant of wondering, she tried to picture what lay ahead.

Well, she thought flatly, she wouldn't know until she saw it.

Chapter Two

Alone in his study, Jason pulled at his black tie and then swallowed his second whiskey. Felice hated his habit of drinking straight whiskey. She preferred he drink something more "refined," like martinis, brandy or fine champagne. And all of it high-dollar stuff. She judged the quality of something by how much it cost. It seemed a trait of someone who'd been denied as a child, not someone who'd grown up as Felice had, a member of the affluent and privileged Rischard family. You'd think she'd have learned better.

Thinking these thoughts now, Jason experienced a twinge of guilt. She did so much to make his and Tony's life comfortable. The guilt grew deeper.

They'd had words earlier. Jason was irritated at her for telling Senator Dan Collins that he'd made up his mind to run for office. She'd protested that it'd been some mistake, that she'd never said such.

Raking his hand through his thick hair, he recalled the argument. He shouldn't have been so short with her. She was only doing what she thought was helpful for him.

And it wasn't her fault he found himself hedged in on every side by responsibilities and commitments. By life itself, he thought tiredly. No, it was his own. He'd made all the choices that put him where he was today: conscrvative, traditional, highly successful. But with all he had, he felt something missing—a big part of himself.

Dampening the urge for another drink, Jason straightened his tie and left the quiet sanctuary of his study. There was a party beginning after all, in his home, supposedly for him.

Felice looked beautiful, he admitted when he saw her at the door greeting two arriving couples. Her soft champagne-pale curls framed her face, and her pale green dress floated with every movement. Jason joined her, quickly flashing her a warm smile that pleaded forgiveness. She nodded, smiling in return.

"Where's Tony?" he asked as he escorted her into the spacious living room.

Felice pursed her delicately etched red lips. "On his way, I hope. He had to pick up his date, but he promised to be here early." Her green eyes flashed excitedly. "I've invited Garrett Baker—of Baker Corporation," she clarified, though there was no need. Jason knew very well who the man was and Felice's reason for inviting him. "With him and Tony playing tennis twice a month, I thought it would be good to have him here. You two could—" She broke off at Jason's look.

"I told you, Felice. I haven't made up my mind to run," he said, feeling the irritation rise at her efforts to maneuver him.

"I know, darling. But if you see just how many powerful people you'll have in your corner, it will give you an idea of how successful you can be."

Before Jason could reply, Felice swept away to join guests, and the doorbell rang, signaling the arrival of more people. He went to the door to do his duty as a cordial host, wondering how he'd ended up hosting a dinner party he'd never wanted to have in the first place.

Several minutes later he turned from the guests to see Tony enter the hall from the direction of the kitchen. Idly Jason noticed Tony's date, a slim woman in white. He took a second glance, his curiosity rising.

The woman's back was toward him as she removed a pale fur cape and handed it to Tony. She shook her head, laughing maybe, and her smooth hair, like rich sable, shone warmly in the light. While not short, she appeared petite, her shoulders small beneath a gleaming white gown that flowed almost straight downward, giving no impression of her shape other than sleek.

The hairs on the back of his neck tingled, and Jason found himself walking toward them, his gaze glued to the young woman, his heart picking up tempo as recognition played at the edges of his mind. It can't be, he thought. *Don't be foolish.* But still he walked toward them, wondering.

Tony spied him and, sending a welcoming grin, placed his hand on the arm of the woman at his side, turning her toward Jason.

And Jason knew. He knew by the light that touched her vibrant brown hair. He knew by her slow, graceful turn. By the slope of her shoulders as she stood there, waiting.

It was his mystery woman from across the street. His woman in the white coat. He was certain, beyond any doubt. The reality hit him almost like a punch in the stomach.

Then some part of his brain remaining rational nudged him, and Jason, realizing he was staring, did his best to regain his composure. Smiling, he glanced briefly to Tony, then returned his gaze to the woman at his brother's side.

"My brother, Jason," Tony was saying. "Jason, this is Lauren Howard."

She extended her hand, her dress shimmering as she moved. "Hello," she said.

Her smile was warm, with just a trace of shyness, but that disappeared in a second as the spark that people share when they immediately like one another flowed between them.

Her voice was deeper than he'd thought it would be, and pleasant sounding. Her eyes were so brown they showed no pupil. They were soft as velvet, wide and round, dominating her face. Her skin was like that of a fine china doll, and she seemed equally fragile. But her grip on Jason's was firm, and he had the impression of a very substantial woman, though not in body.

She had a smile that coaxed a person to smile back, and Jason felt the vibrance of her, the femininity—the woman she was. Even as he consciously recognized the imperfections—the nose a little too long, the eyebrows a bit thick, the sharply squared chin—she was at that moment the most beautiful woman he'd ever seen. There was simply a quiet, lovely air about her that drew a person. And for precious seconds, he allowed himself the pleasure of looking at her, and knowing that she was all he'd imagined she'd be...and more.

A long table covered with a fine linen cloth dominated the large and airy antebellum-style dining room. Shining silver clinked against decorated bone china. Paper-thin, gold-trimmed crystal glittered in the light from two antique chandeliers. A bubble of voices filled the air.

Lauren listened to the conversation around the table more than she talked. She was finding it all fascinating. Money, she thought. Looking at these people one thought of money; they smelled of it. And of rushing ambition, like salmon swimming out to sea, all wanting to get there first.

She relaxed a bit, consciously. Her hand and the rest of her muscles had been behaving themselves, although she was glad when the call to dinner was announced and she was able to sit down.

Feeling someone's eyes upon her, she glanced to Jason Kenyon. He sat at the head of the table, herself next to him, and Tony on her left. She thought she'd noticed Jason's speculative gaze upon her more than once that evening—or had she simply been imagining it because she found herself fascinated by the man?

Jason Kenyon was every bit as handsome as his younger brother, though in a totally different fashion. Where Tony was almost classically good-looking, Jason held a hint of a rugged edge, much like a chunk of granite that has been polished to a sheen on the top, leaving the lines and layers beneath just as raw as nature had devised.

Lauren noticed first his eyes: ocean gray in color and distinctly piercing. A small ragged scar edged the outer corner of his left eye and crinkled when his stern face broke into a smile, one that came slowly and quietly. There wasn't a hint of rushing about this man.

His thick black hair held a silver cast with a tracing of snow white at his temples. His build was larger, less refined than Tony's, and Lauren suspected his well-fitting evening suit concealed shoulders much broader than they appeared. When she happened to notice the darkly gleaming shoes he wore were actually cowboy boots, and no doubt expensive ones, she smiled inwardly. The boots went well with the man.

She put his age at perhaps forty-three, only because Tony had said his brother was much older than himself. Yes, she mused, and also because of the air about him—Jason Kenyon held an aura of quiet power. He didn't say a lot, but seemed content to sit back and observe, even to prefer it.

Tony proved to be a most charming date, the life of the party, keeping the conversation peppered with his witty remarks. Several other women there were clearly enamored of him. But it was almost as if he needed to be on show, as if he thrived on the attention, not for thought of anyone else.

When he smiled at her and winked, Lauren found herself smiling back. He was like an endearing small boy, who greedily took all the cookies and knew no one would scold him.

And his sister-in-law, Felice, was much the same, Lauren thought. She was quite lovely, the height of sophistication, knowing exactly what to say and how to say it. But for some mystifying reason, Lauren sensed a coldness from the woman. She tried to lay the notion aside as simple nerves on her part. First impressions between strangers were often misleading. But this impression hovered.

"Tony said you're working for Ian Walsh." Jason's quiet, steely voice made Lauren start. He'd spoken low, for her ears only.

"Yes," she said, turning her gaze to his, speaking just as low, and noting the quiet hint of a smile in his gray eyes. This seemed their private conversation. Though Tony's elbow brushed hers, he was busy bantering with Garrett Baker's wife.

"How is old Ian? I haven't seen him in quite a while, but I understand he goes through secretaries like cowboys do chewing tobacco." There was nothing provincial in his speech, and the comparison was clearly apt and to the point. Lauren found herself grinning.

"Yes, he does rather chew them up and spit them out," she said. A warmness from his shadowy eyes touched her. "But I'm learning to handle him. Besides, I'm an old family friend. He takes it easier on me."

Jason chuckled. "I can't imagine Ian taking it easy on anyone." His eyes grew darker. "Except maybe you." He spoke so softly, she barely heard him but was warmed by his tone and the intense look in his eyes.

"Do you know Ian well?" She forced a lightness to her voice. The vibrations she sensed were bewildering her—they were too strong, too overpowering. She barely knew this man, and yet...

Jason nodded. "He and my father were good friends. But then, I guess Ian Walsh knows half the people in Kansas and Missouri. What's he doing now? I'd have thought he'd be getting a bit old to practice law."

"Oh, no, Ian will never be too old. Though he does mostly advising now." They both spoke quietly, almost like conspirators. She lowered her voice even further to a whisper, as if sharing a secret. "He's writing a book."

One of Jason's thick eyebrows arched. "A book?"

Lauren nodded, smiling. "On lawyers of the Old West. He intends, he says, to blow a few reputations out of the murky rivers."

Jason chuckled, though made no sound. "And if anyone knows the skeletons in not a few of our more prominent citizens' closets, living or dead, Ian Walsh does."

"Jason, darling." It was Felice's voice. Her sultry tone jarred Lauren's consciousness. Seeing a flash of long lacquered fingernails flutter upon Jason's arm, she looked across into Felice's glittering green eyes. "Shall we retire to the living room for cocktails?" She smiled at Jason, yet Lauren sensed icy daggers being thrown in her direction.

Suddenly fully aware of the private mood that had surrounded Jason and herself, she felt terribly self-conscious, as if she'd been caught picking the loveliest flowers in a show garden. Catching a quick glance of faces, she noted several people were looking at them curiously. "Yes...fine," Jason was saying as guests began to rise. Lauren averted her gaze from everyone.

Tony stood at her elbow. He was making some witty, teasing remark to Felice. Still averting her gaze, she slid back her chair, then stood and smoothed her dress.

Tony held a glass of pale wine toward her, lightly saying, "We'll take these along."

Her mind still on her discomfiture, Lauren reached absently for the glass. Her fingers closed loosely around its delicate stem. The next instant the glass slipped from her fingers and crashed against the edge of the table, shattering into a thousand pieces and spattering both the fine table and her dress with golden wine.

Her right hand, Lauren thought helplessly, feeling an embarrassing hot flush creep across her cheeks. "Oh, I'm so sorry..." In dismay, she watched golden drops stream down the tablecloth and drip upon the intricately designed wool rug.

"No problem," Tony said easily. With his hand at her shoulder, he moved her a step backward from the table.

Immediately Jason was at her other side, dabbing a linen napkin to her dress at her thigh where the wine had spattered. A servant appeared with a wet cloth and wiped the rug. The rest of the guests, after a quick curious look, continued on into the living room.

"I'm so sorry..." Lauren said again, mortified at her clumsiness, at breaking what was obviously a very fine glass, and at everyone hovering. Most of all, she regretted her loss of composure. *She was all over this; she should be all over this.* She fought to control her trembling body and the nervous knotting in her lower back.

"No harm done," Tony said again, casting his boyish smile.

Slowly straightening, Jason looked into her eyes. "I hope your dress isn't ruined."

"No...it'll be fine," she said, hating the breathless sound of her voice.

"There's no problem," Felice said, her ultrapolite voice jarring Lauren's gaze from Jason's. "That was Great-grandmother Kenyon's crystal, but we have plenty more." Her words cut like a knife through the air, her eyes hard upon Lauren.

"Yes, we certainly do," Jason said, his gaze resting on Felice, his low voice steely. Looking to Lauren, he gave a soft smile and took her upper arm. "We'll put cold water on that stain in the kitchen." Even as he spoke, he led her from the room.

If it seemed odd, even impolite for Jason to not only leave his other guests but to pay singular attention to his brother's date, he didn't give a damn. A miracle had somehow brought his mystery woman right under his very roof, and he was going to enjoy it.

With Tony right behind them, Jason led Lauren into the brightly lit kitchen. Amid three caterers who worked to clear dishes and fill trays with cocktails, he sat her in a chair and reached for a bottle of ice water from the refrigerator.

Tony shot him a look that was at once both curious and displeased but refrained from arguing, turning instead to get a cloth from the drawer. Jason almost laughed out loud when they both bent near Lauren, he with the water, Tony with the cloth.

With a gentle smile, Lauren slid her gaze from Tony to Jason. "I think this may be a one-person job," she said softly, holding out her hand to take the cloth from Tony.

Did her gaze linger on him? Jason wondered as he stared into her velvety eyes. It came as a shock to realize he wanted very much to touch her soft cheek, to kiss her lips. Moving his attention to the cloth, he dampened it with the cold water.

"I'm sure this is fine," she said. "The cleaners will probably have no trouble getting it out." She gave a low chuckle and wrinkled her nose. "But in the meantime, I bet I smell wonderful."

Though Jason stepped casually away, he couldn't take his eyes from her. With her head bent to the task, the light shone burnished highlights on her sable hair. Even doing such a small task, her movements were graceful. There was a quiet air of equanimity about her now, though he'd recognized her discomfiture in the dining room earlier.

He'd watched her all evening. She seemed warm and friendly, yet aloof. She didn't fit in with these people, she seemed to know that, but was neither intimidated nor bored by it all. She was a watcher, much like himself. And she enjoyed Tony.

His gaze moved to his brother's dark head, which bent close to Lauren's. It struck him then that they were very handsome together. And that Lauren was young—couldn't be over twenty-five.

Though Jason said not one parting word, and Lauren kept her gaze on her dress, she was very aware of when he left the room. She finished wiping her dress several seconds later.

Tony gave a charming smile. "Feel like joining in on the party again?" he asked.

"Yes, of course. It was just a little spill, can hardly notice it now—see."

His lips twitched. "Yes . . . I see." His eyes met hers flirtingly. Then he said, "You're enjoying tonight?" It was half question, half surprised statement.

"Yes, I am. Very much," Lauren said. "These people are fascinating—I'm getting inside stories on the country club, the best tennis instructors, the finest dress shops and where to go for a face-lift.''

She laughed lightly, but she spoke the truth. She was enjoying herself, simply watching people, feeling quite beautiful, if a bit clumsy, and feeling the object of a handsome gentleman's attention. Involuntarily her mind flitted to Jason at this thought.

The only blemish to the evening was Felice. The woman clearly didn't like her. Recalling this, Lauren almost changed her mind and asked Tony to take her home even as he led her back to the living room. But that would be rude, she thought, and upsetting to him. She didn't want that. And deep inside, she didn't want to give Felice even the slightest impression that the older woman could in anyway diminish her. The best thing would be to join the others quietly, as if nothing had happened.

When they entered the room, her gaze instinctively sought out Jason. She hadn't meant to and was surprised at herself. He stood near the flickering fireplace talking with Garrett Baker and another man. Or more aptly, listening. Felice was at his side, her hand in the crook of his arm.

Lauren sat in a large firmly stuffed chair. Tony brought them each a glass of wine, which she was careful to hold in her left hand. Sitting on the arm of the chair, Tony soon had a conversation going, entertaining them all with anecdotes of his experiences at the bank. But again and again Lauren found her attention, as well as her gaze, roaming discreetly to Jason. Once she found him looking at her. Their eyes met for several long seconds. Then very slowly he smiled. The rest of the people in the room faded from her conscious thought in that moment as his warmth touched her. It was as if they shared a secret.

Then reality returned, and she quickly averted her gaze, though the ghost of a smile played upon her lips—and she knew he saw.

An hour and a half later, she and Tony prepared to leave. Jason joined them, walking with them through the house and out onto the wide sweep of a patio at the back.

"Thank you for joining us tonight." Jason spoke the polite words looking down at her from his greater height. Fine snowflakes lit upon his hair.

"I enjoyed it," Lauren murmured, terribly aware of Mr. Jason Kenyon.

"I may be a while," Tony called back to his brother as he led Lauren away. "The roads and all."

When they drove away, Lauren saw Jason's large figure standing near the double doors. He hadn't gone back inside even then. Something told Lauren he hadn't wanted to be inside all evening.

She declined Tony's invitation to stop for a quiet drink, pleading fatigue, which was totally true. Tonight had been enjoyable, but it had taken a lot out of her, as well. It was hard on a person's body and mind, striving to jump into life, doing so many new things.

She was grateful when Tony didn't insist. Nor did he suggest he come in for a while. He pressed his lips fleetingly to her forehead and smiled charmingly down at her for a second before he left. It wasn't until she'd closed the door after him that she realized there'd been a questioning light in his eyes.

Lauren hung the fox cape in the closet, running her hand lovingly down its softness before closing the door. She remembered buying it four years earlier, on credit that had stretched her purse to the limit. She smiled. Yes, she did love the cape, but she was different now. Now she could resist. She had become more disciplined.

It was discipline that kept her diet strictly on bodybuilding foods, that kept her getting seven to eight hours of sleep a night and thirty minutes of meditation each day and that led her now to slipping into lavender tights and leotard instead of a nightgown. It was discipline that had led her to walk again and would enable her to keep walking.

Though it'd happened over a year and a half ago, the accident was as fresh in her mind as yesterday. It had all been so sudden. Scott had come to Kansas City for his first visit in years. Their mother had been so happy to have both her children with her. Lauren and Scott had slipped away to buy her a present, a mother's ring. They were riding down the interstate; a large tractor-trailer truck came up beside them. The car rocked suddenly. The steering wheel jerked to the right, and Lauren couldn't stop it. She'd tried. But it had just all been too fast.

Yes, the memory remained, and she dreaded it. But she also accepted it, learned to live with it.

Her pelvis had been crushed, and her right wrist, as well, odd though it seemed. She'd been close to death, indeed had believed herself dead and surrounded by the brightest light, with absolutely no pain at all. She'd even wanted to stay with that light, knowing there she was safe and secure. But then someone, or something, had told her no. It wasn't time. There was more left to do. And she'd begun spinning back into a world of reality, a world of pain.

Into that pain had come great sorrow with the knowledge that Scott was dead. And an almost overwhelming guilt that she'd caused his death.

The pain was to be with her for months. It was what she'd come to dread and fear the most. It'd seemed to ta⸱e forever for her body to rid itself of it, but at long last she'd won the battle and was left with only the scars—on both on her body and in memory.

She'd benefited from a new procedure that pinned the bones of her pelvis back into place, but even then the doctors had been skeptical she would ever walk normally again. And only time would tell the extent to which her hand would regain its use.

But she'd devised her own therapy, forcing herself to fight the pain and drowning despair, filling her mind with only positive thought. Guilt hung over her like a black umbrella drenched with rain. She fought this, too.

She'd vowed to herself, though she'd practically refused to talk at all to others, that she would walk, and without a cane or aid of any kind. And she'd told herself, then, that she would even dance again.

But gradually, and even bitterly at times, she'd had to accept that it was not for her to dance again. That it could no longer be her life, her love. That part of the desire would not be fulfilled. It was a disappointment, one she'd fiercely fought against, refused to believe for a long time. And even now it saddened her.

But she could walk, wonderfully, and it was exciting—as only someone who'd been denied the action could imagine. For this gift, she gave heartfelt thanks. She was healed and very much alive. Now she waited to see what she would be led to do with this precious life she'd been given. Perhaps this was the hardest of all. Her dancer's life was over—what would she do now? The question always caused an empty ache inside her. She fit nowhere.

Leaving several lights on to help fill the apartment, Lauren stepped into a darkened second bedroom. She flipped the light switch, and immediately her image reflected from mirrors covering the better part of two walls. The room was empty except for a six-foot balance bar, the scarred oak floor bare and shiny. With one hand on the bar, Lauren slowly and gracefully began the exercises she'd done since her early teens. The exercises that had given her back her ability to walk and that she hoped would continue to build her body back to near total health.

But with that, what? *What?* The question echoed within her, plaguing her. She wanted all life had to give her, intended to have it. If she could just figure out what *it* was.

* * *

Leaning back in the old leather desk chair that had been his grandfather's, Jason tiredly slipped the obnoxious black tie from around his neck. The house was quiet, all guests gone. Thank God, Jason thought. The people Felice had invited were not those he generally chose to socialize with.

They were Felice's friends, if one could call them that. They'd been chosen for the purpose of sounding out his supposed considerations on running for the Senate. Most were self-serving people, at least as Jason saw them, impressed with their positions, their money, in some cases their family names. Garrett Baker had been all right, though, Jason mused briefly. He and Garrett had even made an appointment to meet and talk later in the week.

And then his thoughts turned to Lauren Howard. What fantastic set of coincidences had brought about her showing up at his house tonight? What angel had sent her? he wondered, recalling her exquisite face. He'd missed her that very afternoon after running like a crazy man to meet her. And then she'd shown right up at his house, like an answer to a prayer. How incredible—and wonderful, one of those once in a lifetime things that actually do happen.

The image of Lauren and Tony together brought him up short. How stupid of him. Good grief, what could he be thinking? She'd been Tony's date and, by all observations, he was quite taken with her. But then, Tony was like that with all women.

And he, Jason Kirk Kenyon, was old enough to be her father. The thought entered and sat there, big and bold, tearing at him. His stomach knotted, and he clenched his fist. Yet even while he acknowledged the fact, a small part of him realized he hadn't been this attracted to another woman in years. Not since Jeanne had died.

He was lost in all these confusing thoughts when Felice's voice sounded behind him. At first, he couldn't seem to bring himself back to the present. Partly because he was so far away and partly because he didn't want to talk to anyone, least of all Felice.

"Join me in a nightcap?" she was saying.

Very slowly, with a resigned sigh, Jason turned his chair to face her. Smiling sweetly, she placed a small glass of amber liquid on the desk in front of him. He knew it was brandy.

"Thanks," he said, and managed a smile. She was happy, he could see by the look of contentment on her face. Felice was a beautiful woman even as she approached forty-five.

She stretched, then slid onto the edge of his desk and sipped her drink. "It was a lovely evening, Jason," she said. "And I think it went very well."

Only half listening, he agreed. "You were the perfect hostess," he said.

"And you were the perfect host." She smiled at him, and Jason just looked at her, knowing full well he hadn't been the perfect host; at times he'd been next to rude. "Well, all right," Felice conceded, "maybe not perfect." She gave a light, high-pitched laugh. "But you were very impressive. That was more important. These people will join your team, should you decide to run."

Her words grated on his nerves, but he didn't say anything. There was no need to snap at her just because he was on edge. Lapsing into silence, he dropped his gaze to the shining polished wood of the desk. It reminded him of Lauren Howard's hair.

Catching Tony's name, Jason realized that Felice was speaking of Tony and Lauren. He started, feeling uneasy, as if Felice had been able to read the direction of his thoughts.

"They made a nice couple, didn't they?" she said. "But then, Tony only dates beautiful women. *Young*, beautiful women," she emphasized. "I don't know why he can't find a woman more his own age—and of better family." She paused, and her words hung in the air.

Glancing up, Jason saw her looking at him. She seemed to be waiting for him to speak, but he had nothing to say. Or more precisely, he didn't trust himself to speak at that moment. Anything he'd say would reveal too much, start another quarrel.

Felice shrugged. "Well, for all her beauty, she really was a bit clumsy. I'm awfully sorry about Great-grandmother Kenyon's crystal. Perhaps I shouldn't have used it."

Jason remembered Felice's caustic remark in the dining room. It had angered him then, though he'd chosen to ignore it out of concern for all involved. But it angered him again now.

"We will never put our concern for any object in our home above that of the comfort of our guests." He spoke low, hot anger smoldering in his chest. And even as he saw Felice's eyes widen in dismay, he couldn't stem the words. "I don't give a damn if every piece of crystal is smashed to bits. Now, I'm going to bed."

He'd stepped into the hall when he heard her small, cultured voice call after him.

Chapter Three

He stopped, emotions churning within him. He didn't want to hurt her; he really didn't.

"I'm sorry, Jason." Felice's mouth turned down into a pout. "I only tried to give you a good evening. I always try to do my best for you and Tony."

Jason sighed. "I'm sorry I was sharp with you," he said, feeling defeated by the entire world. "But I certainly don't see any reason for a young woman's feelings to be hurt for such a thing as a glass." He averted his gaze from her accusing eyes. "I'm just tired. Please, let's drop it."

Felice nodded. "Fine," she said, sulking, her voice small and hurt.

Turning, Jason continued on to his room, anger fueled by guilt propelling him as he mounted the stairs. He wanted to be away from her, from lingering images of the evening, from his whole confining world at the moment. As he walked he jerked off his evening jacket as if it were confining him, too.

Later, still too restless to climb into bed, he rifled through some drawers in a closet and came up with an old pack of cigarettes. He'd given up the habit some fifteen years ago, but selected one now and lit it. He stood looking out at the winter night, watching fine snowflakes blow beneath the shine of the back pole light.

He thought of Lauren and wondered what she was doing. Was she sitting snuggled with Tony by some cozy fire? His brother had yet to come home. Jason resisted the possibility of an accident. Tony often didn't come home at night.

Sharp disappointment touched him. He hadn't thought Lauren would be the type to jump so quickly into bed with his brother. He'd thought her different from the usual women Tony could charm. Somehow, she just seemed . . .

Angrily Jason tore his thoughts away. What in the hell did he know about her? He'd seen her five times from a distance and had spoken less than ten minutes with her. And he didn't need to be dwelling on his brother's love life. It was none of his business.

But Lauren *is* your business, his mind whispered.

He shook the thought away, though his mind had no more pleasant a subject to dwell on. He felt guilty about Felice; he often did, mostly because she did so much for him and Tony. She'd seemed to give up much of her life for them, living there with them, keeping their home running smoothly and comfortably. That she was a help in the social end of business was an understatement. She planned and executed all the social engagements, big, small and in between. And she did it superbly. He regretted speaking to her as if she were one of the hired help. Surely he could have rebuked her more gently.

It was just that she got on his nerves so often, more often than not lately with all this senator business. Not that Jason wasn't seriously considering running for the office. He was. The idea appealed to him, the excitement of the challenge, something new to tackle. But in his own time. When he'd considered all the aspects.

His mind moved back over the years, recalling when Jeanne had died and Felice had come to stay. Jason's mother, Ardis, had been here then, too, and had stayed a full month before returning to Mexico City. That was her native home and, at the death of her husband several years before, she'd returned there to live in the company of all the brothers, sisters, aunts and uncles of her family. Her sons had their own life now, she said, and they must live it without interference from her. And, Jason knew, she was much more comfortable with the life she led in Mexico. She came to Kansas City once a year to visit, and they talked often by telephone.

Felice's visit was to have been temporary, too, just to get Jason and the household settled. But "temporary" had turned into nearly ten years. It was only later, when he'd worked through much of the grief of losing Jeanne, that Jason had come to realize Felice needed to be there and feel useful. She really had no other place to go. The elder Rischards were terribly old and did little but sit on the porch at their elaborate Florida retirement home. After one disastrous marriage—and several affairs, Jason was pretty certain—Felice had no other family to call her own except Tony and himself. Jason looked on her as a sister.

Over the years, she'd gradually taken full control of the house. It was a relief not to be bothered, and he'd settled into the comfortable routine of having the house staff competently supervised, his meals ready when he came home, his clothes appearing clean in his closet, even his shoes shined whenever they needed it without him having to alert a soul.

For entertaining, he'd simply tell Felice his need, and it would be taken care of.

One evening he'd come home to find her working with carpet samples, intent on redecorating the living room. She hadn't asked his permission. The house had become hers. And still he hadn't said anything. It needed it, he'd told himself then.

He thought now that, without meaning to, he'd taken advantage of Felice. Deep in his mind he must have known, must have realized what was happening, but it'd seemed easier to let it lie. She was happy; he and Tony were comfortable.

A good deal of the predicament he was now in was his own fault. He'd let her get into the habit of running not only the house, but his life, as well. The last three dinner parties had been her idea—she'd gone ahead without even consulting him, and he'd allowed it. He'd let the situation get out of hand, and he'd have to fix it. How, he wondered, was he going to do that without hurting her?

But it wasn't Felice, Tony, senatorial races or the many-faceted financial world that finally filled his thoughts as he struggled to find sleep in the dark early hours of a winter morning. It was a woman. A flesh and blood young woman with hair the color of sable. And Jason thought wryly that, while he was on the down side of forty-five, he was definitely very much alive.

Because of her later-than-usual night before, it was past nine when Lauren awoke. Looking from her living room window across Ward Parkway, she delighted in the lovely winter-bare park, blanketed in glistening white. Snow lay as a white carpet and coated every bare tree, branch and shrub. An evergreen drooped under the weight of the white fluff. And it sparkled in the rising sunlight.

As with everything she'd done since the accident, trying to add any small bit of strength to her life, she'd chosen this apartment because of the eastern view from the front window. For a few minutes she quieted for meditation, greeting the new day. For Lauren, who had lost so much, every day was precious and filled with wonder. She often grasped at the minutes of her life, wanting to wring from them all she could, realizing only too well how fleeting they really were.

This morning Jason Kenyon's image inserted itself into her meditation. She pushed it out, yet within seconds there it came again. How strange, she thought, she'd made such small contact with him the previous night. But he'd lingered in her thoughts as she'd exercised and even as she'd fallen asleep. And now here he was again.

She saw ocean-gray eyes with laugh lines at their edges, the ragged scar on his temple, his shiny silvery hair. No, it wasn't so strange, she thought, emitting a faint throaty chuckle. Jason Kenyon was enough to cause any woman's blood to heat and mind to turn to more basic physical pleasures. Jason Kenyon wasn't a man to be easily forgotten.

She saw strength, yet sensed a tenderness in him. He was singularly aloof, with a sense of aloneness. He seemed a troubled man.

A rumbling stomach sent further musings about Jason Kenyon from Lauren's mind. She was pleased to find herself hungry and managed to eat a poached egg and two pieces of wheat toast, washed down with a small glass of fresh-squeezed orange juice. It was substantial for her. After cleaning up, she searched through boxes for several books she'd bought while still living at her mother's house. She'd moved to her own apartment only ten days ago and hadn't unpacked everything. Her exercises, mental as well as physical, came first. And with her days spent at the office, that left her scant time for other things.

She made tea in a fine china pot she'd bought for an outrageous price at a specialty shop in San Francisco. She had many such possessions; she'd always been a free spender. Even though she'd worked her way up to commanding quite a good salary, she'd always seemed broke. She loved buying clothes and fine antiques and novelty pieces for her home. As a result, at the time of the accident, she'd had very little in savings. And now there was no free spending.

Even though there was plenty of money. Scott's money.

That's how she saw what she'd received at his death. It would never be hers; her guilt kept it from her. His will had left her half of everything he owned, and his bank accounts had been an amazement to her. The other half had gone to their mother.

But Lauren had not been able to bring herself to touch the money for her own needs. She'd given some away to people she knew needed it, and of all Scott's possessions had only consented to keep a marvelous watercolor by Wyeth.

Lighting the log in the fireplace, she curled in the corner of the couch with an old novel, a first edition that she'd found at a favored used bookstore haunt near the university. She'd lost herself thoroughly in the emotions of the book when the telephone rang.

It was her mother calling from Cancun, Mexico. Widowed after twenty-five years of marriage to Lauren's father, Sybil Howard had remarried a moderately successful travel writer who had columns in several newspapers and a number of books to his credit. She traveled with him to all parts of the world at least eight months of the year.

Sybil Howard loved her daughter dearly, clung to her after losing a son she'd never really been close to. Even after months nursing Lauren, Sybil hadn't wanted to leave to go on this trip. But Lauren had insisted it was time they both got back into their own lives. She certainly no longer needed a nurse. Still, Sybil telephoned every few days just to make certain.

"I'm fine, Momma," Lauren said, laughter and love tracing her voice. Though she'd traveled far since her early years in Kansas City, she'd never lost that soft accent that, like the character of the city itself, was somewhere between North and South, yet very distinctive.

"Are you having much pain?" Sybil asked. "I told you about those stairs to your apartment."

"I'm on the first floor, Momma. There're maybe five steps to get up to the porch," Lauren replied, then for the next several minutes patiently allayed her mother's fears.

Her health was good, the apartment was perfect and she was even enjoying working for Ian Walsh.

"You have grown stronger," Sybil commented.

Lauren knew the fact that she and Ian were hitting it off really wouldn't come as a big surprise to her mother. It was through Sybil that she'd gotten the job with him. Sybil and Ian had been lifelong friends. "Don't let it out of the bag that you've discovered his soft spot," Sybil said. "He'll never forgive you."

They talked for a few minutes more, Sybil speaking of the luxurious new hotel they were staying at in Cancun and sights they'd seen. Lauren found she simply couldn't keep quiet about her date the previous evening, telling her mother of the people she'd met and her impressions and of the faux pas with the wineglass, as well, but that she'd handled it. Her mother had to know every detail.

"I must hang up now, Lauren dear," Sybil said at last. "Oh, tell me, has this Jason Kenyon asked you out again?"

"Tony Kenyon, Momma," Lauren clarified. "I was out with Tony. And no, he hasn't asked me out again. It's nothing serious."

"Oh," her mother said, the one word and definite pause speaking volumes. "But, dear, you spoke in much more detail about Jason." Her tone was that of a wise, between-the-lines-reading mother. Before Lauren could think of what to say, Sybil gave her love and rang off.

She sat looking at the telephone. Yes, she'd found Jason Kenyon very interesting, much more so than his rakishly handsome brother. There was substance to Jason and many fascinating facets hidden beneath his cool, guarded exterior.

Lauren shook her head. She'd probably never see him again, so what did it matter? But then, she thought, so few things in life were certain. Perhaps neither was not seeing Jason Kenyon.

Tony telephoned the office Tuesday and asked her to lunch. She was surprised, mostly because she hadn't thought about him at all.

Lauren accepted. Tony bantered with her and kept her chuckling. He tried to flirt outrageously, but Lauren backed off. She could never be more than friends with Tony and didn't want him to think otherwise. He seemed to accept agreeably.

As the days passed into another week, Lauren found herself thinking often of Jason Kenyon, wondering about him, about his life. What did someone like him do when not at his office or elegant dinners or cocktail parties? Was he interested in anyone special? Were he and Felice close, even intimate? She didn't believe she'd been wrong in sensing Felice's possessiveness of Jason. Would she herself ever see him again?

Two weeks had passed when Tony appeared at the office with some financial legal papers for Ian to study for one of his clients. "Come on to lunch?" he asked easily as he stepped from Ian's office after their meeting. He flashed her his winning grin.

"Don't tell me you don't have an eager woman lined up for a lunch date today," she teased him. It was an easy joke that had sprung between them.

"Oversight on my part," Tony shot back. "So have pity. You know I hate to eat alone." This was true, Lauren suspected. Tony seemed to spend very little time alone—there was no one to watch his show.

"Okay," she said with an indulgent smile. And she really did look forward to the time with him. She was finding her life quite lonely. Aside from an occasional lunch with several women co-workers, her social life was barren. During off-hours these women had their own lives, husbands, boyfriends. And after so long a time of forced confinement and inactivity, she was longing more than ever for company.

Lauren pulled her scarf tightly against the cold as they walked the few blocks to the restaurant that was situated on the ground floor within a newly renovated office building. It seemed all of Kansas City was undergoing restoration in a last attempt to save many of its graceful historic buildings.

A place apparently always awaited Mr. Tony Kenyon even though the restaurant was packed. After they were shown to the table, Tony excused himself to make a telephone call. "It takes forever to get a phone brought to you," he said, "and I really do need to keep a check on some prices. Order me some cognac." Giving a parting wink, he turned away.

Lauren ordered Tony his drink and a cup of tea for herself, then sat casually and discreetly studying those around her. Sitting at the far end of the room, she had a good view and felt somewhat like she was swimming in a sea of blue, gray and black three-piece suits, with an occasional splash of feminine color. Slowly her gaze moved in a circle, resting on the entrance, watching for Tony's return. A tall man stepped into view. She studied him, sensing something familiar in the slope of his wide shoulders. Recognition dawned, sending a small electric charge up her spine.

It was Jason Kenyon, standing alone and quite visible though the room was filled with perhaps fifty men in the same shade of gray business suits with silver touching their hair.

As if feeling her gaze, he looked across the room toward her. He seemed to watch her for a long moment. Wondering if he could truly be looking at her, she smiled. There was no flicker of recognition on his stern face. She couldn't clearly see his eyes at such a distance and in the dim light. He bent toward the hostess, spoke, then Lauren saw him make his way across the room in her direction. She sat there, somewhat in amazement, watching him weave his way between the tables, coming ever closer. A sense of anticipation lit her heart.

She waited, watching him unabashedly. His stern face cracked into a smile twice as he greeted people he knew along the way. Then he stood there looking down at her. He smiled slightly.

"Hello, Miss Howard." There was a trace of teasing in his tone as he used the formal address. "It's nice to see you again. Apparently Ian released you from the lion's den."

"Hello," she said, feeling herself smiling widely as pleasure swept her. "Yes, he does let me out from time to time." Jason glanced to the place setting and the drink across from her, and she remembered about Tony then. "Oh—" she waved a hand toward Tony's chair "—Tony's here. He had to go make a telephone call. Please join us."

There was a twitch of a smile around his hard mouth, but Lauren sensed no humor. It seemed a coldness slipped over the man. "Thank you, but no," he said with a shake of his head. "I think my brother would prefer to keep your company to himself."

Lauren nodded slightly, feeling suddenly quite shy, even rebuked. "I'm sure he'd enjoy your company, as well," she murmured, more as a politeness than anything else. She had the distinct impression that for whatever reason, Jason Kenyon would rather not join them. She was sorely disappointed.

Jason nodded, and just as he moved to turn away, Tony hailed him from the middle of the room. Rapidly he made his way around tables and people toward them.

"I'm glad to see you, big brother." Edgy excitement etched Tony's features. "Please, do me this big favor. I need to get back to the office right away. Treat Lauren to lunch for me, will you?"

Lauren was stunned. "Oh, there's no need—"

But Tony cut her off, giving her his winning smile. "I'm sorry to duck out, beautiful. But some business just won't wait—happened faster than I anticipated." He was already backing away. "Please...stay with Jason. I'm sure he'll enjoy it. And I'll make it up to you, sweetheart. I promise." She was left watching his tall, slender back as he hurried away.

Lauren glanced quickly up at Jason, then averted her eyes in embarrassment. He didn't want to have lunch with her; she'd already seen that.

"There's no need to stay with me," she said. "I'm not a child who needs a baby-sitter." She laughed as she picked up her purse. "And I'm not all that hungry—besides Ian doesn't give me all afternoon for lunch."

"Nonsense," Jason said in a low voice, but forceful enough to cause Lauren to jump slightly and to look at him. His face broke into a smile. "Please have lunch with me, Lauren," he said.

For a moment Jason wondered if she was going to. There certainly was no reason why she should. She'd come to have lunch with Tony. But then that lovely smile slipped across her lips and she nodded. "Thank you." Her voice was very soft.

Giving the waiter Tony's drink, Jason ordered coffee and steak for himself and lamb stew for Lauren. There were a few awkward minutes when neither could think of what to say. Lauren played with her napkin. Jason looked at her, glad to do so. He couldn't ever remember seeing hair quite the shade of hers, nor as shiny. Sleek and smooth, it turned under just below her chin and brushed the collar of her shiny blue blouse. Then he noticed her youth again, and the sour thought hit him that he was sitting where Tony had been. He was lunching with Tony's intended date—the woman with whom Tony'd stayed all night only weeks before. And who knew how many times since.

But these bleak thoughts faded when Lauren said, "I guess you men of high finance have many meals interrupted." She spoke lightly, looking for something to say.

Jason found himself drawn to her warm expression. "I used to. But over the years I've learned what to consider seriously as an emergency and what not to. It's a talent."

"Oh? And what do you consider an emergency?" Her brown eyes twinkled with delight.

Jason pretended to give the question undue consideration before answering. "Missing the comics out of my paper, running out of coffee and losing my season's pass to the Royals' games." He remained perfectly serious, enjoying the look of surprised delight that slipped across Lauren's face. "Certainly," he added, "never money. Money comes and goes. Always."

She laughed then, a warm, melodious laugh that drew a few appreciative glances, he noticed.

"You're a very wise man, Mr. Kenyon," she told him.

"I think so," he said dryly, allowing a trace of a teasing smile.

They talked of the food and the restaurant, of Ian
Walsh—where Lauren's fondness for the older man came
out—and of the fact that they were both native Kansas
Citians. Jason noticed three small scars at Lauren's wrist,
and halfway into the meal it occurred to him that she never
lifted her glass with her right hand and seemed to have a bit
of trouble with her fork. She held it differently than most
people, he realized after careful and discreet study.

They left soon after finishing their meal, Lauren insist-
ing that unlike Jason, who was the boss, she had to get back
to work. "I can go alone," she said, rising. "Stay and have
a second cup of coffee. We don't want any emergencies."
She laughed again that melodious laugh.

But of course he wouldn't let her. He wanted to be with
her all the precious time he could. He felt somewhat foolish, thinking of the craziness of it all, of how he'd longed for
her from afar like some moonstruck adolescent. It was all
so absurd yet so damned pleasurable, he couldn't let it go.

There were several small specialty shops within the lobby
of the building—tobacco, magazines, flowers and cookies.
As they passed the last, Lauren stopped, tugging Jason over
like a child. He laughed with a lightness he hadn't felt in
years. She chose enough cookies to fill a small bag and re-
vealed that one of the secrets she'd discovered about Ian
Walsh was his love of cookies. Then she chose one each for
herself and Jason. "Two for the road," she said, laughing
as she held one up for Jason to take a bite.

She was very close, and he caught a whiff of her per-
fume, a light, alluring fragrance he couldn't place. Her eyes
were dark and twinkled with life and joy. Very slowly, unable to take his gaze from hers, Jason bit the cookie she offered. His arms threatened to close around her, though he
resisted, leaving them hanging at his sides. A shadow of
uncertainty touched her face, and she backed away. As she
bit into her own cookie, she looked at him from beneath the

shelter of her long lashes. The effect was enough to tighten a knot inside Jason's stomach.

She was beautiful, and she made him feel things he thought had dried up within him long ago.

But she belonged to his brother. The thought shoved itself into his brain.

"I need to be getting back, too," he said shortly. Taking her arm, he hurried her through the revolving glass door. She was lovely, he thought hotly, and here she was flirting with two brothers. Apparently the night she'd spent with Tony meant very little.

"Please go on ahead," Lauren said when they stopped at the first corner.

Large snowflakes fell from the gray sky above. The sidewalk had grown quite frosty, and Lauren stepped carefully to the corner's edge. She was puffing. Her legs and back simply couldn't keep up the swift pace Jason was setting. Why, she wondered, had he suddenly turned so stern? Had she said something? She couldn't imagine what, and for the last seconds her temper had been rising. Why in the world, she thought in irritation, should she have to sprint beside him?

"I'll see you on to your building," Jason said, taking her hand into the crook of his arm. "The sidewalks are getting slippery." He gave her what amounted to a bitter smile. "Tony did leave you in my care."

Short of jerking her hand away and demanding to be left alone, there was little she could do but walk beside him. Thankfully he slowed his pace.

"I didn't know I was in the care of anyone," she said, more sharply than she intended, "other than myself."

He certainly was an odd man, she thought, irritated. One minute he'd been quite warm and the next minute he'd acted as if he were angry with her. She saw it as rude and didn't care for it at all.

A sharp stab of dejection touched her spirit. She'd been thoroughly enjoying herself with him. And had hoped, had thought, that he had, too.

They had reached the service alley that ran beside her building and were halfway across it when a quick movement caught Lauren's eye. Taking a second look, she saw a tiny gray animal limping beside the gray stone foundation of the building. A bedraggled cat, she realized, hunching its body and trying in vain to escape the snow. Lauren's heart tugged, and she would have stopped then and there, except for the hardness of Jason's profile.

When they stepped onto the sidewalk at the building's corner, she stopped, forcing Jason to stop, also. "Thank you. I'm safely returned," she said firmly. "You can cross here."

He looked about to argue, but hunched against the cold, snowflakes fluttering onto his shiny hair, he nodded with a goodbye and turned away. Then he waited a moment for traffic to thin so he could cross in the middle of the block.

As soon as he'd stepped into the street, Lauren turned and peeked down the alley. The cat, a kitten really, that looked like a scrappy battered bit of gray against the grimy black of the alley, was sniffing at a scrap of paper. When delivery men's voices boomed from far down the alley, its head jerked up, and it turned to run right toward Lauren.

She bent to catch it, calling, "Kitty, kitty." Just before it reached her, the kitten swerved, doing its best to run away with an injured leg. Lauren ran after it, haltingly as her muscles and the slippery surface would permit, only partially aware of someone calling her name from behind. She easily gained on the injured animal and was within reach when the feeble thing tried to jump up onto the nearby fire escape. It hadn't the strength to make it and fell very neatly right into Lauren's grasp as she lunged, striving to save the kitten from further harm.

But in her effort to propel herself forward, Lauren teetered off balance and fell, her knees taking the full force against the cold alleyway, one knee landing hard and square upon the edge of a street grate.

Pain shot through both knees and traveled up her thigh bones to her hips like fire upon an electric line. She felt her lower back pop. Involuntarily she squeezed her eyes closed, gasping at the intense pain and thinking: *Oh, Lord, I've done it now*. And still the pain seared as a hot dagger plunged into her hips. Her head spun; her vision blurred.

Chapter Four

Seeing Lauren crumple to the ground, Jason sprinted toward her. *"Lauren?"* What in the hell was she doing? It'd been chance, as well as some inner instinct still longing for her, that had led him to glance back to see her one more time and had curiously found her entering the alleyway. Now he reached her and bent close.

"Lauren?" He raised a hand to touch her shoulder, then hesitated, feeling helpless and uncertain, afraid of being too familiar, worried that he might hurt her. Finally, he swept the shiny curtain of hair from her face to take a look. Immediately he read the pain in her expression. Her face was bleached white, her eyes pinched shut. "What happened?" Jason demanded.

"I . . . I fell . . ." She spoke soft and slow and breathless.

"Good Lord . . . here, let's get you up." Gently holding her shoulders, Jason tried to help her stand.

A small cry of pain sounded from her lips, startling him. "Lauren? What is it?"

"My back," she answered in a pain-filled whisper. She opened her eyes then, and he saw the agony written there. "Give me a minute . . . let me get my breath." She tried a small smile and patted his arm as if to give him comfort.

It was then he spied a small furry creature nestled close to her stomach, clutched above the now-crumpled bag of cookies. "What in the hell is that?" he asked gruffly.

"A kitten. Its leg's hurt." She spoke so softly, Jason had to bend close to catch her words. Then even softer, "Just like me."

"Lauren . . . just relax," Jason said, then standing, he bent and slipped one arm behind her knees, the other high on her back. "I'm going to lift you. Don't try to move," he ordered.

In a gentle, fluid motion, he lifted her from the ground, hearing her sharp intake of breath as he did so. Her eyes were open, dark pinpoints in a pale face etched with strain. She dug her teeth into her bottom lip; her body was rigid. And she still clutched that stupid cat.

She was a feather in his arms, and he carried her easily up the street to the doors of her building. A woman coming out eyed them curiously and held first the outer door for him, then the inner door, as well. Inside the wide lobby, the concierge hurried forward.

"Miss Howard . . . oh, Miss Howard, what happened?" the man prattled, fluttering his hands.

"She's had a little accident," Jason tossed to the concerned man, without taking his gaze from Lauren. He lowered her as gently as possible into one of the chairs against the wall. Bending in front of her, he studied her face. Satisfied she no longer seemed about to faint, he turned his attention to her legs. Carefully he lifted her coat aside, prepared for the sight because he'd already spotted the drops of blood twirling down the shreds of her nylon hose and now spattering on the polished floor. Even so, he winced at the gaping wound he saw where the metal grate had dug into the flesh of her left knee. Miraculously the other knee was only scratched.

"Get me some towels—tissues—something," he said to the concierge as he pulled a handkerchief from his inner coat pocket. He heard Lauren breathing deeply as he pressed the cloth to the wound and tried to stem the flow of blood. "Are you doing okay?" he asked her.

She nodded, even managing a little smile.

"Liar," he said softly, gratified to see her smile widen. And he was quite impressed. She was calm and attempting to control her body's reaction with slow and rhythmic breathing.

The concierge returned with the towels, and Jason pressed them against the wound atop his own handkerchief. "You're going to require a trip to the hospital, m'lady," he said.

"Oh, no, Jason," Lauren protested immediately. "I'm sure a Band-Aid will do. The bleeding is stopping." Lifting her leg for a better view, a grimace of pain shot across her face.

"The bleeding is only slowed by all that wadding there," he replied gently, yet firmly. "You're going to require stitches, I'm afraid. Now, I'm going for my car. I'll only be a few minutes." He squeezed her arm, and she nodded. She still held that horrible-looking little animal. Turning to the concierge, he saw the man gazing at the kitten uncertainly. "Stay here with her," Jason told him.

Lauren continued to hold that stupid, pitiful cat all the way to the hospital. Jason suggested they drop it off in the small park adjoining the hospital, and she looked aghast, as if he'd suggested they murder it with their bare hands. He said no more, partly because it occurred to him it amounted to the same thing and partly because he didn't want to upset Lauren. She was so pale, so fragile.

When they wheeled her into the emergency treatment room, he was given custody of the mangy kitten, which had remained docile for Lauren, but spit and clawed weakly the instant he took it. A good deal of its fur was off in patches, and its front right paw turned inward, appearing permanently deformed. Jason didn't altogether care to be holding it.

With the help of a nurse, whose private opinion was that the animal wouldn't live the night, Jason secured a saucer of milk, a discarded though clean towel to warm the scruffy animal and a small box to put it in. It lapped several times at the milk, then closed its eyes. The nurse just shook her head and walked away.

Sitting on a molded plastic chair in the emergency room, Jason leaned forward, rested his arms on his thighs, interlocking his fingers. And waited. His thoughts drifted from Lauren back in time to Jeanne. He hated hospitals. It seemed a place for interminable waiting. His gaze kept returning to the swinging doors, looking for Lauren to return. Then there she was, and an unaccountable surge of relief swept over him.

When her gaze fell on him, a smile that seemed to glow spread across her face. It was a welcoming smile, one that said she was glad to see him. And Jason felt the ties wrapping around his heart. There was no denying the way she made him feel—things he'd thought had withered and died long ago. Gentleness, protectiveness, a deepening sense of life. He was so aware of himself as a human being. As a man. It was almost painful, this process of coming alive again.

It had taken nine stitches. It could have been worse, Lauren knew, and it may very well prove to be. Her back and hips throbbed. She'd strained her weakened body in the fall and could have pinched a disk in her back. In which case, she'd spend days in bed. She knew the procedure. They wouldn't know until the disk swelled.

She felt much better after pain medication but had declined the offer of a prescription, explaining she had plenty at home and relating her medical history to the doctor. He agreed to postpone X rays if Lauren promised to call her own physician the following day and arrange to have them then.

She hadn't wanted to face Jason. She was self-conscious and embarrassed. Adult women just weren't supposed to get into situations like this. What an idiot she must seem, so awkward, so childish. But when they wheeled her out and there he was . . . something broke over her, and she was so very glad to see him.

Jason carried her home, literally, from the hospital to his car, snowflakes dusting their heads, and then from his car into her apartment. His arms were strong, and he carried her easily. It embarrassed her a bit, made her feel like such a nuisance. But then her embarrassment gave way to blessed acceptance. She felt so cared for, so pampered. She held around his neck and breathed in the warm, musky scent of him. Her gaze lit upon the curious scar that edged his eye, and she wondered briefly about it. Snowflakes brushed her face, and she closed her eyes, allowing her head to rest upon his strong shoulder. It occurred to her she was being a bit intimate with a man she hardly knew. Yet it felt too good to resist. She liked Jason Kenyon's arms around her.

They could hear the telephone ringing inside her apartment, but by the time they'd juggled the box with the kitten, found the key and unlocked the door, it had stopped.

"To the couch," Jason ordered, taking the kitten's box from her, holding it with one hand and clasping Lauren's arm with the other. "They should have given you some crutches."

"Oh, I have some," she said sinking gratefully to the couch. She didn't meet Jason's gaze. What could she say? Thank you? You've been most kind? In her heart she wanted to ask him to stay and knew she couldn't. He'd done enough. She wouldn't impose further.

Jason helped slide her coat from her shoulders and with extreme care, as if she were delicate china, he removed her shoes and lifted her legs, resting them straight out upon the cushions. She observed herself with dismay, seeing her wrinkled skirt splotched with mud, her bare feet. She'd discarded her torn panty hose at the hospital, and now her legs were bare and bone white. Sticks, she thought, looking at them. Her left knee was swathed in yards of bandage, her right one bearing several scratches. Her entire being felt rumpled and exhausted. She was a mess, and Jason was seeing it all.

"Where are they?" Jason asked.

"What?"

"The crutches," he said with impatient patience as she reached to take the kitten from its box. "And a blanket and pillows."

Lauren blinked, feeling acutely self-conscious. It all seemed so terribly intimate—him carrying her, removing her shoes, seeing her pitifully pale legs. He was doing so much for her, and they hardly knew one another. And earlier, after lunch, he'd acted aloof and cool, as if he didn't want anything to do with her. What a klutz he must think her, she thought, recalling the night when she'd broken the fine crystal glass at his home. But even while all these thoughts flashed through her mind, she sensed he didn't want to hear any nonsense about her being fine and able to do for herself now, especially when she so obviously couldn't.

"In my bedroom closet," she said quietly, watching with wonder as he jerked off his tie. "The room at the end of the hall." Now he was slipping from his coat and unbuttoning his vest. "The crutches are pushed in the back left corner," she added as he dropped coat, tie and vest on the back of the chair and walked from the room.

She looked at his clothes for several seconds, then scooted down farther on the couch to relieve the strain on her back. Her hips ached like a dull throb just under the surface of pain medication. After partially opening its eyes and attempting to hiss, the kitten slept again, nestled down in its towel. Lauren would've taken it to a veterinarian, but that was impossible now. She simply couldn't ask one more thing of Jason. But she'd taken on the responsibility of the little animal, and she'd do what she could. At least now it was dry and warm, and Jason had said it'd had some milk.

With a large sigh she leaned her head against the wing of the couch. She'd pressed the bag of cookies on the concierge at the office building and requested he take them up to Ian along with the message that she'd had a slight accident and wouldn't return for the day. She thought of calling Ian now to explain in detail. She had to, she knew, but she was exhausted and couldn't reach the telephone at the moment. Such a blessed excuse.

There was no way she could get to work tomorrow, but she would the following day, she vowed to herself, even if in a wheelchair. She wouldn't let anything keep her bed-bound again. Besides, she needed the job. She had no income except that weekly paycheck at the moment. Her mind skimmed over the thought of the account containing Scott's money. It was untouchable, always would be.

Then Lauren thought of her mother, and her spirits sank even further. She hoped Sybil didn't find out about this accident, or she'd be home on the next flight, and more than likely insist Lauren move home again. Or she'd move in here herself.

Jason returned with the crutches, pillow, blanket and her robe. "You'll be more comfortable in this," he said, tossing the robe beside her. Leaning the crutches at the end of the couch, he plopped the pillows and blanket at her feet. She picked up the robe, embarrassed and uncertain until he said, "I'll make us some coffee." She caught sight of a knowing smile on his lips as he turned away.

At first she could do nothing but stare at the robe. Make coffee? He was going to make coffee? And what else? Perhaps, she thought dryly, whip up some cake? *Hadn't he done enough?* Her shoulders sagged as she thought of her predicament. Then realizing he wouldn't be out of the room forever, she moved as quickly as her bruised body would allow to remove her clothes and don the blue velour robe. She was bending awkwardly to place her pile of neatly folded clothes on a nearby chair when Jason returned, bearing a tray with two cups of coffee.

"Here, I'll get it. You just sit down before you fall and do further damage." His deep voice was gruff and commanding.

Lauren complied, feeling her screaming muscles give a sigh of relief as she sank onto the couch. Jason's hands were adept at placing two pillows behind her and easing her back against them. He went so far as to tuck a blanket around her. Like a child, she thought glumly.

When she reached for the kitten, he handed it to her, laying it gently on her lap. He leaned very close, and Lauren found herself self-conscious in all this, extremely aware of his repeated soft touch. A lump rose in her throat. Because of her own stupidity, she was a burden, couldn't fulfill her job with Ian, was of no use to anyone. And dear Lord, she'd broken this man's crystal and ruined his entire afternoon.

Good heavens, the man was a damn executive, president of a bank of all things—not a nurse.

The thoughts came as incoherent admissions and regrets. And although she tried to choke them back, tears blurred her vision, and then, mortified, she felt them brim over and roll down her cheeks. She saw Jason's arm, a blurry white shirt-sleeve, stiffen—and then his face swam before her eyes. Hoping in vain to hide her tears, she looked down.

"Lauren? Are you all right?" he asked, his voice anxious. "Are you hurting?"

She shook her head, trying with all her frail strength at the moment to hold back sobs. She simply couldn't cry before him. She wouldn't give in to the defeatist emotions of the moment. *She wouldn't!*

Then Jason placed a strong hand beneath her chin and forced her face upward. She felt his intense gaze. The tears streamed through her closed eyelids. The next instant he wrapped his arms around her, cradling her in his strength and warmth. The sobs came in full force then.

"I'm sorry," she mumbled into his shirt. "I'm so sorry."

"Shushh...shushh." Stroking her hair, Jason rocked her gently.

"I just hate being so much trouble... and it hurts... and I don't want to hurt anymore. I'm so tired of the pain." Her clenched fists tapped at his chest. It all flowed out of her, the frustration, the anger, the despair. But Jason's arms were around her, speaking in motion much louder than words, freely offering comfort and strength.

Gradually Lauren quieted, feeling drained, but purged, as well. She'd emptied herself of all the troubling extra baggage and was now ready to face her predicament once more. But, oh, how could she face him now? Hearing a faint meowing, she realized the kitten was being squished between them.

"Oh, the kitten," she murmured, pushing from Jason's chest. Their heads touching, they both looked down at the animal. "It looks pretty small," she whispered, stroking the kitten's gray head. One of its ears was torn.

"It may not make it." Jason's voice was gentle, as if trying to prepare her.

Lauren could only nod, a lump in her throat choking her voice. At least the small one was comfortable now. It closed its eyes once more, breathing shallowly.

Slowly, hesitantly, Lauren looked up and found Jason's eyes only inches from her own. They were the color of storm clouds and shimmered with something that reached out and wrapped around her, drawing her to him. She was here, with him, alone, and in a most intimate fashion.

The next instant Jason blinked, straightening, and the spell was broken.

Her gaze fell to his shirt. There were huge damp splotches and traces of mascara across the front. "I... I ruined your shirt," she said. Involuntarily her hand tentatively reached to touch his shirt, then drew back. Again she felt despair trying to edge its way in again. What had she done now?

But a wide smile slipped across his lips. "It'll wash—or I'll buy another. It's not an emergency," he said, reminding her of his remarks at lunch. He reached for a nearby tissue.

Taking it, Lauren blew her nose, chuckling then at the picture she made, and pleasured to hear Jason's laughter. She wiped beneath her eyes and hoped she looked somewhat better. Then she found herself smiling at him, her heart lifting as he smiled back. He had such a handsome face, a strong, almost rugged face—not the kind of face she'd imagine a man in his position having. And she liked looking at him, liked the way it made her feel.

Suddenly there came a hard and rapid rapping at the door. "Lauren, are you in there?" Ian Walsh's gravelly voice demanded.

There was no mistaking the look of surprise that swept Ian's face when Jason opened the door wide. The old man's eyes moved sharply from Jason to Lauren on the couch. And Lauren was no less amazed to find the husky, white-haired man leaning upon his thick cane in the center of her living room and demanding to know what had happened.

"I called here three times," he boomed heatedly. "That fool in the lobby said you'd split your leg wide open. Couldn't walk, he said. Told me Kenyon had taken you to the hospital." His hawkish, pale eyes perused her carefully. "I thought it was Tony," he said, casting a highly speculative glance at Jason. Jason's lips twitched as he extended his arm. Ian clasped it tightly. "Hello, Jace."

"Hello, Ian." There was respect and fondness in his expression. "As you can see, Lauren is off her feet for a few days, but she's alive. Please join us in having coffee."

"Fine," Ian said, walking farther into the room, looking around as he did so. "Jump on down to the street and tell my driver to return in an hour, will you, Jason?"

Giving an indulgent smile, Jason nodded.

Still quite amazed, Lauren watched Ian stiffly lower himself into a chair. "Devil of a thing, having to drive out in this weather. We'll have four feet of snow before it's over." He gestured toward the lumpy towel still on her abdomen. "What the hell is that?"

"A kitten," Lauren replied, remembering it then and the part it had played in her downfall. "I was trying to catch it when I fell," she said ruefully. She looked sheepishly at Ian. "I'll be out tomorrow, too, I think. But I promise to be back the next day." Her heart sank when the elderly man scowled.

"No you won't," he barked, sending Lauren's spirits into a nosedive.

He was firing her, she thought.

"Damn women," he continued, giving his cane a tap on the floor. "Can't get a one of you trained. You'll take the rest of the week off. Won't heal properly if you don't. I'll expect you Monday morning—half hour early," he said, matching Lauren's astonishment with an expression of satisfaction. "To make up for all this." He scowled even more. "And quit that damn grinning."

Lauren tried to remove the smile but couldn't quite make it. Ian's concern was all too apparent, at least to her, if to no one else, and it made her feel so good. It made her feel wanted. That was everyone's need, and perhaps the thing Ian Walsh lacked most in his life—the feeling of being wanted. But that's what Lauren had been able to give him these past weeks. And it had ended up bringing about some sort of relationship although she wasn't exactly sure what kind.

"You won't tell Mother?" she asked in a hushed voice.

"What in the hell would I be doing talking to Sybil?" Ian cut his eyes away. Lauren suspected even more than before that he was keeping tabs on her for her mother. She allowed the suspicion to show plainly on her face. Ian scowled.

Jason returned with another cup of coffee as well as a fresh pot. Ian barked at him to start a fire in the fireplace. "Looks to be ample wood there," he said, indicating the large wood box. "Too cold in here for an old man."

As the small flames flickered in the fireplace, they all talked for a while. It was evident Jason and Ian had known each other for a long time. They spoke of Jason's father, of shared acquaintances and of memories. Though very much aware of the present, Ian tended to dwell on the past. He told Jason a little about the book he was working on and mentioned several people he intended to include in it. Exactly an hour later, nearly as abruptly as he'd come, Ian left, and Lauren and Jason were alone once more.

She expected Jason to leave now. After all, she was safely tended and snuggled in at home. She could manage for herself. And yet, she disliked the thought of his leaving. Pushing this emotion aside, she smiled at him as he stretched. "Thank you for all you've done for me, Jason," she said.

He nodded. "You're welcome."

There was a long pause in which Lauren wondered what else should be said and found herself wishing so very much that Jason would stay. Whatever for? she asked herself, shifting her gaze to the kitten. Stroking its head, she tried to appear casual. Jason had stayed with her long enough; it was time he went home. And she shouldn't let him know her dread of his leaving. She wouldn't. It would be unkind to him, embarrassing to her.

Bending to the coffee table, he began gathering the cups and placing them on the tray. Cleaning up, for goodness sake, Lauren thought with embarrassment.

"I can get that later, Jason," she said, wanting to bend forward and stop him.

"Think I'll make more coffee." He looked at her a long moment. "Would you like some?"

Lauren looked back at him, into his stormy gray eyes. A sweet surge of pleasure stole over her. "I...yes, that would be wonderful."

He was going to stay. For a little while more, he would stay.

Chapter Five

Her apartment was warm and welcoming. Floor-to-ceiling shelves on either side of the fireplace were filled with books. The walls were liberally decorated: classic movie and circus posters, antique photographs and paintings, even a famous original watercolor among them, Jason thought, surprised. In the brightly colored kitchen, his eye was drawn to the refrigerator that also served as a background for small pieces of paper bearing numerous pithy quotes.

While the coffee maker did its job, he leaned against the kitchen counter and stared at a poster-size photograph hanging in the hall, that of a woman wearing some sort of costume and a mask. Though he couldn't be sure, he sensed the woman was Lauren. The hair was dark, the shape much the same. And she appeared to be in the middle of a dance.

His gaze moved to the curious room opposite that he'd noticed earlier. It was obviously an exercise room, a studio for dancing, he realized. A place for practice, with sleekly polished flooring, large mirrors and a free-standing bar.

Lauren? he wondered. It wasn't hard to believe and would surely explain the reason she moved with uncommon grace. Was it a hobby, or had she at one time been a professional? It certainly fit her more than being a secretary for Ian Walsh did.

His mind moved on to puzzle over other things, like the scars on her wrist he'd noticed that afternoon in the restaurant. And during the time Ian was visiting, he'd again noticed Lauren always lifted and held her coffee cup in her left hand, just as she'd done at the restaurant that afternoon. Remembering that she'd already had crutches, he suspected she'd been in some sort of accident, perhaps recently.

Jason found he wanted to know about her, everything he could. He needed to know about her.

No, he thought, raking at his hair. He didn't need to know anything about her. This was just one rare afternoon. He'd only stayed because he couldn't very well leave her here alone; she could barely walk. And he was the only one available, he told himself, knowing even then he was hedging.

He was doing this for himself as much as for her. How long, he wondered suddenly, had it been since he'd taken an afternoon away from work? Since he'd shaken the demands and the cares of that highly tense business environment? A wry grin touched his lips as he realized no one, absolutely no one, neither at his office nor his home, knew where he was. There were no telephones ringing, no decisions clamoring for immediate attention, no one asking advice or giving it.

And, he thought quietly, he was in a most comfortable apartment with a most beautiful woman.

Staring out the window, he saw snow thickly covering the sill outside. Though not yet four, it was beginning to grow dark. His conscience tugged at him. He probably should leave.

But there was time yet, he thought.

Lauren had plainly been glad when he'd stayed. He smiled now, recalling the look of almost childish delight on her face. Recalling his own pleasure at the decision. Then Tony's image inserted itself into his thoughts, and he remembered that his brother had failed to return that night from taking Lauren home. Had Tony stayed here with her? Had she made morning coffee for him? Where else would Tony have gone if he hadn't stayed? Jason couldn't help wondering. Somehow it just didn't fit. Why it didn't, he wasn't certain, just that Lauren didn't fit with Tony. Or was it simple wish fulfillment on his part? He hated the idea of Lauren with Tony.

Because he was attracted to her.

The thought sat heavily on him. What in the hell could he be thinking? He was from a different generation—damn, they'd have nothing in common.

Yet, it wouldn't hurt to stay a while longer. She shouldn't be alone. And he didn't want to go back to work, he admitted. Or even home. He didn't want to go back to the world outside. He would take the time now, this precious time. The world certainly wouldn't fall apart without him.

He placed the coffeepot and cups on the tray. It was somewhat comical; he wasn't used to doing such things, hadn't done them since the early years of his marriage to Jeanne.

At the entry to the living room he paused and looked at Lauren. She was intent on studying the kitten. Her shiny sable-colored hair fell across her cheeks as she looked downward. Her face reminded Jason of a china doll's. Square in shape, her face had full cheeks of pearly-white skin, smooth and soft like velvet. In that moment, she looked exceedingly fragile, exceedingly young.

Emotions tore at him. In this moment he longed to protect her, to take care of her, but in the back of his mind was the distinct realization of other, basic male desires that lay tauntingly beneath the surface. And for this he felt anger at himself for being so juvenile. And for being drawn to something that would be no good for Lauren, nor for himself.

But when he set the tray upon the table in front of the couch and Lauren looked up at him, a strange warmth touched his shoulders. He was looking directly into her wide, brown eyes. Deep, fathomless eyes that seemed to hold years of knowledge. They were searching him. And they were the eyes of a woman, not a child.

"She's so weak," Lauren said. Dark lashes brushed her cheek as she turned her attention to the kitten, stroking a finger over its head.

"You sure it's a she?" He slid the table back a fraction and crouched near, taking a better look at the animal.

Lauren's eyebrows were drawn together. "Reasonably sure." With the tip of her finger she lifted the kitten's deformed paw, then let it go. It dropped limply. "I wonder what happened to it?" she said in a small voice.

"She was probably trying to get warm in a car engine—got caught in the fan belt." Jason crouched there, looking at the kitten, but more aware of Lauren, her thin, graceful fingers, her fragrance, the way she was mothering the kitten, comforting it.

"What a strange place to find it," she said. "The middle of a big city."

"There are a number of apartment buildings and restaurant kitchens around," he said.

Lauren nodded. She glanced to him; he caught her hesitancy. "Would you bring a saucer of milk from the kitchen?

Maybe we can coax her to eat." Her eyes widened. "Maybe we could try some oatmeal."

"Oatmeal?"

"I have instant. All it needs is hot water..." She looked at him as if she'd like to withdraw the words.

"Coming right up," Jason quipped, pleased to see her smile. He reached for her cup of coffee. "And while I'm about it, here, you relax." Remembering the fact she always used her left hand, he turned the handle for her to take it easily.

She reached for the cup, then hesitated. Her wide brown eyes flew to his, questioning. Slowly her fingers slipped into the handle. "Thank you," she said softly.

"It's in the refrigerator," Lauren called to Jason as he left the room.

He knew, she thought, watching his retreating back. Jason knew something was wrong with her right hand. She'd read the knowledge in his eyes. He was the first person to ever guess she had physical problems. The first person perceptive enough to see past her careful pretense.

She thought of his eyes, recalling that first night she'd met him and the way he'd looked at her then, as if he were trying to imprint her image on his mind. And she remembered the way he'd watched those around him, quietly, as if distancing himself from everyone while remaining keenly aware of every small detail. Her lips twitched into a wry grin. No, Jason Kenyon didn't miss much.

He was such a mixture, this man. He was at once commanding, even a bit stern, yet he was gentle, too. Although Lauren sensed he was more gentle with her than most. Perhaps, she sensed, the gentleness didn't come easy to him.

They tried to get the kitten to eat some. After hissing and spitting a bit, it took three laps at the oatmeal mixture, then closed its eyes again. Lauren gently wrapped it in the towel, and Jason laid it on the tile hearth close to the fire. They'd done all they could now.

Jason turned on the table lamp and added several logs to the fire as darkness began to close in. Again, bent on his haunches, he jabbed at the logs with the long poker. His arms below the rolled-up sleeves of his shirt were strong, the hair dark and coarse. The flickering firelight lit his features, playing upon the small scar at his temple, sparkling in his somber gray eyes, highlighting both the dark and silver in his hair.

He was terribly handsome, carrying a sense of strength. Lauren liked looking at him, felt drawn to his strength. Even as she wondered why he'd stayed with her, she shook the question away. She didn't want wonderings to mar the pleasure she felt. The outside world was far away at this moment. She liked it that way and sensed that Jason did, too.

Watching the movement of his shoulder muscles beneath his crisp white shirt as he continued to poke absently at the logs, she sensed a heaviness deep within him. Something close to sadness, maybe even closer to quiet despair. A feeling of empathy swept her. She, too, knew such feelings. In that instant she wanted to reach out and take his away.

He shifted his position, not sitting in the chair, but resting his back against it as he sat on the floor, his legs stretched out in front of him. Lauren noticed his boots were shiny black lizard skin. He poured another cup of coffee for them both, and they drank it even though it was reaching the tepid stage.

They began to talk. It was easy between them, not at all stilted. They laughed and joked at first, all the while each seeming to quietly watch the other. Lauren admitted he didn't seem to fit the image she had of a banker. Jason said she didn't fit his image of a secretary. When she admitted she really wasn't much of one, he raised an eyebrow. But instead of explaining, she asked him about the scar at his temple, telling him it made him look more like a roughneck who'd prospered in oil, a casino owner or sailor.

Chuckling at her images, Jason told her how he'd come by the scar. In his younger days—his much younger days, he said with a chuckle—he'd been a rodeo cowboy, no less. He'd even seriously considered a career in rodeo. He hadn't needed to worry about money if he lost, he joked. But he was destined for the bank. He was the oldest male; it was tradition. He didn't elaborate, but Lauren sensed the heaviness settle upon him again.

They talked of their childhood, Jason speaking of Tony and his parents. His father had been forty, his mother thirty-five when Jason was born. They'd been thrilled to have Jason, near overcome with amazement when Tony was born. His mother, Ardis, was from Mexico City, he said, and Lauren realized where he and Tony had received their dark, Latin looks. Ardis had returned to Mexico to live after the death of Jason's father.

Then adroitly, she noticed, Jason managed to turn the conversation toward her own background. She found herself telling of her own family—average, middle class. Her father had been a lawyer, her mother a homemaker, and one brother, who'd also become a lawyer. Then, almost haltingly, Lauren began to speak of herself and the way she'd rather grown into dancing and the moderate success she'd attained.

"I've seen you in those!" Jason said, looking thunderstruck when she mentioned a commercial for a popular soft drink she'd participated in. "I didn't pay all that much attention." He spoke almost apologetically, and she laughed.

"You'd probably be hard-pressed to recognize me," she said. "I was dressed as a gum-chewing teen from the fifties. My mother was none too impressed. She always hoped I'd become a prima ballerina. But you have to be driven to attain that—or any great success—with dance. I never was quite dedicated enough. I just enjoyed, and I truly did prefer modern dance.''

"But why...this?" he asked, puzzled, his sharp gray eyes appraising her.

"An accident," she said quietly. She told him then of the car crash that had killed her brother and of the injuries to herself. She told him of the doctors' prognoses that she might never walk unaided again and of her efforts to do so. She spoke of it all in few words and found it wasn't so hard. A river of understanding flowed between them. Many words weren't needed.

When Jason announced he was hungry—and that she was too thin and needed to eat—Lauren insisted on helping prepare something. This time she refused to give in to his bullying command to remain on the couch. He helped her get into position on the crutches, and his hands brushed her body as he did so. Lauren liked even that small contact. And she nearly ended up sprawled across the couch because in positioning crutches, four hands were not better than two.

Preparation of the simple meal—eggs, toast and canned fruit—was somewhat a comedy of errors. Though she knew her "helping" was more getting in the way, Lauren also knew she was enjoying it and suspected Jason did, too.

On one crutch, she had succeeded in pulling the orange juice from the refrigerator when she lost her balance and began to wobble. Jason, frying pan in hand as he scraped scrambled eggs into the plates, dropped the fork he was holding and tried to grab her. Falling against his chest, she found herself staring up into his gray eyes. He was laughing—and then he wasn't. He was simply looking at her.

She felt his heartbeat thudding beneath his shirt. Or was it her own? Lauren thought he was going to kiss her. She waited, wanting to kiss him. Anticipation stirring, she looked to his firm lips.

But then Jason pulled back, placed the pan in the sink, and carefully helped her to straighten up. With precise movements he reached for her other crutch and handed it to her. His expression was cold and unreadable.

"You go on ahead," he said. "I'll bring the rest of this on a tray."

The warm understanding that had existed between them seemed to fizzle into the air. Lauren settled again on the couch, feeling her heart dip. She'd been enjoying these hours with Jason. She knew they had to end, but she dreaded the coming of that end. And she very much hoped it wasn't now.

Jason was quiet when he came and settled himself again on the floor. They ate, making occasional comments. Lauren didn't push him. She wanted him to feel free with her. Instinct told her this was his need. If he wanted to talk, he would; if not, she would accept. How could she think him interested in her, in kissing her? She was hardly attractive at this moment, on crutches, her leg and back stiff. How silly and fanciful she was being. Jason Kenyon was being kind; that was all. Their worlds were far apart.

But gradually their easy association returned, and Lauren forgot all these thoughts. They talked of inconsequential things—the refurbishing of the building that housed Ian Walsh's law firm and others throughout the city, the Stockman's Bank and anecdotes about its flamboyant architect, a television weatherman they both found amusing, sights they'd each seen, books they'd each read.

Lauren watched Jason's face, noticing the lines of strain round his eyes had eased, the sense of heaviness lightened.

How long they talked, she didn't know. She thought once of how late it was becoming, marveling that Jason was still there. But she wouldn't turn her wrist to look at her watch. She didn't want to know the hour. She simply wanted to enjoy this point in time, to hold it for as long as possible, as a person does when he or she know the moment is special, fleeting and will never come again.

Jason had made another pot of coffee, and Lauren was just shifting position to reach for the cup he held toward her when a searing flash of pain shot across her hips. She gasped and froze.

"What is it?" Jason's voice was sharp with concern as he took the cup from her hand and knelt beside her.

"It's all right." Smiling weakly, Lauren gingerly straightened a leg. "I've just been in one position too long." When she moved to stand, Jason took her elbow and helped her up. She moved slowly, achingly, but refused to let on to Jason how much it hurt. She hoped she simply looked graceful. She hated for him to see her like this. Glancing to him, she gave a small smile. "See? Much better." She sank back to the couch, feeling his keen gaze as she punched the pillows and appeared to recline easily on one side. Though it wasn't easy.

"Do you have some medicine? Something for the pain?" His voice was sharp.

"Yes." Lauren looked at him. There was no fooling him. "In the bathroom medicine cabinet. The bottle with the pink lid."

He brought her two capsules, and she knew he'd read the directions on the bottle. She took them, with him watching.

Jason tossed another log on the fire, then settled again into his position in front of it. They continued talking, but long pauses interspersed their conversation now. Their time was coming to an end, and Lauren knew Jason felt it as much as she. Was he as loath to let go as she was? It was a wonder, but he seemed so.

It had to be very late, though still Lauren refused to check the clock. She felt herself growing groggy and knew the pain medication was the main culprit. She never should have taken it; it was shortening her time with him. She suggested another pot of coffee, even though they'd already had three. Jason agreed and went to make it.

Lauren turned her head to watch the flames in the fireplace and listened to Jason stirring in the kitchen. She laid her head against the pillow and then closed her eyes, just for a few seconds.

With quiet movements, Jason added several split logs to the fire, then closed the protective glass doors to the fireplace. He checked the kitten, finding it still breathing lightly. He very much hoped the animal made it, for Lauren. He adjusted the blanket around her shoulder but refrained from brushing her cheek with his fingers. The action could wake her. He turned out the lamp; the fire lit the room with a flickering glow.

And very quietly Jason left. The ticking of the lock behind him reverberated in the silent hallway and throughout his body, as well. This special interval in his life was over.

Fastening his overcoat, he lowered his eyes against falling snowflakes. The Corvette was surrounded by mounded snow where the plows had been through. Parked on a small hill, it refused to go forward, so he had to back out onto the road in order to find enough pavement for traction. It was past three in the morning, the road nearly deserted. Streetlights lit the darkness with a fuzzy glow. With his foot pressing lightly on the accelerator, he started for home, but his thoughts remained on the woman who lay sleeping before the fire.

She was older than he'd figured. Twenty-eight he'd-pieced together from various things she'd said. He smiled dryly—not much older. He pictured her, her shiny dark hair, the way it fell across her cheeks, the way her dark eyes seemed to hold some sort of understanding, some wonderful secret. A special warmth, he decided, that drew him. He remembered the things they'd said, the laughter they'd shared.

He hadn't left immediately after finding her asleep. He'd finished his cup of coffee, then had actually dozed off himself for nearly two hours. He hadn't wanted to let this episode in his life end.

But it had to. He knew that. And it had ended the moment he'd stepped from her apartment, he told himself. If he saw Lauren Howard again, it would be an accidental encounter, a fleeting hello and nod sort of thing. That was best. Though it was a hard and depressing decision.

His spirits sank even lower when he saw light glowing within the kitchen as he drove around to the back of the house. Felice would be the probable one to wait up for him, and he prayed she hadn't. He just didn't want to face her now, didn't want to face anyone. Doing so would completely take from him what little joy lingered from the hours spent with Lauren. Perhaps, he hoped, the light had just been left on.

Using the remote control, he opened the garage door and drove into the black, empty space.

"Where have you been?" Felice demanded when he entered the kitchen.

He blinked as his eyes adjusted to the harsh brighter light. And to the bombarding anger. Felice's eyes seemed to flash as much as did her pink satin robe. Regarding her, Jason let out a sigh.

"I didn't mean to worry you, Felice," he said, slipping from his coat. "I've been out. Forgive me for not telephoning."

"Beth said you left for lunch and didn't come back." The cluster of diamonds on her finger sparkled in the light and drew his gaze as she gestured. "Tony said the last time he saw you, he'd left you having lunch with his friend, Lauren

Howard." Her eyes narrowed. "It's going on four in the morning, Jason."

"I know what time it is, Felice. I apologize. I should have called. But I can't change that now." He looked pointedly at her. "I am a grown man. I believe I can come and go as I choose. Now, I'm going to bed, and I intend to sleep past nine. Good night."

He left her there, in the kitchen, anger shooting from her eyes. He supposed he should feel grateful for her concern over his whereabouts. But all he felt was smothered. She wanted to know where he'd been. More to the point, whom he'd been with. He knew this. And he couldn't altogether blame her for it. But he had no intention of telling her. It was his business, and no one else's. Perhaps least of all Felice's.

It struck him then that there may be a much larger problem with Felice than he'd realized. She never waited up for Tony, never worried over his frequent nights out, nor questioned him as to where he spent those nights.

"Jason." Tony, dressed in loose sweatpants and shirt, his finger marking a place in a book, stepped into the hallway just as Jason reached his own bedroom door.

"Yes," Jason said, experiencing mild surprise and continuing on into his room.

He halfway expected to see their maid Grace poke her head from his closet. He'd simply been gone one night, he thought in irritation. It wasn't as if he'd never done it. What was the problem with everyone?

Hearing Tony's muffled footsteps follow him into the room, he glanced over his shoulder. "Is it something important? If it can wait, let it. I'm beat." He didn't want to talk about Lauren, not now, though he knew he'd have to tell Tony sometime.

Tony leaned against the dresser, watching as Jason slipped from his suit coat. "Felice was worried."

"So I discovered." Jason tossed his coat to the chair back and pulled his tie from the pocket. "I should have called her. I just didn't think." He spoke as he hung his tie in the closet.

Tony regarded him sharply and raised an eyebrow. "Were you with Lauren all this time?"

"Yes," he answered after a moment. He guessed now was as good a time as any. Tiredly he pulled off his still-unbuttoned vest and tossed it atop his coat. "She had an accident this afternoon."

"Lauren? How?" Tony shot in quick succession.

Jason sighed as he slipped the heel of a boot into the bootjack. "She was trying to save this injured cat and fell." He plopped the boot to the floor and worked on the other. "She gashed her knee and jarred her back, maybe pinched a disk. Can't be sure yet, but she did some damage, anyway, to those muscles which haven't fully healed since the automobile accident." He began unbuttoning his shirt.

"A cat? What for?" Tony said. "And what accident?"

Jason paused to look at his brother. "A stray kitten—she wanted to help it." He studied Tony. "Lauren was in a bad car wreck eighteen months ago. You didn't know?" he asked, although he knew by Tony's expression that he didn't. And he'd sensed when he was with Lauren that very few people knew. It was a private matter with her. And it wasn't unlike Tony not to notice. Tony's world and mind generally moved too fast to notice anything like that, especially when Lauren didn't intend for him to.

Tony shook his head.

"It crushed her pelvis, injured several vertebrae, broke her wrist," Jason said quietly. "That's why she has trouble with her right hand. Her brother was killed in the wreck," he added, stripping off his shirt. "They stitched her leg at the hospital this afternoon, then I took her home. But she can hardly walk, has to use crutches when she does. And she's in a lot of pain. I didn't want to leave her alone.'' He began emptying his pants pockets.

Tony sat on the end of the bed. "When did this happen?"

"What?"

"Her fall—today."

Glancing over, Jason found Tony's speculative gaze upon him. And he knew the questions going on within his brother's mind. "On the way home from lunch—the lunch you had me sit in for you," he couldn't resist pointing out.

"And you needed to stay with her until nearly four in the morning?"

"I stayed with her until three in the morning," Jason said evenly. "If it is any of your business. She needed someone. And I happen to enjoy her company. I'm sorry if you have a problem with that.'' He watched Tony's expression closely. "It's my understanding that there's nothing serious between you. Am I wrong?"

Tony glanced down, then back up. "No, there's nothing serious—yet." He paused. "But, Jason, don't you think she may be a bit young for you?" The words, the tone, were deliberately cutting.

Jason allowed a caustic laugh. "Tony, I spent an evening with her. I didn't get engaged. And she is quite nice to look at,'' he pointed out, as if that said it all.

Tony gave a crooked grin. "She is that.'' He rose and walked to the door. He stopped and half turned around. "Think I'll stop by her place tomorrow. See if she needs anything.''

Something cold and hard ran down Jason's spine. "Probably a good idea,'' he said, not looking up.

Tomorrow. For him the thought came as a dread. Tomorrow held only days that ran together, one after another. Where was it all leading? His mind raced ahead, listing the things he'd need to do to make up for his afternoon away from the office, as well as appointments already set. *Where was it all leading?* Bleakly, the thought returned.

Chapter Six

Felice quietly closed the bedroom door, then leaned against it. Her body shook. Her nails bit into her palms.

Jason was hers. He was hers. Her mind burned with the thought. It was a protest, a statement, a vow all in one.

As she'd stood outside Jason's bedroom and listened to him speak to Tony, she'd wanted to burst in there and tell them both. She hadn't worked all these years to have Jason finally emerge from where he'd buried himself in his work to turn to another woman. He was supposed to turn to her! To Felice!

She'd tried those years after her sister's death to make those words come completely true. But Jason had just never been able to see. He'd mourned for Jeanne and then buried himself in his work.

Jutting her chin, Felice walked to her dressing table. She sat and looked into the mirror. She looked nearly the same as she had when she first came to this house, she thought, picking up a hairbrush and attacking her short curls with almost vicious strokes. There was a bit more silver among the blond, but frosting only highlighted this. She had few wrinkles; she'd taken care of herself and at forty-four she knew she could pass for ten years younger. Though fairly short, she was sleek and trim. Many a man's eye turned at her figure.

When she'd first come back to Kansas City, when she'd realized the vacancy at the Kenyon home, she'd determined to fill it. She'd been divorced two years by then and was living in New York with her fourth lover. That was how she remembered them, by numbers. She remembered only one of their names, a Leon Cotton. He'd been a boisterous painter who'd eventually made a small name for himself. She'd been happy with him, but in those days he hadn't made much money. They'd lived on Felice's allowance from her father. It'd been enough, but not as much as Felice wanted. And Leon still didn't make enough. Leaving him hadn't been a mistake.

There'd been occasional affairs in the past years, of course. But she was very careful, very discreet, only indulging in a pleasant little fling when she was vacationing out of the city. She never took a chance on these interludes reaching Jason's attention. She never, ever, jeopardized her position.

She was right where she wanted to be, living how she wished. She'd never had a real job, a career. Her station in life was her career, she supposed. In Jason's house, she lived quite well on the allowance from her father. There was nothing for her to spend the money on except clothes and trips. And with Jeanne dead, she was the only one left to inherit a respectable fortune.

While the fortune was still pretty well intact, the family name, the Rischard name, didn't carry as much weight as it once had. But that didn't matter, Felice thought, because she was part of the Kenyons. That opened any and every door. And being a Rischard made her a perfect match for Jason. It made good sense. She knew his ways, had been brought up in the same fashion. She would be good for him—much better than her sister Jeanne ever was, Felice thought even years ago.

She'd always believed Jason would come to her eventually. And she'd stayed, she said proudly to herself. She'd stayed and become invaluable to him. If she hadn't succeeded in becoming Jason's wife in a full sense of the word, she had succeeded in carving a place in his life. She'd made the Kenyon home her own. She was the perfect hostess and a force in the best social circles in Kansas City. Jason was her escort to the theater, to luncheons, to a whole host of functions. If he occasionally spent a night away or there was mention of his various "other women" as she called them, she overlooked it. Those women weren't in the position she was. And she intended to see that no one ever took her place.

Least of all that clumsy little mouse of a child, she thought savagely.

But Jason's face tonight, his words—who was this girl to him? For the first time in the years since she'd come to her place in the Kenyon home, Felice felt a distinct threat. A threat to her position, her way of life. In an effort to deal with the fear, her mind cast about for things that offered reassurance.

Again assessing her image, her confidence returned.

The girl was pretty, Felice conceded, bluntly surveying the facts. Maybe even beautiful. And she had an inordinate amount of grace. But she was just that—a girl. A child, without the polish, the strength it would take to capture Jason, at least for very long. She was even vapid, hardly saying a word the night Tony had brought her to the dinner party. She'd seemed content to let Tony charm her, and everyone else.

The girl couldn't compete, Felice thought. There simply was no way. She, Felice, was the stronger one. She hadn't gotten where she was by being stupid and meek. Lauren Howard might have her sights set on Jason Kenyon, but she was in for a big disappointment.

She slipped into bed and switched off the lamp. She pulled the sheet and fluffy silk comforter snugly around her neck, conscious of the cool smoothness touching the bare skin of her shoulders. Her silk gown warmed slowly against her body. She longed for Jason, for his hands to rub the silk against her body, for his hands to touch her intimately.

He cared for her. She knew he did. She'd seen his looks of admiration numerous times. Her mind went back to a time nearly a year after Jeanne's death. She'd chanced upon Jason late at night in the kitchen. He'd kissed her, passionately. She'd wanted more, so much more, and she'd made it plain.

But Jason had broken away, shaking her from him with an expression of revulsion. She shrank momentarily from that painful memory.

But he had wanted her, she consoled herself. Of that she'd been certain. On that occasion and several since. Oh, Jason Kenyon thought himself so noble, she thought impatiently. He wasn't any different from the rest of them, though he liked to think so. He was a man after all—and she'd gotten what she wanted from many a man. Even much from Jason.

She could do much for him. He was beginning to immerse himself in politics, just as he had in the financial world. And she could help him achieve this new dream. He knew it; it would draw him to her. And she'd be at his side when he went to Washington, the fresh new senator from Kansas.

* * *

Lauren thought of Jason. He was with her when she awoke each morning. While she stretched and exercised her muscles so they would move smoothly. And he even intruded, delightfully so, into her meditation. He was there while she applied makeup and wondered how she would look to him. While she searched her closet and drawers for just the right clothes, just the right colors to make herself beautiful for him. He was there when she alighted from the bus in town and looked up to the bank and wondered which window was his. And every time a telephone rang, a door opened or her doorbell chimed, her heartbeat jumped in eager anticipation.

But the days passed, and he didn't come, he didn't telephone. Not to her home, not to the office.

When she awakened the morning following her accident and evening with Jason, the apartment seemed singularly empty. She lay very still, listening for his footsteps. It seemed he should be there. But, no, their moment in time was over, she reminded herself, recalling with a twinge of embarrassment mingled with regret how he'd had to leave with her asleep.

But her heart had never felt fuller, brimming with something she wasn't quite sure of. Love, she guessed, but was hesitant to say. Could someone truly fall in love in such a short time? Well, they could certainly begin to fall in love, she decided, smiling at her joyful thoughts. Whatever it was, she intended to grasp and hold it, for all it was worth.

The first thing she did was check the kitten, wanting to feel its warm and responsively alive body. Something with which to share her new feelings of joy, something living to give to.

But the kitten no longer breathed even shallowly. It had died.

Lauren sat for a long time holding its still-warm body in her lap, wondering just what she could do, wishing Jason were there. Its death hurt her very deeply. She'd felt like maybe she'd found someone to care for just as everyone had been taking care of her for so long. She'd hoped the kitten would make her apartment less lonely.

She consoled herself that she'd done what she could for the animal. At least it seemed peaceful now. Carefully, reverently, she folded the kitten into the towel and then into a brightly colored scarf. She wasn't physically up to getting out in the snow and digging through the frozen ground, but surely Jason would call or come by soon. He would help her bury it. It would help to share this with him. And thinking of him, the joy flickered again into her soul.

Even the pain in her back and knee, so severe that she had to soak in the bath for an hour and a half and take more anti-inflammatory medication, could not dampen her rising spirits. She felt more womanly, more alive than she could ever remember feeling before.

She cleansed and rebandaged her knee, stretched her muscles very gently so that at least she could walk in an upright manner, if haltingly, and dressed in a vivid blue thick velvet shirt and pants outfit her mother had given her. She brushed her hair and applied makeup, all the while listening for the telephone, for footsteps outside her door. She scolded herself for such silly behavior. The man had to work, after all. But still, she couldn't keep the hopeful expectancy away. She called Dr. Walter's office and made an appointment for the early afternoon, and she hoped Jason wouldn't call while she was out.

Just before noon the doorbell chimed, and Lauren hurried toward the door, clumping along as fast as the one crutch she'd given in to would allow, ignoring her protesting back muscles. She swung open the door, smiling, already imagining Jason's flinty expression.

But Tony stood there.

Disappointment stabbed her. She didn't know what to say, could hardly rearrange her thoughts.

"I came to see how you were," Tony said. He smiled, yet his eyes regarded her sharply. "May I come in?" He raised two white bags. "I brought lunch. Like Chinese?"

"Oh... y-yes," Lauren stammered, stepping back, searching for her welcoming smile and spirit. Her heart couldn't seem to push through the disappointment. Why wasn't it Jason? "Please—come in." She managed a smile then.

Tony stepped into the apartment, asking, "Have you eaten?"

Lauren shook her head. "No... and I love Chinese. It's very kind of you. Please, come on into the kitchen." She led the way, awkwardly on the crutch, but unconcerned any longer of how she appeared.

It was a pleasant lunch; Tony was unusually attentive. At her directions, he prepared the coffee maker and insisted on putting out the plates and silverware. He said Jason had told him of the accident yesterday, and he questioned her a bit about the car wreck of her past and the extent of her injuries. She answered the questions briefly, volunteering no extra information, relieved when he let the subject drop. She really didn't feel like talking. Tony didn't seem to notice, being his usual talkative and charming self. And Lauren did enjoy listening to him. Her mind wandered, though, as she picked at the food. She just wasn't that hungry, she told him.

Remembering the kitten, Lauren had to ask him to help her bury it. What if Jason didn't come? The thought struck bleakly, and she shied away from the prospect. Of course Tony didn't understand and offered to take the animal's tiny body down to the trash can. Lauren didn't know what to say, couldn't bring herself to explain how she felt, that a trash can simply wouldn't do. She told him not to bother, she'd take care of it later, and tried to hide her aversion. It certainly wasn't Tony's fault that she was incapacitated or that the cat had died or that Jason hadn't come as she hoped so much he would. She felt so alone. So terribly alone, even with Tony sitting right there.

Tony generously drove her to her doctor's appointment and then home again. And exhausted, she allowed him to help her up the stairs. After he'd settled her on the couch and helped her off with her coat, she assured him she was fine, that she simply needed to rest. The air was strained between them. Tony seemed to want attention she just couldn't give him. She pulled into herself, needing to, in her battle to deal with the ache—in both her body and her heart. Tony appeared relieved to leave.

Dr. Walter had examined her, but had ruled out the need for elaborate tests. They could quite possibly cause more pain and discomfort than necessary. She did believe Lauren had injured a disk, though not seriously. It would just take time. She very much hoped Lauren could return to work the following week, but cautioned against forcing her body to exercise. Rest, in bed, for days.

Jason did not come. He did not call. Just as the light of day began to dim, Lauren found a trowel and, balancing and hobbling with one crutch, she made her way outside. The cold air slapped her face and painfully knotted her muscles. She knew she was being deliberately stubborn, that she could have asked her upstairs neighbors to help her or simply thrown the kitten away. But she persisted, angrily, if slowly and with excruciating pain.

With tears streaming down her cheeks, she leaned down and stabbed at the frozen ground beneath the snow, over and over, digging deeper and deeper. She cursed her injured body, accusing it for making everything ten times harder to do and for being the reason Jason hadn't returned. And knowing she was being unreasonable at the same time.

She covered the small bundle with dirt and packed it tight. Then she hobbled back to her apartment and collapsed on the couch, where she fell soundly and blessedly asleep.

Each morning thereafter Lauren awoke with the hope that maybe today would be the day Jason would contact her. But he didn't.

Tony called twice. Their conversations were brief. Lauren just couldn't think of anything to say.

On Monday, despite a lingering stiffness, and wearing wool trousers to cover her bandaged knee, she returned to work. Her recovery had been good. She was exercising again, moderately, and walked only with a slight limp. The stitches were healing well and would be removed in another few days.

To her surprise, Tony came to the office that day, to check on her, he told her. He called the office on Wednesday. They bantered easily with each other, keeping conversation strictly on a casual level. Lauren puzzled over it. Tony seemed to want to develop a relationship with her but to keep a distance at the same time. And for Lauren's part, she wasn't interested in anything other than friendship.

As the days passed and no word came from Jason, it was her heart that suffered. The hope, the expectancy faded bit by bit.

It had been a special time, she told herself, striving to be terribly practical about it all—one of those out-of-the-ordinary times. Apparently it wasn't meant to evolve into anything more. If Jason were interested in more, he would've called. And why should he be interested? What in the world could she have that he'd find attractive, more so than the numerous elegant, exciting and physically perfect women he was bound to know within the circle of his life? There was Felice. Perhaps she and Jason . . .

But she'd felt his attraction to her, Lauren puzzled. Perhaps she'd been mistaken. Or else it'd been one of those fleeting things. Just as that night had. She strove to put all "fancies" as she saw them out of her mind. She needed to concentrate on her job. It took a lot of energy every day to do it, and now her body had been set back. She had to work again to regain strength and smoothness of movement.

She was very purposeful about setting her mind away from Jason Kenyon, and yet he didn't disappear totally. Lauren began to wonder if perhaps she should just go over to see him. At least to thank him. She really should do that.

Jason automatically answered his secretary's goodbye, finished the sentence he was reading, then tossed the report to his desk. Five o'clock already. It'd been one hectic day. As he had every day this week, he rose and moved to the window, looking down at the evening rush of people and automobiles moving along below. It was cold and clear, with lingering snow that had turned mostly gray from the grime of the city.

He was looking for her and knew it was foolish.

Tony had gone to visit Lauren the next day, just as he'd proposed. He'd made a point of telling Jason. Of that time and the times he'd called her since. Jason sensed his brother telling him very clearly: hands off.

Jason had wanted to see her, had wanted so very much to sit with her again in her welcoming living room. To see her smile, feel the warmth from her eyes. It had taken every scrap of discipline he possessed not to go to her, not to call her. Once he'd driven by her apartment. It had been evening and a cozy yellow glow had shone from inside. Three times he'd reached for the telephone, had actually dialed once.

But, he told himself, it wouldn't work. It wasn't right. He had no right.

Tony had met her first, was interested in her. Tony was his brother. And Lauren was so young. He wasn't right for her. It occurred to him he was being a bit too serious, too intense about it all. But a strong intuition told him that with Lauren it would be serious, very serious. It was best not to let it get that far.

He saw her then; she was several minutes late. She wore her white coat, gray slacks showing beneath. Her hair blew in the wind as she stepped from the building's elaborate doorway. And she was not alone. Jason's heart thudded as he saw Lauren slip her hand into the crook of a man's arm and lean familiarly toward him. Laughing, Jason imagined. The next instant he recognized the man, and he smiled, sadly, chiding his foolish reactions of jealousy and relief. What difference should it make to him who Lauren was with? The man was Ian Walsh. He had trouble believing it, but it surely was. The man swung a polished knobby cane in his other hand and walked stiffly.

"Jason?"

The voice sounding in the quiet of his office startled him from deep concentration. He turned to see Felice walking toward him. She wore a dark fur hat atop her fair hair and a crimson wool cape adorned with matching fur at the neck. The cape floated around her as she moved. She looked elegant and purposeful.

Jason sought to pull his thoughts away from Lauren, feeling an ache as he did. "Hi," he greeted Felice. "Is it that time already?" She stopped and leaned against the front of his large desk as he glanced to his watch, wondering if it were truly later than he'd thought.

"No, Jason," Felice answered with a wry smile and exaggerated patience. "I came early. I knew you'd be involved..." She waved a hand at his cluttered desk. "I came to make sure you didn't forget."

"I haven't forgotten," he told her with dry amusement. And I knew you wouldn't let me, he added to himself, mild annoyance touching him. He averted his eyes, running his gaze over the stack of folders, the thick report and his notes before him. He'd intended to work until six and then meet Felice. They had a seven-thirty dinner date with Senator Dan Collins and his wife.

He heard Felice's movements toward the wall cabinet and the soft click of the door as she opened the enclosed bar. "I'll be quiet as a mouse," she said over her shoulder. "Can I pour you something?"

His annoyance passed as he glanced up from his cluttered desk. She faced him, expectant, happy. She was very lovely, was smiling at him. He knew she loved dinner at the Top of the Crown and was looking forward to dining with Dan and his wife.

And Jason was, too. He was eager to hear what Dan could tell him about the prospect of running for senator, about everything connected with the endeavor. He and Garrett Baker, who had influence in the political vein, had gotten together several times in the past weeks to discuss the idea. It was a new direction, a new challenge, and he'd decided to throw himself into it. He hoped it would prove the remedy to the restlessness that had been plaguing him for the past year.

Suddenly Jason wanted to be away from all this, the sea of paperwork, the enclosing confines of the office. He very much wanted to breathe in the cold fresh air.

"Ah, hell," he said, and strode to the closet. Jerking open the door, he reached inside for his suit coat. "Let's go have a quiet drink."

Felice stared at him with sweet surprise. Catching her gaze, Jason smiled broadly at her as he rolled down his shirt-sleeves.

"Here, let me help," she said, her heart picking up tempo as she stepped over and held his suit coat for him, catching the pleasant scent of lingering after-shave. Hastily he slipped the coat on, then adjusted his shirt button and tie. Felice straightened his tie, giving it a final satisfied pat. "You're quite handsome, Mr. Kenyon."

"Let's go," he said.

She didn't let his gruff tone bother her. She was too happy and excited about a bit of quiet and intimate time alone with him.

He grabbed for his overcoat and then took Felice's elbow, fairly propelling her from the office. A gay laugh escaped her lips. She'd been right before, she thought. Jason was coming around to being interested in running for the senate. Very interested, unless she missed her guess—which she didn't very often. She'd wisely quit saying anything to prod him. How foolish of her to do so earlier. There were other, more subdued ways. Like getting Anna Collins to issue the invitation for tonight. The men could talk politics while Felice and Anna visited. Innocent and friendly, as well as a hook for Jason. And a nice opportunity for Felice to be with him, she thought with a high sense of contentment.

She'd also been very foolish to be upset about Lauren Howard. Jason had not even so much as mentioned the young woman. It'd been nothing after all. Felice knew Tony had been seeing Lauren; he'd made a point of telling her. And Jason would never consider stepping on his brother's toes. She should've known, Felice told herself, glancing to Jason's hard profile. After all these years.

Jason found the evening a pleasant one. Dan Collins was a near generation older than himself, and they'd never been close friends, but Jason had always respected the man. Now he found that respect growing as he and Dan talked. By the time they called it a night, Jason had committed himself to running for the senate seat Dan was vacating, but he wanted to keep the announcement between the two of them until he'd had time to talk to Tony and Garrett Baker and other associates who would be helping him. He wanted to firm up plans.

He was in mellow spirits as he and Felice went home. He felt invigorated by these new, challenging thoughts. But when he looked at the wide expanse of bed waiting for him, a hollow spot opened within him. He thought of Lauren. Then he firmly shook the image, the longing, away. For a change, and thankfully so, sleep came easily and deeply.

Lauren didn't make up her mind to go until she'd stepped out on the sidewalk, intending on catching a late lunch. She and Ian had spent a busy morning. Ian was pleased with the third chapter of his book. And he was pleased with her— actually had said so, in his gruff and reluctant manner. The fact was they were growing closer. Lauren had become a great help to Ian. Her artistic talent, he told her. She'd been so absorbed with the work that she'd not even thought of Jason since she'd entered her office that morning.

Now the cold, brisk air brushed her cheeks, and she turned her face toward the bank building across the street. Doing so had become a habit, she thought wryly.

It was the end of the week. And still she'd not seen nor talked to Jason. She'd not had the chance to thank him again for all he'd done for her. Not only did she want to see him, but not speaking to him seemed terribly rude. She really should take the time, she told herself, even as she was already crossing the street and heading for the revolving glass doors of the bank, drawn along as if by a powerful, unseen force.

Her steps echoed on marble flooring as she entered the lobby and walked toward the elevators. It was a high-ceilinged area, the low hum of computers mingling with the enduring banking atmosphere of impressive carved marble and polished oak of yesteryear. The banking lobby was separated from the main lobby of the building by glass doors that could be closed in off-hours, leaving continual access to the business offices above.

On the wall between the two elevator doors was a listing of names and offices. Lauren scanned the listing and found Jason's name, his office just listed as third floor. Hesitantly she pressed for an elevator. He probably wouldn't be in, she thought. He was probably out to lunch. She didn't want to speak to his secretary. What would she say? And why was she being so silly about all this? She almost laughed out loud at her frantic thoughts.

She was still debating her actions as she stepped into the elevator and the grand oak doors whooshed closed behind her. She could turn around now, she told herself. But she really must thank him, and it was a perfectly plausible excuse to see him. That was all. Just see him.

The elevator doors opened at the third floor. Slowly she stepped out into a wide, carpeted area and looked uncertainly around. It was quiet, a few people moving about and murmuring. There were several offices, but Lauren presumed Jason's was beyond the tall, wide double doors.

She walked through the doors to a spacious office, conscious of the thick carpeting beneath her feet and taking in her surroundings: white walls, ornate ceiling dating from the period when the building was built, sleekly polished doors and woodwork. A woman looked up from her desk and smiled. "May I help you?"

"I'd like to see Mr. Kenyon," Lauren said, and then added, "My name's Lauren Howard. I don't have an appointment."

The woman simply nodded, giving another friendly smile. "I'll see." Apparently people often didn't have an appointment, Lauren thought.

Just as the woman reached the door leading into Jason's office, it flew open and Jason appeared. His vest was unbuttoned partway down, shirt-sleeves rolled up, collar unfastened and tic loosened. His attention concentrated on papers in his hand, he barely looked up, saying, "Beth, get Henderson on the phone. There are some mistakes in this proposal—and I don't think they're unintentional." He raked a hand through his thick, silver-tinged hair. "And get someone up here to take a look at my extension. I'm having trouble getting calls through again."

The woman, Beth, was regarding him patiently and waited for him to pause before she spoke. "Jason, there's a Lauren Howard to see you."

Lauren took several steps toward him as Jason glanced to his secretary.

"What?" he said. Those thick eyebrows came together, and then he looked beyond the woman to Lauren.

She didn't know why, but her breath stopped in her throat. She looked at him, and he looked back.

"Hello," she managed finally.

Chapter Seven

"Hello, Lauren," Jason said. Surprise was evident on his face, in his voice. But so, also, was pleasure as his gaze moved swiftly over her.

Lauren's heart rose. Having difficulty thinking any coherent thought, she searched her mind for the reason she'd come.

Jason stepped back then, indicating his office. "Come in," he said.

"Oh, no," Lauren said hurriedly, knowing she was interrupting his work. "I won't take up your time." She felt suddenly quite shy. "I just wanted to thank you for all you did for me last week. I surely couldn't have managed without you."

Jason leaned an arm against the doorjamb. Lauren was conscious that his secretary had discreetly left. They were very much alone.

"You don't owe me any thanks," he said, giving a wave of his hand. "But you're welcome," he added as she began to protest. He looked at her a moment, and Lauren saw a shadow come into his gray eyes. He rubbed a hand to the back of his neck. "To tell you the truth, I enjoyed having an afternoon off for a change. I rarely get a chance to do that." His shoulders tensed, and Lauren sensed a peculiar guard come over him. "Is your leg—" He broke off, his gaze moving downward.

"I'm fine." She felt his probing gray eyes. "Really. The knee still looks pretty hideous, so I wear slacks, but it's healing."

He nodded.

"Well, I just wanted to say thanks. I'll let you get back to it all..." Inclining her head toward his office, she gave a small, understanding smile. Feeling as if she were the cause of his sudden discomfort, for whatever reason, she wanted to flee, wished she'd never come. But curiously, her feet wouldn't move.

"How's the kitten?" he asked, his voice reaching out to stop her as she turned.

She took a small breath. "She died."

The shadows in Jason's eyes deepened. "I'm sorry."

"We knew her chances weren't good." Why in the world did she want to run into his arms?

"Maybe you'll find another." His eyes seemed to pierce her.

"There are pet shops," she said, intent on looking into his eyes, not even paying attention to her words. They seemed to come out of her mouth, yet from far away. "And someone's always advertising to give away kittens."

Jason nodded. Awkwardly she stood there, uncertain of what to say, wishing Jason would say something. Just what, she wasn't quite sure.

She forced herself to move to the door. "I'd better be going," she said, deliberately giving a casual smile. "I told Ian I'd make it a quick lunch."

He moved beside her. "Ian still keeping you hopping?" he asked, falling in step with her.

"Yes, more than ever. He's going to have to make a few trips soon for research. I thought I'd get a nice holiday then, but now he says he wants me to go with him." She paused at the double doors. "Well—goodbye." She looked full at him, giving him time to say something, anything, to ask to go with her, or for her to stay.

"Goodbye, Lauren," Jason said, his deep tone low. "I'm glad you stopped by." And Lauren knew he meant it.

She walked away with that incredibly graceful walk of hers, not looking back. He was probably the only one who would notice the bare hint of stiffness, Jason thought, or know the reason she moved so slowly. He watched as the elevator appeared immediately at her summons. She stepped in, turned, then catching him looking after her, cast him a small parting wave. The elevator doors closed.

He'd used all his willpower to simply let her walk away like that. It would have been so easy to walk with her, to join her for lunch. And so harmless, he told himself, though he knew he was lying.

Slowly he walked back to his office and went to the window to look down upon the sidewalk. He was still watching for her to appear below when Beth called his name and entered his office.

"She's very lovely," Beth said with a wide smile. Jason could see the direction of her thoughts. It both hurt and pleased him.

"Yes, she is," he answered, Lauren's image playing teasingly across his mind. "But don't go jumping ahead of yourself. She's Tony's girl. And she's a bit too young for me." He chuckled as he said this, trying to sound light. He shifted papers on his desk, as if drawing his mind back to his work.

"A bit young, maybe. I don't know about too young," Beth said. Looking up, he saw her eyebrow raised. She shook her head and clucked. "She definitely doesn't fit with Tony."

"Oh?" Jason said, amused at her forwardness. Beth had been his secretary for fifteen years. At times he wasn't sure who bossed whom.

"No," Beth said firmly. "Jason, sometimes I can't understand how such an intelligent man can be so blind. And I mean you. You've had several lovely women interested in you in the past years. Yet you've never realized. Wake up and look!" She slapped a folder hard upon his desk at her last word. "The repairman will be here for the telephone in twenty minutes. And Henderson was out to a long lunch."

That was the trouble, Jason thought as he sat perusing the pages in front of him, unseeing. He was perfectly aware of Lauren's attraction to him and of his to her. *But she was young enough to be his daughter, damn it!* Couldn't Beth see that? It was all very romantic—but not very practical in the real world. Lauren deserved someone more her own age. Someone who could give her children.

A whisper came across his mind that older men than he had fathered children. He sat there a moment, lost in rare regrets. He and Jeanne had wanted a family, but Jeanne had never been able to carry a baby to term. She'd suffered two miscarriages. For a brief few seconds Jason again felt the pain of that loss, remembering his wife's cries in the night. And how he'd not been able to help her. Then Jeanne had required surgery, the complete removal of one ovary. There was still a chance for them, the doctors had said, but the months had gone by... and then Jeanne had died.

He thought again of Lauren, seeing her pale face, her coaxing smile. But twenty years divided them. So what? his brain argued. What's so important about that? He was healthy. But, he countered, for how long?

And, Jason thought firmly, there was no forgetting that Tony was interested in her. It wasn't right for him to break into their relationship. What relationship? something within countered stubbornly. Tony had been home early every evening this week. That didn't seem like a sign of a serious relationship.

Impatiently, with effort, Jason brought his mind under control, pushing aside his musings, just as he'd learned to do when Jeanne had died, and turned his attention to the work before him.

The day passed, and so did the next, and Lauren played upon the edges of his thoughts. Almost without realizing it, he argued with himself reasons he should and should not see her. When he did finally realize he was doing so, he did it more deliberately, seeking to think it all out. Reasons for not seeing her became less sound.

A week later, on his way to his bedroom after coming in late from the office, he heard Tony whistling around in his room. Stopping at Tony's door, he looked in to see his brother pulling on a sweater. The old affection of brother for brother swept over him. Rapping his knuckles against the doorframe, he leaned against it, holding his coat over his shoulder.

"Friday night on the town?" he asked, his heart giving an odd squeeze, suddenly envious of Tony's mood and intentions, and suspecting the object of his brother's intentions was Lauren.

"Yep," Tony said, casting Jason a charming smile as he straightened his shirt collar above the sweater. "How'd it go with Henderson? Get it straight?"

Jason shrugged. "Pretty much, after a few threats." His brother's unending energy made him feel suddenly tired—and old.

"What are you doing tonight?" Tony asked. "Felice said something about dinner at the Colony."

"I told her to go on. I just don't feel like it." Jason watched Tony check his pants pockets. He knew chances were good Tony had only half heard what he'd said. "Seeing Lauren?" he asked, careful to keep his tone casual and friendly, his lips offering a teasing smile.

Tony glanced at him and then away, and puzzled, Jason sensed a reticence. "No..." Tony answered, fiddling with the sleeves of his sweater. "Camie Pearson." Turning, he picked up a brush and raked it through his dark hair. "We're just going to a small gathering of the bunch." Jason caught an unmistakable hint of guardedness in his tone.

He studied Tony, who didn't meet his gaze. "I thought you were pretty interested in Lauren," Jason said slowly.

Tony glanced at Jason, then away. "I am interested in her. She's a wonderful woman," he said, checking his image in the mirror. Turning, he cast Jason a wide smile as he reached for his coat. "Don't wait up," he said easily.

"Do I ever?" Jason gave a rueful grin, and together they walked out into the hall.

Suddenly Jason felt very lonely. Earlier he'd wanted to be alone, had craved it in fact, and had told Felice to go without him with friends to dinner. He'd known Tony would be going out; Tony always went out. But now the prospect of the big empty house didn't sit too well.

He stepped away, saying over his shoulder, "Have a good time. Maybe we can catch a game of racquetball tomorrow."

"Yes, sure," Tony called after him.

It wasn't serious, Jason thought as he entered his large, empty-feeling bedroom. The thought started small, then grew and hardened into a clearly recognized truth. *Tony didn't feel toward Lauren any differently than he had any other woman all his adult life.*

* * *

The next morning, Tony and Felice slept in after their late hours of the night before. And Jason was glad. He showered, dressed and was downstairs by nine. He spent a few minutes drinking a cup of coffee, leaning against the counter and talking to the housekeeper, who told him there was a pet shop at the small shopping center not far from the house.

He was there when the shop opened and, after careful deliberation, chose a gray-striped kitten without a tail, a Manx, the shop owner told him. It was the smallest and appeared to shrink from the others. Enthusiastically, Jason purchased everything that could possibly go along with the small feline. He fairly bounced around the shop, choosing things as he saw them, plunking them down on the counter for the clerk to add to the bill: a blue collar with a bell, a cat-scratching post, a wicker basket and cushion, vitamins, catnip mouse, grooming brush, litter box, gourmet food and a fancy dish.

"Anything else I ought to get?" Jason asked the clerk.

The man looked at the array on the counter and said dryly, "If there is, it hasn't been made yet." He held his hand poised above the register, hesitant to push for the total.

A plaid blanket caught Jason's eye, and he reached for it. "This, too." He looked at the clerk. "I guess that'll be all," he said, feeling rather like a sheepish young boy. "No, hand me those little balls. It may like to play with those."

"It's a he," the clerk said in his sour voice as he plopped the packet of colorful balls on the counter. "Now, are we ready?"

Jason nodded, reaching for the kitten.

"Are we sure?" The clerk persisted.

"Yes," Jason said with a tolerant grin.

He was insane, he told himself as he drove the streets heavy with Saturday-morning traffic. The kitten let out small cries from the travel box the pet shop clerk had provided. Jason told the tiny critter that all his discomfort would be worth it when he got to his new home. Then he laughed aloud at himself for talking to a cat.

And yes, he was insane, he admitted, but it felt so damn good. He'd been taking everything too seriously. Tony was obviously not solely intent on Lauren, so he couldn't be stepping that hard on his brother's toes. And what was wrong with seeing her? Enjoying her company? Hell, yes, insanity felt damn good at this moment.

Lauren awoke grumpy and with the sniffles. Looking out the window, she glowered at the rising sun. Settling for a lone piece of toast and strong tea for breakfast, she sat at the table and moped. She knew very well she was moping and deliberately allowed herself to do so. There came a time when a person got tired of being sunny and optimistic.

The apartment seemed so empty. For once, Lauren almost wished herself back at her mother's house. Her mother and stepfather had returned from their trip the first of the week. Right about now, they'd be rising for breakfast. The house would be filled with the aroma of rich coffee and sweet cinnamon rolls.

With a sigh, she rose and placed her cup in the sink. Changing into a faded blue sweatshirt and pants, she tied her hair back with a scarf and began to clean the bathroom. The only thing to do when one felt positively hideous was to do something equally hideous in the hope it would make you feel better. It wasn't exactly straight-thinking logic, but from past experience Lauren knew it could work.

When the doorbell chimed, she was bending over the tub and was sorely tempted not to answer it; she didn't want to talk to anyone. But having second thoughts, she rose stiffly to her feet. If it were her mother, appearing unannounced as she often did, she'd worry if Lauren didn't answer.

"Just a minute," she called as the doorbell rang again. Releasing the safety chain, she opened the door, prepared in her mind to see her mother.

It was Jason.

Lauren just stared up at him, delight flooding her, mortification right on its heels. She groaned silently within. She was a mess, a total horrifying mess. Water dripped from the yellow plastic gloves she wore, her shirt and pants were splotched with water, her hair resembled dark broom straw sticking from beneath her scarf, no makeup, no shoes.

Jason didn't smile. "Don't you check through the peep-hole first?"

"I..." Lauren ran her gaze over his face. It still didn't seem possible. Hadn't she told herself she'd never see him again? That obviously he wasn't interested in her? "I usually do," she said in a small voice. "I was just expecting you to be my mother."

"I hope I didn't disappoint you." He spoke earnestly, and his eyebrows knitted.

"Oh, no, of course not. Please come in." Lauren moved back so he could enter. Her attention was drawn to the large box in his arms.

As he walked past her into the room, she hurriedly removed the gloves and laid them aside on the nearby glass-topped accent table. When she turned back, Jason stood in the middle of the room looking a bit ill-at-ease, yet happily so. Lauren couldn't help smiling in answer to his smile. She forgot then how she must look. Her gaze slipped from his face to the box he still held. Glancing back up, she cast him a questioning look.

"I brought you something," he said, bending to set the box on the carpet. She could sense his delight in the surprise, and it transferred to her.

She stepped closer, conscious of her bare feet, as he reached into the big box and pulled out another, smaller box that had curious round holes on the side. At once Lauren suspected, and when she heard what sounded very much like a faint baby's cry, she knew.

"A kitten," she said, breathless wonder filling her.

She watched his large hands reach gently into the box and pull out a small ball of gray fur, handing it to her. She cuddled it against her and rubbed the top of his head with her cheek.

"For me?"

"Yes."

Her vision seemed to glisten, and she was very close to full tears. She smiled at Jason. His normally stern face had a soft edge to it.

"Thank you," she said, feeling more than a little amazed at the intensity of her pleasure in seeing the tall, powerful man standing there in her living room. It was as if the brightest of suns had broken through the thick, impenetrable clouds of her heart.

Later, they sat watching the kitten play while sipping coffee, which Jason had made. Lauren had already cleaned herself up. She felt much better after putting on a bit of makeup, brushing her hair, and donning her blue velvet pants, matching shirt and a pair of shoes. As she'd dressed, she'd recalled the last time she'd put the outfit on, hoping, believing that Jason would come, only to be disappointed. But he was here now, and her heart seemed to sing.

She wondered what in the world had brought him as she found her attention divided between the small, tailless kitten and the large, handsome man. The last time they'd spoken, she'd distinctly believed he wanted nothing else to do with her. It had hurt, but she'd tried to push it aside. And now... now here he sat.

Jason was a study in contrasts as he sat upon the floor, dressed in dark slacks, a thick ivory-colored fisherman knit sweater and obviously expensive, dark snakeskin Western boots, his large hands tossing the small plastic balls for the tiny animal to chase. His low chuckle sounded several times, touching some inner place within Lauren.

He smiled at her now as he tossed one of the balls into her lap and the kitten scampered after it.

She laughed easily as the kitten rubbed up against her. Her gaze met Jason's and his seemed to hold hers. Time stopped, and it was as if Jason had reached out to draw her to him. Her gaze didn't waver from his; it could not. He rose, then bent toward her. She knew he was going to kiss her. Involuntarily she closed her eyes and lifted her face. Her breath stopped as his hand brushed her cheek, his lips touched hers.

His mouth was warm and, though the kiss was brief, she felt the strength of the man. And sweet desire slipped into her veins.

He drew away, and Lauren gazed up at him. For the instant she wasn't even thinking, only feeling something magically sensual. But then she saw Jason pulling away, physically, yes, but also spiritually, the same reticence coming over him that she'd noticed at his office.

Embarrassed then, Lauren strove to hide it. She didn't want to make a fool of herself or cause Jason any discomfort. It was hardly a kiss anyway, she told herself, just a small brush of his lips.

"Let's go for something to eat," Jason said. "I'm starved. I haven't had any breakfast. Have you?"

"No," she said, giving a shake of her head. And quite suddenly she was very hungry. "And I'm starved, too."

"Good." He seemed eager again. "Get your coat, and I'll take you to a place that makes the best omelets and sweet rolls in town."

Lauren rose, happy excitement touching her. But then the kitten playfully sent one of the toy balls rolling across the floor, reminding her of her new companion. "Oh, we can't leave,'' she said, casting Jason a worried frown. "The kitten—he'll be frightened left all alone. He's only been here a little while."

Even in that moment, she thought she must be a bit daft and even a bit childish, which she definitely didn't want to be. But she couldn't bring herself to leave the kitten alone in a strange place. He was so small and hadn't even been there a whole hour yet. Either Jason would understand or he wouldn't.

Jason cast the kitten a skeptical glance. It rubbed against his pant leg. "Got any eggs?" he asked, cocking an eyebrow.

"Yes." Lauren's gaze met his and held. It was as if he'd touched her in a peculiar, even intimate fashion. And she very much desired to be alone with this very special man. "Instead," she ventured, "why don't we send out for a pizza? We could even have an indoor picnic."

Jason looked incredulous. "It's not even eleven-thirty in the morning."

"Oh," she said, wondering if she'd proposed something terribly outlandish, but unable to see anything wrong with the idea. "Does that matter? Don't you like pizza?"

He didn't answer right away. Then his firm mouth turned into a half grin. "I love pizza." The light in his eyes warmed. "And I know a place I think we can go ahead and order it from, even if it isn't noon yet."

Lauren's spirit sang. She felt beautiful, and frivolous, and very attracted to an extremely handsome man. She felt very much a vibrant woman, a feeling that had been denied her for such a long time.

He asked her preference in pizza toppings, then placed the call, dialing the number, Lauren noticed curiously, from memory. He ordered easily, obviously knowing well the place he'd called. Lauren's eyes widened when she heard him request a very fine Chardonnay.

And she was thoroughly astounded when thirty minutes later she opened the door not to any simple pizza delivery boy, but to a young man wearing a dark suit and bearing an enormous wicker basket. He smiled at Lauren, then gave Jason a knowing wink as he handed over the basket and received several bills for his trouble.

Lauren could do no more than stare at Jason, watching him close the door and bring the basket to the coffee table.

Jason's lips twitched upward. "Might as well go all out," he said, giving a teasing wink.

"Have you ever had an indoor picnic?" she asked as Jason helped her spread a blanket on the carpet, where the bright winter sunshine streamed through the front windows.

"Once, years ago, with my wife," he said. He reached for the large floor pillows Lauren kept beside the fireplace. "We were in college—I'd forgotten until you asked." He looked thoughtful, as if he were remembering.

"Were you married long?" she asked, bending carefully to her knees, mindful of her fresh-healed cut. It occurred to her she may have overstepped the boundaries Jason seemed to need.

But he answered readily. "Sixteen years." He looked fully at her, and suddenly the apartment seemed very quiet. Lauren became aware of the kitten rubbing against her thigh, but didn't break her gaze from Jason's. "I'm old enough to be your father," he said.

Lauren knew a moment of amazement when she realized it was so. "I guess you are," she said after a moment. Her gaze ran over his hair and his face, finding a handsome, strong man. "But I just never thought about it."

Her eyes were wide, looking at him in wonder. Jason knew she wasn't kidding—she'd really never thought of it. He caught the sweet fragrance of her. And he certainly didn't feel in any way fatherly toward her. In that moment he was more alive than he'd been in years.

They sat on the blanket in the warm sunlight, eating pizza and drinking wine. It was another moment caught in time, and Jason wondered how many such moments a person was allowed in his life.

They clinked their glasses together in several nonsensical toasts. Lauren's hair glistened, swaying with her every movement. Her eyes sparkled warmly. And Jason knew sweet contentment—as well as tempting desire. It was a very good sensation.

They talked and talked, Jason speaking of Jeanne for the first time ever to another woman. Lauren asked questions without a hint of embarrassment. Jason felt he was emptying himself of a lot of dead weight, dark shadows that had been pressing him down.

Their conversation turned to Lauren and her struggle to be whole again. She spoke of her guilt over feeling responsible for her brother's death. And of her pain, of her fears, of her determination. And Jason became aware of a woman with great strengths as well as a fragility that went beyond her body to deep within her gentle spirit. She tried to protect herself from the blows life had dealt her, but there were cracks in the armor. The realization made him want to shield her, to take care of her.

Somewhere in the hours they relaxed upon the pillows, they pushed aside the empty pizza box, the drained bottle of wine and smudged crystal glasses. Lauren lay with her head on his thigh, the kitten curled against her. She was a warm and alluring weight, and he savored it, savored the tone of her voice, the fragrance of her. He was aware of her as a woman, and more aware of himself as a man than he could remember being in a long time.

He allowed his hand to stroke her dark and shiny hair; it felt like silk beneath his fingers. Slowly he stroked down her shoulder and then rested his hand at her rib cage. She felt so fragile beneath his touch. She was so thin, he could have counted each one of her ribs.

His hand ached to slip beneath the plush blue fabric of her shirt and caress the skin he knew would be like velvet. Her large round eyes regarded him warmly, and he suspected she'd allow him that, even briefly imagined her response. Then he firmly pushed the images aside.

His iron discipline held. They weren't ready for that. He wasn't ready for that. He'd told himself it was all right to see her, to enjoy her company—but nothing beyond. There could be no serious relationship between them. It was best not to do anything that could lead to more. This was the price he would have to pay for just seeing her.

And yet, a whisper came into the back of his mind: he was involved with Lauren. And, he suspected, quite seriously.

The shrill ringing of the telephone jarred the stillness. Lauren smiled wryly, saying, "It's probably my mother."

She rolled to her side in order to rise, but Jason put a restraining hand on her shoulder. "Stay," he said, smiling indulgently and tucking a pillow behind her head. "I'll bring the phone." He knew she was still stiff, perhaps sore, though she'd never admit it. He would have answered the telephone himself, but it occurred to him it might be unwise if it was her mother. He gave a silent chuckle at the old-fashioned thought.

Bringing the ringing telephone, he placed it and himself back down beside her. As she answered the kitten scampered up into Jason's lap.

"Why, hello, Tony," Lauren said after a moment. A chill cut Jason's spine. He looked up to see Lauren's eyes upon him, dark with apprehension.

Chapter Eight

Immediately Lauren felt Jason pulling away from her, though he didn't move so much as a fraction. Even not touching him, she sensed his muscles tense, saw his jawline tighten. Though she knew perfectly well she'd done nothing wrong, she felt extremely uncomfortable. It was definitely awkward with one brother on the telephone and the other right there in her living room.

Tony asked how she was, and she answered, hardly aware of what she said. She glanced cautiously beneath her lashes toward Jason. His expression was totally unreadable, as if he had no emotions at all.

When Tony asked if she was busy, Lauren said the only thing she could, what she thought best in that moment.

"Yes," she told him, softly and slowly, gathering all her poise. "As a matter of fact, Jason is here."

She wouldn't have had to tell Tony; she could have simply said she had company at the moment. Mentioned no names. But Lauren did it deliberately, refusing to be in the least less than direct, and by doing so made it plain to both men where her interest lay.

Why in the world she felt that both men would like to smack her, she wasn't quite certain. There was silence on the telephone line, and Lauren raised her eyes to Jason's, anxious at what she would find there. The thought that she was being ridiculous, blowing it all out of proportion flashed through her mind. Yet a strong inner instinct knew this moment was vitally important.

Jason's mouth crooked into a wry grin, but a low glimmer of exultance shone in his deep gray eyes.

She heard Tony exhale a long breath. "I see," he said. "Then I'll talk to you later, Lauren. Goodbye." Very formal, very stiff. She knew she'd hurt him and felt profound regret. Even as she gazed still into Jason's eyes.

"Yes . . ." she replied. "Goodbye."

Slowly she replaced the receiver, her gaze searching Jason's face, uncertain, even unaware of what she was looking for. He leaned forward, placed both hands on either side of her cheeks, raking his fingers into her hair, and brought his mouth down to hers in a full, hard, probing kiss. She quivered within, her mouth parting, seeking onto his. To balance herself, she pressed her hands to his waist, feeling the steely muscles beneath his sweater. He smelled of rich cologne and fine wool and male warmth. And his lips drew upon hers with a rough, strong sweetness.

Tony looked at the telephone with smoldering anger and resentment. Pushing quickly to his feet, he walked to the family room window and stared out at the yard still edged with frosty snow in the shady places.

Jason. Older brother, Jason, Tony thought dryly. He owned the house Tony lived in, governed the bank where Tony worked, even ran Tony's share in that bank. He owned half of their vacation home on St. Thomas and the family ranch in Kansas. And now it appeared he'd captured the attention of a woman Tony had been interested in—yes, it had been a casual interest, he admitted, but at that moment it didn't matter. The old rivalry he'd always felt toward his older brother had surfaced, strong and full.

He'd always loved Jason, respected him, yet envied and resented him, too. Where the resentment came from, Tony wasn't certain, shied away from analyzing, but it was a rivalry that went deep into his being, sometimes fueled by the fact that Jason didn't reciprocate the rivalry in the least, had never seemed to recognize it even existed. Tony was perfectly aware of the times Jason went out of his way to give to him—as a big brother should, he thought now, scornfully. Jason's brotherly regard had touched his heart many times, and probably just as many times in the past he'd resented it, used it.

Jason was the first born, self-assured, responsible. So much like their father, aware of duty, always doing the right thing. It had been ordained at his birth that he would eventually become the president of the bank. At their father's death, he'd been appointed executor of the estate, even to taking care of their mother's inheritance. It had hurt then. Surely their father could have split the duty between them, even though Tony had been very young at the time.

That he'd been the pampered one, Tony was fully aware. He was the youngest, born after their mother had believed she would have no more children. So much had always been expected of Jason, so little demanded of himself. To Tony it was as if they thought maybe he couldn't do it. Tony'd received their father's gold watch; he'd received the majority of the family money. But he'd never been able to have what he wanted most—to be the oldest, to be the firstborn. Perhaps more, to be Jason.

And he hated the fact now that he hadn't been the one to charm Lauren. Bitterly he pictured her face. There was only one reason she would prefer Jason, he thought hotly. She was after money and position. Jason was one step farther up the ladder than he, and quite possibly she considered Jason easier prey. Tony never leaned toward marriage.

Oh, she'd been a good actress, he had to give her that. He never would have thought it, and obviously Jason couldn't see it. But why else would she have turned from him? Tony thought of the cool send-off she'd given him the night of their first date. No woman had ever turned away from him.

It fueled his anger now just to remember that night. He'd cooled his anger and his frustration with Lacey Thornton in whose bed he was always welcome.

Tony didn't like what was going on between Jason and Lauren. *And he wasn't going to accept it.*

Hearing Felice's soft footsteps behind him, he turned. She flopped gracefully to the couch and tucked her shapely legs beneath her, saying, ''I wonder where Jason is. It's boring around here today.''

Tony thought of telling her, then resisted. He strongly suspected all hell would break loose if Felice knew. There was a bit of regard for his brother in the decision. Besides, this bit with Lauren would end quickly. Jason, ever the practical one, would see how foolish it was. And, Tony vowed, he would point it out to him.

Jason unlocked the apartment door but didn't follow Lauren in. Instead he leaned against the doorjamb while she switched on the lamp and hurriedly found the kitten, cuddling it to her.

''He's fine,'' she said.

''Yes, he's fine.'' Jason's tone was exceedingly low. His gaze moved from the kitten to Lauren's eyes. His eyes smiled at her. Then he kissed her quickly and commanded she lock the door after he left. She complied, warmed by his regard for her. Leaning against the locked door, she called goodnight, picturing his face and strong body as she heard his muffled answer and then the rattle of the outer door. Racing to the window, she watched him walk in long strides to the red Corvette and slip behind the wheel. She watched until he'd driven out of sight.

Turning back to the living room, she stroked the purring Leo, as they had named the kitten, thoughts of Jason still filling her mind.

She was in love. Totally. It had come so quickly, she marveled. But it was here, strong, full, overflowing. Lauren Marie Howard loves Jason Kenyon. She wondered what his middle name was. There was still so much she didn't know about him, she mused with a sigh as she walked slowly down the hallway to her bedroom.

She was vibrantly aware of every breath she took, the very pulse beneath her skin. It had been this way when she'd discovered she would live after the accident. The sensation had returned now, in full force and more. And she was so very grateful to be alive, to be able to experience this stupendous and marvelous feeling of being in love. With Jason Kenyon.

Setting Leo on the bed, she deliberately recalled Jason's kiss of the afternoon. Her blood grew warm, and the pulse threaded from her heart to deep within her stomach as she felt in memory his lips on hers, the sensations his hands had caused upon her tender skin. The memory was too sweet, made her long for him almost unbearably at that moment.

The kitten pushed onto her lap and nuzzled up against her chest. Laughing softly, Lauren again set the animal aside and searched through her drawers for leotard and tights. Even tonight she would not deviate from her discipline of exercises. Perhaps tonight she needed them more than ever before to take the edge off her body's throbbing energy.

Assured that Leo had come to feel at home, Jason had taken her to a quiet restaurant for dinner, and then they'd gone to a movie. Lauren hadn't kept her mind on the picture, however. She was too caught up in her hand being within Jason's, his deep voice, his laugh, his dry sense of humor. She thoroughly enjoyed the time, and her pleasure was centered in the fact that she knew Jason had enjoyed it all, too.

They'd returned to the apartment, but instead of coming right up they'd walked along the sidewalks, hand in hand, in the cold hush of winter nighttime, darkness broken here and there by streetlamps and porch lights. They'd talked, or simply fell into an easy silence.

He'd not kissed her again the rest of the afternoon and evening, had only touched her to take her hand. With feminine instinct, she'd sensed his control, knowing that he'd been as aroused as she'd been throughout their time together. She smiled now with the thought.

It was his way. Jason was basically a cautious man, a thoughtful man, who would rarely do anything without thinking it all out. He would not be one to fall into bed at the first rise of passion. Nor would she. By allowing desire to burn fully too soon, one could end up scorching the tender first buds of love. It was better to let them grow, to see if indeed they would grow.

In the workout room, Lauren sought to push all thoughts from her mind and to focus on her few exercises. She had not worked back up to her full routine as yet. But even as she stretched and willed her muscles to relax and work, Jason's image lurked in her mind. Because of these thoughts, and some playful help from Leo, she quickly ended the workout, changed into a thin, brushed flannel gown and snuggled beneath the plush comforter. The bed felt so large. She was grateful when Leo hopped upon the bed, purring loudly, and curled down at her shoulder. She stroked his soft fur and wondered what Jason was doing, how he looked in sleep.

She tossed restlessly, sleep eluding her as she reflected on the happenings of the day. Her surprise at seeing Jason, her delight in the kitten. Tony's telephone call, Jason's guarded expression, her own regret over the situation. But she would not let false impressions stand. She'd made it perfectly clear to Tony from the beginning that she wanted nothing but a casual, friendly relationship. She'd believed he understood, felt the same. And she would hide nothing from him. It was imperative, with his being Jason's brother, that he knew where she stood.

And that Jason knew, too. She was interested in him, didn't believe in playing games.

She'd been surprised when Jason had mentioned his age, had admonished herself for not thinking of it before. How could she not have thought of it? It was just that he was so strong and vibrant. She'd seen his maturity—but not as a great age difference between them. And it wasn't as if he was so ancient. She chuckled aloud at the thought.

Did it even matter, the age difference? It seemed such a silly thing. But not to Jason, she reminded herself. It bothered him. Her heart squeezed at the thought of anything in the world hurting him. And it didn't seem to fit; Jason seemed above such things. She smiled softly in the darkness. His concern for her, for his age, showed the warm, vulnerable side of the man. Would it be a problem? A whisper within told her that it could very well be.

But she was good for him, she told herself, and the realization warmed her heart. She was good for him. He'd laughed with her, had seemed to break out of the dark shell she'd sensed from the very first. She could give him so much, if only he would let her.

Was love always this puzzling, she wondered, this threatening? It certainly did make a human so very vulnerable.

But then, without that vulnerability, that openness to all of life, one might as well be dead. Lauren wasn't afraid, but she did worry. Perhaps this, too, was a part of love.

Finally the kitten sat right atop her chest, as if to force her to stop twisting and turning. And Lauren slipped into sleep.

The telephone woke her the next morning. Groggily she reached for it, wondering what time it was.

"Wake up, sleepyhead."

Hearing Jason's low voice startled Lauren fully awake. Pleasure swept over her, dismay following immediately as she glanced at the clock and saw the time. She'd overslept. For the first time, her inner alarm had not gone off. It was well after nine.

"I'm awake," she said to Jason. Would she see him today? Her hopes rose.

"Have lunch with me today," he said. "It's a beautiful Sunday."

Lauren glanced quickly to the window. Though the blinds were closed, she had the distinct impression it was raining. She smiled and refrained from pointing that out.

"I'd love to," she said. "How shall I dress?"

"Casual—and warm," he answered, a pleased tone to his low voice.

He wanted to see her. It had not been a mirage after all.

They went to the Crown Center for lunch, then wandered through the mall there, looking in at all the novel shops, like lovers on a Sunday afternoon, Lauren thought. Extremely conscious of Jason's large, rougher hand enclosing her own, she was aware of his every movement beside her, his thigh occasionally brushing hers, the heady scent of his musky after-shave.

They purchased fresh fudge and delicate sugar cookies, and in one shop Jason bought her a scarf of beautiful blue colors. Then he bought an umbrella so they could walk to the Liberty Memorial. Lauren wished she could run, but her back and legs were still too stiff. From the top of the memorial, they could see nearly the entire city dusted now with misty rain.

She snuggled into the crook of his arm, her own arm wrapped around the back of his waist. She felt somewhat dizzy. A fear of heights, she confessed sheepishly to Jason. He chuckled and held her closer, rubbing his hand firmly up and down her back. His sweater was rough beneath her cheek; his arm a comforting strength for her.

Day was fading when he took her home. Leo ran to meet them the minute Lauren opened the door. Delighted, she reached down and picked the kitten up. Jason stood very close, seeming as loath to leave as Lauren was to have him go. But he'd pass on the coffee this time, he told her, his eyes dark as the sky of the moment. Gazing into them, Lauren immediately sensed his desire, felt her own body respond, a heat growing deep within her. Bending, she placed Leo on the floor.

She waited, uncertain of what to say, of even what she wanted to say. Her body seemed to cry out for Jason's touch.

He gazed down at her. His hand came up and stroked her cheek. She thought perhaps he would kiss her, wanted him to kiss her ... but what then?

When his kiss came it was light and fleeting, and she experienced a disappointment, only to have her breath leave her the next instant when Jason turned back and grabbed her to him, pressing his lips roughly to hers. Again he held his hands at her neck, keeping his body a fraction away, as if to enfold her to him would be just too much to bear. She kissed him fully, passionately, sweetly drugged by his lips massaging hers. Every cell in her body longed to press against him, to sample the feel of his hard, strong body against hers. She resisted, fearful of pushing beyond borders Jason had seemed to set—and that she, herself, wasn't certain she was ready to cross.

Jason lifted his head. She struggled to focus, seeing first his firm lips, then daring to lift her eyes to meet his. A gentle, steady warmth glowed there. He smiled softly.

"I had a wonderful afternoon," he said, his tone husky. "Thank you."

"Me, too," she managed, hoping he could read the pleasure in her eyes.

And then he left, promising to call.

Lauren leaned against the closed door, varying emotions tugging at her. She was quite a bit irritated at Jason, at the way he would one minute pull her to him, kiss her, and then pull away, as if to slam down a wall between them. She gave a throaty chuckle. To her own ears she sounded like a woman who was more than a bit frustrated. And yes, she was, she admitted.

She longed for him. As she thought about it, a cautious voice sounded within her. "For heaven's sake, you've just met the man," she muttered aloud.

Sometimes that was all it took, came a whisper into her thoughts.

She wanted to be with Jason. She wanted to share his life and have him share hers. And she would see him again soon, she was sure of it, anticipated it, even though he'd left her only moments before.

And she did see him soon—the following day, Monday. They had lunch together. And Tuesday, as well. Quick, hour meetings, snatched out of each of their busy days.

On Wednesday Lauren flew to Denver with Ian to do research. She missed Jason, was amazed that she could miss someone she'd known such a short time. She sensed Ian's close observation and tried harder to force her attention on the old record books she was supposed to be reviewing.

Ian fumed that he'd brought an empty-headed female along, but Lauren realized it was more bark than anything else. She knew proudly that she was a very good help to him. She was still terrible at note taking and slow at typing and filing, but she was adept at picking out information from the years-old handwriting that Ian's failing eyesight caused him to miss. She saw to keeping his notes in order and within immediate reach. She was becoming better at typing from Ian's tape-recorded notes; at least these she could stop when necessary. And she handled personal things like getting meals when Ian would have forgotten, renting a car and driver and having his suits pressed.

She returned from Denver Saturday afternoon and, despite feeling a bit foolish, couldn't help listening for the telephone, waiting for Jason to call. When he did, a strange relief mixed with eagerness nearly overwhelmed her. It frightened her in its intensity.

They talked for only a few minutes, as if the telephone was definitely unsatisfactory for them both. Jason couldn't get away—a business meeting at his house, he explained apologetically. Lauren hurried to assure him it was fine. After all, she thought, why should he feel he had to run right over to her?

The following week flowers started arriving at her office and at her home. With the delivery on the third day of still another vase of long-stemmed roses, pink this time, Ian boldly demanded to know who they were from. Lauren told him, self-conscious in the revelation, yet unwilling to appear so to Ian.

"Uhmf," was all Ian said, chewing on the end of a cigar and moving his gaze thoughtfully from the flowers to Lauren.

With the fourth arrangement of flowers sent this time to her home, Lauren called Jason's office. Hesitantly she asked for him, nervous because it was the first time she'd ever telephoned him.

"Lauren?" His voice sounded surprised, even anxious.

"Jason," Lauren said, her heart warming when she heard his voice. "You have to quit with the flowers. I love them. Adore them. But flowers do last, a few days at least. I'm running out of room for them."

"Okay," he said, laughing. "I guess I was getting a bit carried away."

For the next two weeks they went to dinner, to lunch, to the theater, spent one Sunday afternoon visiting museums and art galleries, and the other just lazing around Lauren's apartment, playing Monopoly and petting Leo, who gave them not a moment's peace. Discovering Lauren frequently took a cab to church, Jason showed up on Sunday morning and took her himself. It was extremely pleasant to sit close to him for one whole hour. She admonished herself, though not too hard, for letting undisciplined, even sensuous thoughts dwell on Jason, not hearing one word the minister said. She might as well have stayed home, she thought, chuckling. But, no, it was wonderful to be with Jason anywhere.

It was at church that Lauren was forced to introduce Jason to her mother and stepfather. She was reluctant to do so, for some reason wanting to keep her relationship with him to herself, treasured safe within her heart. And also knowing full well the conclusions her mother would jump to. While being perfectly gracious, Sybil appraised Jason keenly. Lauren was surprised when her mother called later and mentioned Jason only in passing. When she hung up, she realized it was her mother's way of trying to let her lead her own life, also realizing that it couldn't be easy for Sybil.

Over this time Lauren was aware of the fact that few people either of them knew saw them together. On several of their outings, Jason greeted people he knew, but they seemed very casual acquaintances at best. And, Lauren realized, she and Jason went few places where they were likely to run into business acquaintances or colleagues. She wondered if Tony or Felice knew how often she and Jason were together, or if they had any inkling of their growing relationship. The thought struck an uneasy chord. For some reason she felt it best that they didn't know.

As the days passed, Lauren knew a growing love for Jason. It was both beautiful and frightening. She was intensely aware of him as a man, of herself as a woman. Sometimes she ached for him to take her in his arms, longed to feel his lips on hers, his body pressing hers. She wanted to make love with him yet faced the prospect uncertainly, too. This uncertainty stemmed partly from a normal feminine nervousness of facing the unknown with this man. Would she please him?

It stemmed also from Jason's own behavior. Though she believed he felt similar longings, had seen the revealing heat in his eyes, he was often withdrawn, guarded with her. He would kiss her, then pull away, hiding any emotion behind his stern expression. She wondered if it had to do with remembrances of his wife. Perhaps he could never fall in love with another woman, simply wanted to have a casual relationship. And yet she certainly didn't get this impression when he kissed her.

She wanted to speak to him about it, to be open with him, but she feared upsetting him, of breaking into his privacy. He was happier, more relaxed than when she'd first met him, but he seemed to keep a tight rein on himself, stepping back whenever he felt himself opening up too much, growing too close.

Once, alone in bed just before falling asleep, a panic assailed her. What if Jason were suddenly to quit seeing her? How would she stand it? Her heart hammered, and she pulled the covers up tight against an invading chill. The moment passed, yet the question remained.

Jason hadn't realized he was whistling until he entered the back hall and looked up to see Tony leaning in the family room entry, an expression of quiet contempt on his face. The whistling died on Jason's lips; a sense of caution took over.

"Have a good afternoon?" Tony questioned sarcastically.

"Yes, thank you," Jason answered quietly. He'd picked Lauren up early from work, and they'd spent the past couple of hours looking at cars for her. She was thinking of driving again. Disregarding Tony's rudeness, he further intended to ignore his brother by going directly into his study. When Tony followed, Jason knew there would be no respite. His brother had that small-boy belligerent air about him.

"You left the office early today," Tony said. His tone was accusing.

"Yes." Jason volunteered no more. He walked to the bar and poured himself a whiskey. He raised the bottle and a questioning eyebrow to Tony, but his brother shook his head.

"Jason," Tony said, "you can't be serious about Lauren."

"How serious I am is none of your business." Jason looked hard and pointedly at his younger brother. This inquisition had gone far enough.

"Come off it," Tony said, his voice rising. "I'm trying to help. You're my brother. I don't want to see you get hurt."

Jason took a sip of whiskey, then nodded. "Thank you. I'll take that into consideration." Placing his glass on the desk, he leveled his gaze to Tony. "For some reason you don't like my seeing Lauren. I kept off when I thought you two had something going. It is now my impression that there never was anything between you two at all. There is no reason why I, or any other man, should not see her."

"Good grief, Jason. She's half your age. Young enough to be your daughter."

"I'm seeing the woman, Tony. I haven't absconded to the islands with her," Jason said, much more blandly than he felt. Though his brother's observation hit a tender spot in his core, he would not for a moment let Tony see it.

He watched Tony, and he could almost see the wheels turning within his brother's brain. Puzzled, he searched for what was actually going on here. He realized his brother opposed his seeing Lauren more strongly than Jason had ever guessed he would. But why?

"Keep an open eye, here, Jason," Tony said, quieting his voice. "She's young. And ask yourself why she's suddenly interested in you. It did come suddenly, didn't it? Do you think it could have anything to do with your being a Kenyon?"

Cold, steel anger slipped into Jason's veins as the reality of what Tony was insinuating came into focus.

"I don't like what you're hinting, little brother." Jason's voice came low, his gaze holding Tony's unwaveringly. "Now, I'll consider it simply that you feel it your duty to say this to me, in private. But you'd better never say it beyond this room—nor to me again."

A flash of fearful uncertainty swept Tony's face. Then the belligerence returned. "You'd better consider what I'm trying to tell you, as well as your chances of getting elected to the Senate if you do get serious with Lauren."

Chapter Nine

A coldness came over Jason as he faced his brother. "I have heard you, Tony. And now I repeat—it is none of your business." His voice cut like a knife through the vibrant tension in the room. He stared sharply at Tony. For a moment his brother looked as if he would argue again. With steely eyes, Jason dared him.

"Fine," Tony said then, as if he had to have the last word. Stuffing his hands into his pockets, he pivoted and strode from the room.

Jason watched Tony's retreating back, then turned his gaze to the personal mail on his desk, impressions of the brother he knew flitting through his mind. He'd known Tony to get belligerent when he didn't get something he wanted, but it'd been a long time since they'd had words. And never over a woman. Then again, this was the first time the same woman had ever captured their separate interests. But Tony had not seemed all that captivated by Lauren, Jason puzzled, recalling the other women his brother had been seeing. Tony's anger went deeper. Rivalry, Jason suspected with a heavy heart. Tony'd always felt such a sense of competition, though Jason had done everything possible to nullify it.

To hell with it, he thought angrily. This is one time he would not pacify his younger brother. He could not.

Then with sharp clarity he remembered Tony's words: *young enough to be your daughter.* The words again stabbed their intended target. They were so very true.

"Is something wrong between you and Tony?"

Felice's voice came to him from far away. Staring at the envelope in his hand, he realized he'd crumpled it in his tight grasp.

"Jason?" Felice said, surveying him sharply. Tony had brushed angrily past her in the hall. Curious, she'd been about to ask him what was wrong when she'd thought better of it. No one talked to Tony when he was in one of these black moods. Since he'd been coming from the study, she suspected the two brothers had had words. An unusual occurrence; usually Jason smoothed Tony's feathers, not ruffled them.

"Yes," he said shortly, casting Felice an irritated glance.

Felice bristled at his manner. "What happened with Tony?"

Jason looked down to the mail on his desk. "Just a difference of opinion."

He obviously wasn't going to tell her what it was about. She sensed he wished her to go but denied the notion. Of course he wouldn't be thinking that. He cared for her. He'd just had a bad day. She stared at him until he looked back up.

"I'm sorry, Felice," he said then, almost absently. "I didn't mean to snap at you."

With a controlled effort, she smiled, pushing aside her annoyance, thinking of her plans for the evening. She didn't want them spoiled. "It's okay. Is there anything I can do?"

Jason, the mail once more capturing his attention, shook his head.

"How about going up and having a nice hot shower," she said, moving to stroke his temple. "Relax before dinner. I've invited a few guests this evening. That'll take your mind off the pressures of today."

Pulling out of her reach, he stared at her. With dismay, Felice saw cold stubbornness slip into his gray eyes.

"I'm sorry, Felice. I'm going out to dinner tonight," he said, his voice very low.

"But Jason, I've invited guests this evening. Garrett Baker and his wife and—"

"Then I hope you have a very good time," he said, cutting into her words.

"But they're looking forward to seeing you. Garrett in particular. You know he'd like to." He couldn't do this to her, she thought, panic choking her throat. He simply couldn't. "You've been out so much these past weeks."

He gave her a long look, and Felice knew she'd erred with her last comment.

"You should've asked me before planning a dinner party that required my presence, Felice," he said. Pulling at his tie, he stepped toward the doorway. "Now, please excuse me. I have a dinner date. I'm not sure what time I'll be home."

Almost unbelieving, she watched him disappear into the hall. Listening, she heard his footsteps thud softly on the carpet as he ascended the stairs. She had the almost overwhelming impulse to run after him and shout obscenities at the top of her lungs. But years of training stood her in good stead, and she simply remained quite still, pressing her fingernails into her palms, until the mad moment passed.

It would be all right, she told herself, struggling for control. It was just a passing phase. He'd get over it—whomever he was meeting tonight.

It was Tony who told her later just who Jason's date for the evening was.

"He's meeting Lauren Howard," Tony said offhandedly after Felice's carefully woven poise had momentarily slipped and she'd voiced displeasure at Jason's absence. Flashing her eyes to him, she sensed he was quite happy to tell her. Immediately she retreated behind a cool guard.

"Oh?" she said. "I thought you were seeing her."

Tony shook his head. "Not for a while now. But Jason has. Nearly every day for over two weeks. I told him tonight that he should think about what this could mean to his political career."

Felice simply turned away. She didn't say anything; she couldn't. Fear and anger swept down her spine like a sharp icy spear.

Throughout the evening she played the perfect hostess. "I'm so sorry," she told her guests. "Jason was called out to an important business meeting."

With pride, she knew no one would see the anger that stewed deep within her. No one but Tony, who cast her his mocking grin. Damn Jason! she thought. He can't do this to me. She would have to do something. But she just didn't know what.

During the last weeks of real winter, Lauren continued to see Jason. At first he seemed perfectly content with quiet candlelight dinners out at restaurants—and he knew the most wonderful places—or at Lauren's apartment, where he delighted in fixing a meal with her. She wasn't the best cook in the world, but she could make a magnificent salad, which she discovered was one of Jason's favorite things to eat.

Often Jason would set a fire in the fireplace, and they would eat their dinner in there, sharing with Leo, who happened to adore spinach. Afterward they would watch television or play cards, rummy or cribbage. After Jason taught her poker, she didn't want to play anything else. He teased her about having a gambling weakness buried deep within.

But after a time Jason began to favor going out, doing things among other people. She was fascinated when he had her join him for several business luncheons. She said little and listened intently, striving to learn all that she could that would help her relate to Jason better. Conscious of her right hand, she was very careful to use mostly her left. She didn't want to do anything to embarrass herself or Jason. They joined several of his friends for dinner, or if alone, he took her to his club, where the lights and people abounded. He never stayed long after taking her home.

Lauren sensed his unease and puzzled over it. Was something wrong with her? She felt so much when around him. Her heart beat faster, her breath came shorter, every cell in her body seemed inordinately alive and humming. Didn't he feel this way? He didn't seem to.

She'd thought at one time that he'd been attracted to her, but now, well she didn't know what to think. He treated her exactly like a very good friend, did nothing more than kiss her forehead lightly when he left her. It hurt and disappointed her. She felt anything but "friendly" toward him. For she'd fallen deeply in love with Jason. Love had formed a strong, sturdy vine within her heart, a vine that every day continued to grow.

It was inevitable that gossip about them would grow to the point of being reported in the social section of the paper. It happened after Jason had taken her to a charity dinner for the children's hospital. The short blurb hinted at Jason's bid for the Senate seat and then called Lauren his current constant companion. She didn't know why, but it made her feel uncomfortable, as if her privacy had been invaded. She didn't want her relationship with Jason to be on public view. What they had was so precious; she feared that the bold observations of others would somehow destroy it.

Some inner instinct realized how very fragile her relationship with Jason really was. More and more she seemed to be holding her breath, expecting him to say it was over. She knew she should talk to him about it, find out what in the world was truly going on. She even pictured scenarios where she asked him point-blank if he cared for her.

But her pride refused to allow her to do such a thing. And she shied away from doing anything she feared would hurt Jason.

Perhaps she should break it off, she thought. Obviously she felt much more for Jason than he for her. Perhaps to end it now would be the best thing. She would face it, get over it. Heaven knew she'd faced much more than this and had survived, she told herself.

But then the telephone would ring, and she would hear his voice, and her heart would pick up tempo in eager anticipation. More and more she longed for him to hold her, to be in his arms. To hear him tell her he loved her—and to express that love. Many times when she opened the door to his knock, she wanted to throw herself ecstatically into his arms. Looking into his deep ocean-gray eyes, she wanted to pull him to her, to kiss his lips and taste his skin, to press her body to his hard, virile frame.

She wanted Jason Kenyon in every sense of the word. She just had no idea what to do about it. She held back because Jason held back. For whatever reason, she knew he wanted this space to remain between them. And she accepted it, hard though it was. For now. *But she couldn't forever.*

And just beneath the surface, she knew the growing hurt of rejection.

On the last Friday in March, Lauren was typing the finishing touches on some notes for Ian and trying to hurry so she could leave early. She was meeting Jason; they were going car hunting again. Her back had given her only morning stiffness and ache for the past two weeks. She'd walked a mile every evening, except two evenings when a cold rain had set in. She knew she was ready to drive.

Jason had not been pleased with any of the cars she'd picked out so far. They'd all been at least five years old for one thing, and he was skeptical of their reliability. But she simply couldn't afford a brand-new one, or one in perfect condition. He'd hinted at buying her a car, and she'd absolutely refused, even been appalled at the idea, though deeply touched. Anyway, it had been his constantly taking her to dinner and lunches, even buying the food to cook at her apartment, that had enabled her to stretch her paycheck further than she'd ever imagined to be able to afford a used car.

She paused, staring at the typewriter, her thoughts turning to Jason. Something was going to have to happen soon. She knew regret. He didn't care for her, she thought sadly. Not like she did him. And she simply couldn't go on seeing him. Of course, she was very aware she'd told herself this a million times in the past weeks. And that no matter how much she tried to face facts as they were, a small nibble of hope remained that she could be totally all wrong. But that hope was dimming. Yes, she told herself now, she had to quit being silly, like an ostrich burying its head in the sand.

She had to face the fact that Jason did not care for her the way she cared for him. She even had the vague, uneasy feeling he thought of her more as a daughter—and she despised the notion. But more than once he'd mentioned the difference in their ages. Though he'd spoken in a teasing fashion, Lauren recognized a seriousness beneath his tone.

She simply couldn't go on seeing him, she decided, wanting something from him that he simply couldn't give.

She jerked the page out of the typewriter, and at that same moment Tony walked into the office. As always, she sensed his animosity. She'd seen him several times in the past weeks. He'd had business with Ian but generally said little to her. She still regretted hurting him but knew she hadn't done anything on purpose. If he'd believed there was anything between them, it had been all in his mind. And he certainly hadn't been giving her any kind of rush.

"I'm sorry," she said to Tony now. "Ian's gone for the day. Is there anything I can do?"

"No," Tony said slowly. "It can wait."

He looked at her, and she looked back, surprised that he didn't just turn around and walk out. She was further amazed when he perched on the edge of her desk. She ventured a smile, a slow hope stirring that Tony could be over his hurt.

"If you need him to call you, I can reach him at home," she offered.

Tony shook his head. He glanced around the office. "You've done okay here," he said, his tone casual and friendly. His gaze returned to her. "You're the first woman to tame old Ian. You must feel pretty proud."

Something in his voice then struck Lauren as almost threatening, taking her off guard.

"We get on well," she replied cautiously. She began clearing her desk, putting things in her top drawer. Suddenly she wanted to be away from Tony.

"You've done well with Jason, too," he said.

Her head coming up with a jerk, she met Tony's gaze. She didn't say anything.

Tony's eyebrows rose speculatively. "If you think Jason's going to marry you and you'll be sitting pretty, you'd better think again. He's no fool. He'll see through your sweet-girl act, if he hasn't already."

"What do you mean?" she said levelly, suspecting exactly what he meant and astounded at his words.

"Just that Jason's no fool. Sooner or later he's going to see what you're really after."

Amazed, angry, hurt, she just stared at him. How could he say such a thing to her? What could she say back? The next instant she heard Jason's voice.

"That's enough!"

Looking beyond Tony, Lauren saw Jason stride across the office. His face was contorted with rage. As she watched, his hands reached out, grasped Tony by the shirt and hauled him from the desk. Then he was throwing his brother up against the wall. The sound of angry voices mingled incoherently with that of scuffling bodies.

"Jason!" Lauren cried, without fully realizing.

The scene was a rapid blur before her. Threads of Jason's silver hair falling to his forehead, the scar on his temple etched with exertion, the clenched shoulder muscles evident beneath the dark sheen of his suit coat. Tony's angry eyes, his thin fingers pushing at Jason's shoulders. It all looked so unreal and out of place in the very proper and staid surroundings, between two men such as these. And Lauren knew only that she had to stop this terrible happening.

In a split second, she rounded the desk. "Jason," she said again, pleadingly, placing a restraining hand on his arm. "Stop it. Stop it, both of you!"

She felt the knotted muscle of Jason's arm quiver, saw the working of his firm jaw as he struggled to regain control. For a moment longer, he and Tony stared at each other, hatred boiling in each of their eyes. Then, relaxing his grip, Jason flung Tony from him and turned away, raking a hand through his thick hair. Lauren watched the tense set of his shoulders as he walked to the window. Her heart squeezed not only with concern but also with something very near resentful anger—at both men.

Tony straightened his suit and tie with hurried fumblings. He looked as if to speak, but meeting Lauren's gaze, he closed his mouth firmly and left the room. Silently she commended his good sense, because she was in no mood to hear any more from him.

As she stood very still next to the desk, her mind replaying the angry scene, she was aware of Jason's husky breathing being the only sound in the room. Her gaze ran unseeing over the green leaves of the philodendron on the top of the oak filing cabinet.

"I'm sorry for what Tony said." Jason's deep voice cut into the silence.

She heard a slight rustle of fabric as he turned from the window. She remained with her back toward him.

"Do you believe him?" she asked in a hoarse whisper.

"No!" He strode over and put his hands on her shoulders, squeezing. "Of course I don't." He would have turned her around, but Lauren pulled away.

Pivoting, she faced him. She searched his face, seeing the caution rising in his eyes. And hating it. It was again the guarded wall that she'd become so familiar with.

"Then why did you show more emotion with Tony a minute ago than you have shown to me in a month?"

His eyes narrowed, the guard rising even higher. "What do you mean?"

How could she explain? It amounted to accusing Jason of not loving her. What a humiliating thing to do. He'd never professed any love for her. There was absolutely no reason why he should. And she wouldn't let him see her hurt. She would not have his pity, his guilt.

"I think I'd like to go home now," she said, stepping to her desk, averting her eyes.

As she reached for her purse Jason's hand closed around her wrist. Her gaze flew to meet his and found his gray eyes glittering with determination.

"We were going to look at cars," he said. His grip bit into her wrist.

"I think we'd best leave it." She met his gaze evenly. Lord, she was so angry at him, and she wasn't even certain why.

"I'll take you home."

They drove the distance in silence. Slowly Lauren recognized her anger. She wanted Jason to explain his relationship with her, explain why he kept her at arm's length. Somehow her desire didn't seem quite fair, and yet, damn it! She deserved an explanation. Didn't she? Did he really suspect her of being after his money? *How could he think such a thing of her?* And if he didn't, what other explanation could there be? A quiet, feminine whisper questioned whether something could be wrong with her. Maybe she wasn't what Jason desired. All the speculations hurt.

She thought for a moment that he would drop her at the sidewalk, almost wished he would, finding the prospect loathsome at the same time. But as she opened the passenger door, Jason slammed the floorshift into Park and turned off the ignition. Walking rapidly up the porch steps, she heard him coming behind her. In the inner hallway she fumbled with her apartment key; his hand closed over hers, taking the key from her and opening the door.

Why in heaven's name, she asked herself, was she so aware of his scent, of his movements, of his aura of strength?

He grabbed her upper arm and whirled her around. She looked at him through blurred vision and realized, mortified, that she was close to tears. She wouldn't cry, she thought. It was all so stupid, so senseless. Why in the world would she cry?

Because she wanted him. She wanted him so badly. She wanted him to love her, *and he didn't.*

"Lauren..." His low voice came softly, traced with despair.

"I'm not in any way interested in your money," she said, her voice coming hoarsely.

"I know that."

"Then why?" She searched his eyes for the truth. "Why do you pull away from me so? Why won't you let me inside?"

Finally she'd voiced the crucial question that had been plaguing her for weeks. She waited to hear his answer, her gaze studying his face, trying to understand what was written in his expression. There was a hardness, a remoteness. Then gradually the remoteness crumbled. Before Lauren could think of what she was seeing, Jason, emitting a low groan, reached for her and pulled her roughly to him. His lips closed rough and demanding over hers. And she welcomed his kiss, all questioning thoughts replaced by a tide of heat rising inside her. A desire too long denied.

All the pent-up, frustrated longing of the past month poured from Jason as he pressed Lauren's quivering body to his and hungrily claimed her lips. Then as if realizing the very preciousness he held in his arms, he gentled, savoring the feel of feminine lips, moist and soft as velvet, beneath his own. Lauren's eager, trembling response set his blood to racing.

Her warm, womanly scent filled his nostrils, her passion seeped into the empty place in his heart. Thoughts of practicalities, of right and wrong slipped away. For just these precious minutes he took solace in her and forgot the reasons he'd kept from doing just this for so long.

Dragging his mouth from hers, he gasped for breath and tasted the softness of her skin from her face to her neck, catching the saltiness of tears.

"Jason... Jason." Her breath teased his own neck, her husky, pleading voice ripping through him. And then he was kissing her again, running his hands feverishly up and down the curves of her body. A body that had been growing slowly fuller with every passing day, right before his eyes. He pressed and kneaded the outline of her breasts, then moved to her hips, savoring every inch of her.

Images flashed through his mind, fanning the flames of a passion too long denied. Lauren's dark eyes, filled with heat. Her slow, gentle, loving smile. Her satiny skin that beckoned for his touch. Her scent that struck a chord deep within him. All the things he'd tried to block from his mind but simply pushed to the back, to simmer, to taunt.

The sweet throbbing in his loins was almost unbearable. Instinctively he pulled Lauren against him, trying to assuage the ache. Rubbing his cheek against her hair, he delighted in the silky feel of it. Through the soft fabric of her dress he felt her pulse beating everywhere his hands touched. She was heavy against him, giving, trusting. She was beautiful, clear through. The most beautiful human being he'd ever known. And he wanted her, more than ever before.

Yet even into this heady, heavenly moment, his sense of discipline spoke. Along with a very real fear. For if he took Lauren to him, he knew he would be bound by her—and he wasn't at all sure that was what he wanted.

If he gave in to his desire, what would he have left of himself? He'd hardly known who he was in months, but he'd managed to hold to a scrap of discipline, a scrap of self-respect, yes, even a scrap of much-needed independence. If he threw aside what he believed to be right, what would he have left?

And it was wrong to take from Lauren and not give back.

The thought rocked him to the core, and he clutched her to him. He didn't know if he loved her. *Oh, Lord, he didn't know anything anymore.* He'd lost himself in some crazy phase of his life. He knew he wanted her, passionately, sensually. He wanted to take all she had to give.

But what could he offer in return? What did he want to offer? Money? Security? An affair? None of this fit Lauren, nor was it in the least worth what she offered him. That she believed herself in love with him had been plain for a long time. He'd tried to deny it to himself, feeling the guilt heavily, but it was deniable no longer.

Oh God, what had he done? What was he to do now?

The inner answer was almost too much to face.

Slowly his strength returned, though when Lauren moved against him, sending a flash of heat throughout his body, he almost lost it all. Then, firmly, he held her from him and with a will of iron forced himself to look at her. She gazed up at him with those fathomless dark eyes; they were glazed with desire, and questions, too. He owed her some answers.

"We can't, Lauren," Jason said, his voice low and husky, anguish written across his face.

Lauren looked at him and tried to bring some sense into her whirling mind. At that moment she could only feel. Her heart pounded, and her body throbbed with heat and longing, a true and vibrant ache that only Jason could soothe. And he'd pulled away. She needed him to touch her, and he'd pulled away. She loved him. But he'd pulled away.

"But I love you," she said. She had to tell him, felt she would have burst if she hadn't said it. And didn't it matter to him?

Jason raked a shaky hand through his thick hair and then looked at her again. She thought she died a little at the look, feeling pain, humiliation.

"I'm sorry, Lauren," he said then. "I didn't mean for you to fall in love."

"What did you mean then?" she asked bluntly, wanting to strike out. She trembled with physical and emotional longing. "Why have you been seeing me? What have all these dinners and lunches and romantic afternoon outings been about?"

He looked at her for a long minute, regret stamped on his face. She shrank from the expression.

"Damn it, Lauren!" He said. "I don't know what it's all about. I don't know what anything's about. I haven't for months. I'm nearly twenty years older than you. It wouldn't change anything if I did love you. It would never work for us."

"If you did love me?"

"I don't know, Lauren. I can't say I do when I just don't know." Heat crept into his deep gray eyes. "I know I want you. It's been all I could do to keep my hands off of you for all these weeks. But that's not love."

He couldn't say that he loved her. As far as Lauren could see, that said it all.

Jason gave a caustic laugh. "Lauren, I'm forty-eight years old. And for the first time in my life I don't know what direction my life is taking. I don't know who I am anymore. I think the popular term is midlife crisis." His eyes turned cold. "And believe me, it is. I've found myself doing things I never thought I'd do, wanting things that I've never wanted before, hating the life I've spent all these years building—feeling trapped by it." His expression softened. "And then I met you. You made me feel things I thought had passed forever. I began to feel alive again. With you I've even begun to believe in life again, and in myself."

Listening to him, Lauren wanted to put her hands over her ears, to deny his words. Because she sensed he was going to tell her goodbye. She'd wanted to hear the truth of what was between them, she told herself. Now he was telling her. That it couldn't be the words of love she longed for was something she was going to have to face. And, damn it, she didn't want to face it. It was asking too much for her to bear one more loss in her life.

"I care for you, Lauren," Jason said then. "But I can't honestly say if it's love or just the result of my craziness at the moment. And I can't live my life depending on you to fill it up. I have to find my own way."

"I can wait, Jason," she offered. If she could just get him to stay with her. Surely in time he would realize he loved her. Together they could face anything.

He shook his head, saying gently, "I can't go on being around you. Not and keep my hands off you."

She hated his gentleness in that moment. He was treating her more like a child than an adult woman. Her gaze locked with his as she listened and absorbed his words. Seeing the heat in his eyes, she felt her own blood pulsing faster through her veins.

"If we made love, I don't think I could tear myself away from you," he said, his voice husky.

His gaze moved then, downward, like a soft caress to her lips, to her throat, sliding down her body. As if feeling his touch, she stood unable to move, her breath caught in the back of her throat.

"I won't go to bed with you." Jason spoke almost defiantly. "I won't settle for an affair with you—and I won't let you settle for that, either." He smiled sadly. "Not with you. I'm no saint, but it would tear us both apart to have an affair. I'd feel guilty every time I left you. And you'd have so much less than you deserve. I just can't. Not with you."

"But . . ." She stopped, uncertain of what to say, if even she should say anything. She could partly understand him; it touched her deeply. He cared for her too much to take from her without feeling he should give. She had to stop herself from degrading them both by begging him to stay with her, begging him to throw aside the principles that made him the very man he was. The man she loved.

If it were possible, his eyes seemed to grow darker. "Lauren," he said, "you deserve so much more than I can give you. Someone your own age, who can give you children, grow old *with* you, not years ahead of you."

So there it was again—the years that separated them, that she couldn't just brush aside and treat as if they didn't exist. She'd known deep inside that the difference in their ages could very well cause trouble.

"You're not old, Jason." The idea was ludicrous. Couldn't he see in himself what any other woman with half an eyesight could see? And couldn't he see that they were two people suited to each other, above and beyond any man-measured years?

"No, I'm not," Jason agreed. "And right now the difference doesn't seem like such a big thing. But the number of years between us could make a great deal of difference in the future still ahead. It won't matter much to me, but for you, Lauren, they could mean the world." He regarded her intensely, stubbornly. "I'm not going to screw up your life, just to please my own."

Lauren felt such helplessness, rejection and heartache. She just stared at him, trying to keep the accusation from her eyes, but knowing it was there. Why did he have to be so stubborn? What could she say to make him change his mind?

"I'm sorry, Lauren."

She hated his regret. She whirled, turning her back to him. Let him go, she thought fervently, filled with overwhelming mixed emotions. There was nothing else to be said. And she couldn't stand for him to see her crumble. She wouldn't stand for his pity.

"Goodbye." His low voice, filled with regret, sounded just before the front door clicked. And he was gone.

Whirling back around, she took a step forward, intending to run after him, to beg him to come back. But, no, she couldn't do that. It would be degrading to Jason, to herself. He'd made himself plain.

His words echoed within her: *I don't know if I love you.*

How that hurt. Because she knew how much she loved him. Totally. Implicitly.

Slowly the tears streamed down her cheeks. She felt them slip into the edges of her mouth and drop from her chin onto her chest as she still stood, staring at the door. She felt Leo rubbing against her ankles, his meows coming to her as if from far away. Gradually she realized he'd been there for some time. Bending, she picked him up and hugged his small warm body to her, trying beyond reason to soothe the ache within her heart. But, of course, nothing and no one could. It could only be endured.

Chapter Ten

Lauren ended her cooling-down stretches, slipped the bright pink sweatband from her head and wiped her face with a towel. Still puffing, she went to the window to pull it down. It was the third week in June and hot. Today she would give in to air-conditioning. In the kitchen she poured a glass of icy lemonade for herself and a saucer of milk for Leo. Reaching for a section of the Sunday paper, she folded it and bent to place it on the floor beneath Leo's feeding dishes. The bold print of an article caught her eye: "Kenyon to leave Stockman's."

Slowly she stood back up, holding the paper before her. With a swift glance to the top, she saw she held the business pages, then she scanned the article, reading that Jason Kenyon, president of the Stockman's Bank of Kansas City, would be resigning his position at the end of the following week as a first step in his candidacy for the U.S. Senate seat. The small article named who would be taking his place, not

Tony, surprisingly, then cited the man's qualifications. It then mentioned a bit of the bank's colorful history, speaking of Jason's great-grandfather as the one who'd actually begun the banking institute that was to become Stockman's.

In the past month Lauren had seen Jason's name in the paper several times, his picture with the announcement of his candidacy and a few more news blurbs since then. Apparently, though, he was keeping a low profile so far.

It'd hurt every time she'd seen his name, his picture. It still hurt now.

And as always, her mind slipped slowly back in time to memories of him. Sometimes it seemed like years ago, sometimes like yesterday. Had it really been months since he'd walked out her apartment door?

Winter had slipped into spring and spring into an early summer. Lauren had again lost weight but continued relatively pain free. She'd purchased a small green Toyota and discovered her back and legs functioned best if she sat upon a thin cushion when driving. She enjoyed a new feeling of freedom, though she often needed to take a breath and push aside the fear of the vehicle, remembering the accident.

Twice she'd had to pull to the side of the road, her breath coming so fast she was hyperventilating. Perspiration traced her palms. All she could see was the grassy embankment and the concrete wall rising before her just as the car slammed into it. And then Scott's bloody face. She fought the memory, cried a little, then sat until her breathing returned to normal and the shaking stopped. She drove home and forced herself to drive again.

Ian's book had progressed into the second draft, and Lauren's typing skills had managed equally as well, even with having to favor her right hand. She and Ian had made numerous trips to cities such as Jefferson, Denver, Amarillo, Tulsa and Dallas. Ian had begun to treat her more as an associate than an employee. He still barked a lot, but generally they found they enjoyed each other's company.

At Dr. Walter's request, Lauren had started visiting a young teenage boy who'd suffered serious injury to his spine in a skateboard accident. The boy was in good health and the prospect for healing was good, but he'd needed a boost to believe in that healing. By her second visit Lauren had gotten the boy to start small exercises from his bed. He was working on parallel bars now, but Lauren continued to see him and to assist his professional therapist when she could. She'd also begun visiting a nine-year-old girl who'd been hurt in an automobile accident. The girl should recover completely if she worked at it, and Lauren felt she had great dancing potential. The result of all this was that Lauren had joined the volunteer staff at the hospital.

At times she felt she benefited much more than the patients she was there to help. She delighted especially in the children, in the free and easy love they poured out to her. In the times small hands would push their way into hers, small arms would wrap around her neck. "You're pretty, Miss Lauren. Maybe I will dance like you someday, Miss Lauren. Thank you, Miss Lauren." Just being before them and walking seemed to spur even the ones with the most severe body injuries onward. And the work, the love, was a help in filling up the giant hole within her. A hole that she privately believed could never be filled.

If only she could share it all with Jason, she thought so often. The fact that she was truly typing now, however slowly; she'd gone beyond hunt and peck. And that she was driving and working with the children. If she could only tell him about how Ian...or about little Ricky's leg...or about Leo...

But she couldn't. And never would. And she tried very hard to accept it.

It had been pure hell at first, always thinking of Jason, longing for him, hoping he would call. Unable to accept what had happened, she'd dared to dream that he would change his mind. But the days passed and no word came from him. She'd toyed with the idea of going to him, just as she had once before, but couldn't bring herself to do it. It would be degrading. Jason had made himself plain—and so had she. She'd told him she loved him. But he'd not wanted her love. There was nothing else for her to do but to go on with her life.

It was hard. Somehow the days shone less brightly, music barely stirred her soul, her limbs even seemed heavier when exercising. It was as if her whole world were now covered with a drab, gray film.

Looking at the article again, she pictured Jason's strong face, his gray eyes the color and vibrancy of a stormy ocean, his shiny, silver-tinged hair, the slow smile that would break across his stern expression.

Maybe someday, she thought, she would forget Jason Kenyon.

It was a phase, just like buying the Corvette, like seeing Lauren Howard, Felice told herself as she watched Jason filling suitcases on his bed. He was moving out to the ranch, had been staying out there every weekend for the past few months. And now he'd taken it in his head to move out there, to that godforsaken place. Granted, the house was grand enough, comfortable, but other than land and a few neighboring ranches and farms there was nothing out there.

"This could all wait for next weekend," Felice said. "You still have this week at the bank, and there's that party Friday evening. It's your first important appearance, you know. And those people are important." Inwardly she cursed his foolishness; outwardly she was smart enough to pretend to understand.

Jason only glanced at her for a second and continued packing. "I'm leaving plenty of clothes." He cast her a patient smile. "No matter what you think of the ranch, Felice, I'm not going to the ends of the earth. Oh, did you have Grace pack those books I wanted from the study? And did she order the liquor?"

"Yes." Felice nodded. "All of it is already in the truck." Her gaze fell to where his shirt stretched tight over his shoulder muscles. If possible, he'd become even more muscular in the past months, but then, he'd been spending every available moment out at the ranch, working cattle or something equally as stupid, or playing racquetball or tennis with Tony.

She knew exactly when he'd quit seeing Lauren Howard. The man she'd hired to follow and investigate the little Miss Howard had reported the exact time Jason had walked out of her apartment. And that he'd never seen her again.

Again she repeated to herself: all a phase. Though she recognized the shakiness within her that questioned this supposition. There was no denying Jason was different. He'd always been strong, determined, but now there was an underlying quiet steel about him. He was more relaxed than he'd been in months, and unshakable. And Felice was finding it much more difficult to weave her life into his, in fact, damn near impossible.

"Thought you were meeting Keri for lunch?" Jason said then, startling her out of her thoughts.

"Yes . . ." She glanced at her watch.

"You'd better get going," he said, rounding the bed. "I can manage fine." He regarded her gently, and Felice's heart jumped. "Thanks, Felice, for everything you've been doing—getting my clothes ready and all the other things. I really can manage now."

"Jason," she said, allowing a sultry look. "We will miss you. I will miss you."

"I'll be around often" was all he said.

He would come home, Felice told herself as she walked down the wide stairs, trailing her fingertips along the gleaming banister. This was the Kenyon home. He would play for a while out at the ranch, just like he used to when he was young, all that rodeo nonsense, and then he would come home.

And Jason Kenyon would be going to Washington, and she would go with him. Maybe not as his wife, she conceded, but she would go. And one day she would be his wife.

Felice was just getting into her convertible when Tony drove up. He sounded a wolf whistle. "Going somewhere special?" he teased.

"Just lunch at the club," she answered, a pleased smile touching her lips. She inclined her head toward the house. "Jason's upstairs packing." Her mouth turned down into a familiar pout. "He's still intent on moving out to that place. Talk to him, Tony. Reason with him. He doesn't need to be going out there just when things will begin picking up around here with the Senate race."

"I have talked with him, Felice," Tony said firmly. They'd been around this before. He was well aware Felice was trying to use him to manipulate Jason, and he wasn't about to do it. He'd done too much to his brother already. "Jace's a big boy. He knows what he wants."

Felice's expression turned cool. "All right. But it's all a big waste. He'll just end up moving back in another month."

Tony only smiled and waved, watching as she backed out the sleek Chrysler. He very much doubted his brother would be turning around and coming back to the town house very soon, though he knew Felice couldn't see it. She saw only what she wanted. And it appeared she was getting tired of waiting for Jason. Tony wondered just how far she would go to try getting his brother. The thought set off a wave of worry. What would Felice do when she finally had to face the fact she'd never have the place that she wanted in Jason's life?

He met Jason coming down the stairs with a couple of suitcases.

"Take these on out to the truck, will you?" Jason said. "While I go up and get the rest."

"Sure." Tony reached for the bags. "Got time for a beer before you go?"

"You bet." Jason smiled at him, and Tony felt the brotherly love.

He turned away, guilt stabbing him. Even now, after all these months, he felt like a heel for what he'd said to Jason about Lauren, for the way he'd behaved toward both of them. And for what it had caused.

Jason had looked like death the night he'd come home after their scuffle at Lauren's office. Tony had known he'd broken off with her. But instead of being triumphant, he'd felt a peculiar sense of remorse.

As he and Jason grappled with coming to terms with one another, Tony had tried to slough off the remorse. He told himself that he'd only been concerned with Jason's welfare—and knew he truly had, which surprised him. But he also knew he'd been mostly concerned with his own ego.

He kept thinking that Jason and Lauren would patch it up and get back together, but it didn't happen. And though it was comforting to see Jason finally coming around, seeming to get a handle on things, Tony still remembered what he'd done. It was one of those embarrassing things that haunted him every time he thought about it. He wished fervently he could erase it from the past. And oftentimes he saw a look come into his brother's eyes, a pained, bleak look Tony suspected was caused from the loss of Lauren. A loss that he, Tony, had done everything he could to bring about.

It was beyond time for him to outgrow jealousy of Jason, he raged at himself. Hell, he was a man of thirty-six years, was extremely successful in his career, respected in finance and investment. It was time he got his personal life together, as well. And he was trying.

Jason hoisted two small duffel bags over the side, dropping them onto the bed of the sleek new pickup. He'd bought it only two weeks before, trading in the Corvette. The truck was top of the line, you name it, it had it—even a television. Damn thing was more luxurious than a limousine and a hell of a lot more fun. That he'd bought it for fun didn't bother him so much anymore. He was getting to know himself a lot better these days. And he was gentler with himself, too, allowing for more enjoyment in his life.

He wasn't really taking that much with him out to the ranch. Just a few of his favored things: clothes, books, the bootjack he'd had since high school. He wasn't even taking a picture of Jeanne; he'd put those away a long time ago. But he did carry in his wallet a small snapshot of Lauren he'd taken on one of those fantastic afternoons they'd spent together. He took it out and looked at it occasionally. Not so much anymore, though. Instead of getting less painful, it was becoming more unbearable to think of her, knowing she was so close. And yet, unreachable for him. How he missed her.

He strode up the steps to sit with Tony on the terrace in the shade of an umbrella. Jason loved the heat, but Tony did not. Grace brought them frosty mugs of beer.

"Mind if I drive your Mercedes once in a while now?" Tony asked, smiling his charming smile. "Like to impress the women, you know. Wish to hell you hadn't gotten rid of that Corvette."

Jason chuckled at the teasing. "Feel free," he said. "You know where the extra keys are kept."

"It's going to seem strange with you not at the bank," Tony commented.

Jason nodded. "You know, I never really wanted that job."

Tony's eyebrows shot up. "No?"

"Well, maybe at first," Jason conceded, thinking back. "It made Dad happy. And it was pretty good for the ego being as young as I was. And it sure allowed me to do a lot of things. But now . . ." He shrugged.

"You may have a hard race for that senatorial seat, but I think you'll win," Tony offered after a moment. "Garrett's certain." He winked. "I'll vote for you."

Jason grinned at his brother. "Thanks."

"What will you do if you lose, Jason?" Tony asked, suddenly turning serious.

"Just what I'm starting on now—working the ranch." He regarded his brother evenly, touched to see a look of real concern on Tony's face. "I need the space, the peace and quiet the place gives me. And for once, the ranch and the Senate are something I want to do. I have some good ideas of what I can accomplish in both areas. Old P.D. Squire has kept the ranch in good shape, but that's all—only maintained. I think I can revive that place and make it again into one of the best ranches in the state. As for the Senate, well, there're a lot of possibilities there."

Tony nodded thoughtfully. "I'll sell you my share in the ranch," he said after a moment.

Jason, surprised, just looked at him.

"I don't need it, Jason. A ranch is no place for me. I've never cared a bit about it."

Jason nodded. "We'll talk about it."

"Jason," Tony said, then looked away, and Jason sensed something was bothering him. He sat very still and listened. "I want to apologize for the things I said to you, and to Lauren, about your relationship. It wasn't any of my business—and it was way off the mark.'' His gaze turned earnest. ''I hate like hell to think you two broke up because of the things I said.''

Jason regarded his brother, then turned his gaze to the tip of his boot. ''Thank you for that, Tony.'' He paused, respect growing for his younger brother. He knew it couldn't have been easy for Tony to apologize. ''It wasn't anything you said,'' he continued slowly, thinking of his words, unwilling to speak too deeply of what had happened between himself and Lauren. ''I just came to my senses. You were right about the age difference.''

''I was correct in the fact, Jason. But that was all. Sometimes the facts don't relate,'' Tony said. Jason felt his keen appraisal. ''Have you seen her lately?''

Jason's gaze shot up. He shook his head. ''No. Have you?'' How was she? Did Tony know something?

Tony nodded. ''I made a point of going to Ian's office yesterday.'' He gave a crooked grin. ''I thought it high time I apologized to her, too. Maybe even more than to you.''

''How did she look?'' Jason couldn't keep himself from asking. In all the months he'd seen her only twice, from a distance. Twice he'd allowed himself to go to his office window and look down at the evening rush, scanning the crowd. He'd seen her as usual come out of the office building across the street. He'd driven past her apartment and seen the light on within. And he'd remembered.

''Thin and pale. But still beautiful, of course,'' Tony said, giving a small grin. ''And as Lauren would, she was very gracious. Even practically pushed aside my apology.'' Again Jason saw Tony's keen regard. ''She's one special lady, Jason. Maybe you two...''

But Jason shook his head. ''The difference is too great, Tony. It wouldn't work. It wouldn't be fair to her.''

It was like speaking about her had opened up the wound all over again, Jason thought as he pulled the pickup from the elegant, curved drive. He headed in the direction of Lauren's apartment, just to pass by on his way from the city. It seemed a silly, childish thing to do. But terribly human, he allowed.

He thought of her silky hair, of her china-smooth skin, of her delicate smile and eyes that seemed to see clear through him, to accept him and still to love him. Would he ever get over it? he wondered.

He knew himself well now. Time could be a great healer, great revealer. And his life was taking on new directions. Directions he was choosing with great deliberation for the first time in his life. It was exciting and stimulating, but sometimes very empty. He had no one with whom he could share the new discoveries about himself. Even as he thought it, he knew that just anyone wouldn't do. He wished very much he could share it all with Lauren. That to do so would somehow magnify it all, make it all perfect.

But he was right, he told himself firmly, shaking aside illusive daydreams. He wasn't the one for her. These things happened sometimes in life, and that's all there was to it. Besides, by now she'd probably already found another, young man. The idea hurt beyond belief.

The summer evening twilight was coming a bit early as purple thunderclouds gathered on the western horizon and billowed toward the city. Lauren sat beside Ian Walsh in the back of his dark limousine as it moved smoothly along the quiet neighborhood streets. Ian was dashing, with his shock of white hair a handsome contrast to the dark suit, black bow tie and white pleated shirt he wore, and Lauren told him so.

"You're too thin," Ian growled.

She felt him giving her a sharp appraisal and simply averted her eyes to her hands that lay in her lap, looking thin and pale against her black dress. She had no rebuttal. She knew she was way too thin. The mirror was testament enough, and Ian, her mother and stepfather nagged her about it often, she thought, frowning. You'd think she was not eating on purpose. But she tried, she truly did, only nothing seemed to taste good, to attract her.

Jason's face came again into her mind, and her thoughts turned to him as she stared unseeing out the tinted window of the car. She'd seen him for the first time yesterday. He'd been coming out of the bank with two other men. She was walking on the sidewalk across the street with several other secretaries. Her breath had stopped when she saw him, and it'd been as if he'd felt her gaze, for he'd looked straight at her for long seconds. She'd yearned so much to see his gray eyes. Then he was walking away, and she was entering her building, the sounds of voices and the city all around her.

She had to forget him, she told herself fervently. This was stupid, this longing for him. Pining, as it were.

She smoothed at the silk dress, recalling her image in the mirror. The dress was black and elegantly simple, the belt at the waist at least giving her a bit of shape.

In an uncommon gentle gesture, Ian covered her hand with his own. "You look lovely, my dear," he said.

She smiled gratefully, even as amazement touched her. Though they'd become friends, good ones, any show of emotion from Ian was rare.

Ian had amazed her quite often in the past three days, she mused, her gaze again moving to stare out the window. She'd been totally shocked when he'd asked her to be his date for the party tonight, a gathering of alumni from his university class. He'd made no explanation, had just waited with his usual scowl. She'd protested that she didn't have anything to wear, but Ian had scowled even further.

"You're my secretary," he'd said, peering over the rim of his glasses. "You will go. Friday evening. Seven o'clock."

Absently, she raised her hand to touch the small, gold and jeweled pin at her waist. Ian had sent it to her apartment with a note thanking her for accepting his invitation. Surely, she thought, it'd been more of an order. But, after all these months, she'd come to learn one thing about Ian Walsh—he was anything but what others considered rational. And that was his charm. And he always had a reason for his actions; no doubt, he did tonight, whether or not they became clear.

Ten minutes later she entered a spacious, brightly lit entry hall of a white columned home, and a young man in a trim suit ushered them into a large adjoining room. Immediately Lauren recognized several faces, men who'd come to see Ian since she'd been working for him. Ian made the introductions, and Lauren caught several speculative gazes. She couldn't keep the smile from her lips—that Ian wanted to tease people by giving them something to gossip about could very well be the reason he'd insisted she come. Ian was like that.

She'd had no idea he could adopt such polish and geniality, she told him, as he guided her about the room, which was rapidly filling with people. He could when he chose, he whispered into her ear, his face breaking into a rare chuckle. Tossing his highly polished cane in the air, he blithely reminded her he'd been in politics.

There appeared to be about thirty people present, Lauren assessed when finally able to take a good look around, with more guests still arriving. The living room was long, like two rooms connected, brightly lit, and it hummed with voices. Ian was greeted with surprise, many commenting on his hermit ways. And more than one eyebrow was raised at him with Lauren on his arm. He glowed in the attention and the quiet gossiping, Lauren thought, greatly amused. Playfully she decided to raise speculation a bit on his behalf and kept her hand nestled into the crook of his arm, repeatedly leaning close. Though his face remained characteristically dour, Ian's gaze met her own, and she read his inward merriment.

For the most part Lauren said little, her attention captured by all around her: the elegant, glowing room that hummed with voices and occasional laughter, the beautifully dressed people, even the waiters who circulated with trays of drinks and elaborate hors d'oeuvres. It looked like an entire dinner was being served.

On about the third introduction to someone who was an ex-politician of some sort, Lauren felt apprehension stir. Her gaze moved from face to face and settled finally on Ian. He was talking, and she had to wait before she could speak to him.

Hearing high-pitched laughter and greetings shouted across the room to latecomers, she automatically turned her gaze in the direction of the entry hall. Immediately she recognized an ultrafeminine voice and puff of curly blond hair as belonging to Felice Rischard. With smiling red lips and breezy manner the petite woman entered the room. Lauren's gaze shot to the man at her side.

It was Jason. Tall, commanding, his silver hair catching the light, his shoulders beneath the black fabric of his evening suit were even broader than she'd remembered them.

It flashed through her mind to hide, and at the same time she was aware of the ridiculousness of the notion. And then she saw his steely gray eyes look right at her, his gaze seeming to capture hers. Her breath stopped in her throat; her heartbeat echoed in her ears. The room was suddenly much too bright. *And how she longed to go to him, to hear his voice, to see him smile at her.*

Instead she turned away.

Ian turned with her, pressing her hand against his side with his arm. He regarded her speculatively.

"You knew, didn't you?" she whispered urgently, wondering why in the world he hadn't told her. Why in the world he'd brought her.

Ian nodded. "This gathering is for Jason and others to discuss his ideas and views," he told her blandly.

She just looked at him, watching him calmly sip his brandy, thinking: at least he could have prepared her! But then, if she'd known, she most certainly wouldn't have come. Order or no damn order! And something in Ian's calm regard told her he knew that. He'd kept his silence on purpose.

"You two need to see each other," Ian said then, astounding her.

Chapter Eleven

"I should think you could leave that decision up to me," Lauren said in a sharp, low voice, only partially aware of Ian guiding her away from others.

"Sometimes more mature, clearer heads should prevail," he answered in a most infuriatingly emotionless tone.

"How dare you do this, Ian. Not even to warn me."

He smiled at someone but spoke to her. "You cannot go on hiding from this, letting it eat you up. After all—how much more weight can you afford to lose? And don't you think you should remember who is paying your salary at the moment?"

"I don't give a damn who's paying me," she answered, seething with the anger of betrayal. "Excuse me..." she said, giving in to the overwhelming urge to flee, if only for a few precious minutes. She turned quickly, and her purse slipped from her grasp. *Her damn right hand!* She'd forgotten. It was almost too much, and her eyes moistened, her throat burned.

She watched as Ian, immediately and stiffly, bent to retrieve it. His gaze met hers.

"I'm sorry, Ian," she said then, finding it a struggle to speak. "Please, just give me a few minutes."

Ian watched her slight, graceful figure weave across the room toward the hallway, being very careful to stay far away from Jason and Felice. His heart squeezed for her. She meant so much to him, like the daughter he'd never had. She could have been his daughter, he thought, not for the first time.

So many years ago, a lifetime ago, he'd stood in much the same predicament as Jason. He'd been in love with Lauren's mother, and she with him. But Sybil had been twenty-two years his junior, a child of eighteen. He'd been on the verge of a very swift and demanding career, one that would have been hard for Sybil to fit into. And then, too, he'd wondered if what he'd had to offer her was in the least what she needed or deserved. He'd had to make a choice. And every once in a while he wondered if he hadn't made the wrong choice.

Lauren took refuge in one of the two guest bathrooms she found at the back of the large hallway. Her mind whirled with emotions: anger, at Ian and herself and even Jason; embarrassment; and a deep, deep yearning. She struggled to sort the emotions out, to deal with them. Muffled voices, piano music, glasses clinking came from beyond the door, reminding her of all she must face.

She had the impulse to leave. It would be the best thing, she thought, staring at her pale image in the mirror. Run away. Why shouldn't she? Ian, damn his hide, had overstepped his bounds by miles. He'd had to try and maneuver her as if he were God. Well, there was a vast difference between Ian Walsh and God, she thought vehemently. God couldn't be half as headstrong.

Yes, she could leave. She didn't care what anyone would think, even if she left Ian standing right in the middle of the hall, which was what he deserved. But what would Jason think?

Jason. Her mind whispered the name. How could it be that she was thrown into such turmoil after all these months, months when she'd done her best to face the fact he would never be hers, she would never lie in his arms? Oh, Lord, she just didn't know how she could go out there to face him with all these feelings in her heart. He would know, she thought, her cheeks growing hot. One look at her face, and he would know—and feel pity. Or guilt. She just couldn't bear for him to know. She would not have his pity. She would not make him feel guilt.

Again she beheld herself in the mirror and jutted her chin. She could not leave, she thought determinedly. It would be running from him, and then he would know her true feelings for sure. And she would not run from herself, either. She would stay and be calm. He would never know how she hurt, she vowed silently. No one would.

With a shaky hand she opened the door and stepped into the hall. Coming, unbelievably, face-to-face with Felice Rischard.

For long seconds Felice simply looked at her, and Lauren looked back, dumbfounded at the pure contempt that swept the older woman's beautiful face. When her quiet poise threatened to crack, Lauren held to it with every scrap of pride she possessed. And told herself she would leave just as soon as she could get her feet to move around Felice Rischard. She would leave this party and to hell with what Jason or anyone else thought.

"Hello, Miss Howard," Felice said at last. A half smile touched her reddened lips, and she gave Lauren a look of superior disdain.

"Hello, Miss Rischard." Lauren matched the woman's tone. She forced herself to continue to meet Felice's gaze, though inwardly she wanted to run from the antagonism she saw there. And the triumph.

She knew instinctively that Felice's strong animosity sprung from a fevered possessiveness of Jason. She felt very much the adversary in that moment, albeit an unwilling one. After all, Felice was the one at Jason's side. And it most definitely had been Jason's choice.

"Are you mourning the loss of someone?" Felice asked then with a carefully raised eyebrow, her gaze raking Lauren.

Icy pain touched Lauren at the comment. To her disgust, she felt her face flush. And damn it! She couldn't think of a comeback. For a split second she just looked at Felice, trying to think of something, wishing she were anywhere but there. Then the next instant the words were on her tongue and out of her mouth.

"Did you mistake this party as one for aging prom queens?" Lauren said quietly, quite pleased with the comparison, and thanking God, however sheepishly, for the thought.

But victory was not sweet, for she caught the reflection of her own image in Felice's bitter green eyes. And she knew that in her insecurity, she'd sunk to Felice's level. Pity for the pretentious, flamboyant woman touched her. How silly Felice's animosities were, how childish, how pathetic. Giving a tight smile, she stepped smoothly around her and walked away.

Mentally gathering her poise, Lauren forced herself to enter the living room. She felt several men's curious and admiring gazes but kept her eyes scanning for Ian and pur-

posely avoiding anyone who in the least resembled Jason.
What would she do when she saw him again? Would she
have to speak to him? Would he speak to her?

She heard snatches of conversations as she crossed the
room, even mention of Jason and something about the
Senate. She kept her mind from thinking of him. She found
Ian, a bit of relief sweeping her. He handed her a cocktail,
and she drank from it uncommonly deeply.

"Ian, I'm leaving," she said then, quietly.

He returned her look with a pure deadpan one of his own,
took her arm and turned to introduce her to a man at his
right. Seething with anger, Lauren smiled, appearing vitally interested. But she had no idea of the man's name or
even what she had said.

Even as she knew Ian was covering for her, she struggled
to bring her mind back from whirling confusion. The man
was a governor, no, wasn't he an ex-mayor of Kansas City?
He looked like a bartender. Good grief, she had to get away.
She was thinking incoherently.

But Ian showed no inclination of leaving the group of
people that had now gathered all around them and were av-
idly listening to what he and Mr. Bartender had to say about
politics. And short of stomping her foot and ripping her arm
from Ian's, Lauren had little choice but to stand there, too.

Jason listened and discussed, every bit the competent and
suave politician, he thought dryly to himself. Yet, all the
while he kept one eye on Lauren. That he would speak to her
he knew. What he would say, he had no idea. But he would
look into her eyes. He would find out if she were as cool and
unconcerned about him as she appeared.

The room was a babble of voices above the low tinkling
of the piano. Occasionally there could be heard the rumble
of thunder outside. Rain spattered hard against the French
doors at Jason's back. The woman to his right was talking

about farm prices and what should be done about them. She seemed to have all the answers.

Felice was at his elbow, another cocktail in her hand, a bit shaky on her feet. She'd had too much to drink and they'd been there barely forty-five minutes. He sensed her heavy scrutiny, her questioning. He ignored it. He knew she was wondering at his reaction to seeing Lauren, a reaction he had yet to show. There'd been a few other curious glances; several of the people here tonight were aware a relationship of some kind had existed between him and Lauren. But no one, not even Felice, would guess the blow that had hit him when he'd stepped into the room and his eyes had been drawn to a familiar head of dark, shining hair.

It'd been a blow that shook him to his very foundation. He'd searched her face to see if she'd been equally touched. But he couldn't tell, couldn't be certain. There'd been something there in her dark eyes, but she'd turned away, closing it to him.

He had no right to know anything about her, of course, he reminded himself. But the ache within him cut at his very breath.

She stood now with Ian Walsh. Very close. Jealousy of the older man nipped at him. Every time Lauren leaned against Ian's arm, the knot grew harder inside of Jason. He was surprised, and further displeased to see a soft sheen enter the craggy old man's pale eyes when he looked at her. And smiled, the damn old goat actually smiled. That, Jason knew, had to be something out of the ordinary with Ian Walsh. But, Jason thought, if anyone could soften the hard old man, it would be Lauren. No one could resist her gentle way forever.

"Miss Howard is quite ambitious," Felice murmured, pressing her hand into the crook of Jason's arm.

"What?" he said sharply.

"Miss Howard." Felice inclined her head. "She doesn't give up. She's found a suitable—" She broke off as Jason glared down at her.

Pulling away from her, leaving her there, he began making his way from group to group, talking, all the while heading toward Lauren.

He was only a few feet from her when Garrett Baker along with Adam Taylor, the man they'd hired as campaign manager, joined him. Adam Taylor at once turned the conversation to farm prices, and immediately several men there had things to say on the subject. With so much of Kansas's economy based on agriculture, it was imperative that Jason make plain his views on what he would do to help the farmers and ranchers. And Jason did have strong views on this subject—but right now he was thinking more strongly of Lauren. And she and Ian were walking across the room toward the hall, perhaps to leave.

Jason simply couldn't let her leave. He had to speak to her. He just had to.

"I'm sorry...excuse me," Jason said to the several men and women around him. One of those men was Frank Kerby, a powerful rancher from south-central Kansas. The Kerby family had done banking with Stockman's for over fifty years; Frank Kerby had been a friend of Jason's father. Jason recognized amazement flit across the older man's face and disapproval on Adam's and Garrett's faces, but he still turned and hurried after Lauren and Ian, ignoring calls from those he passed.

Stepping into the hallway, he glanced quickly around, spying Lauren, alone, standing in the foyer near the front door. Her back was toward him, slim and ramrod straight.

"Lauren."

Her name was from his lips in a moment. As he stepped toward her, she whirled to face him. She looked much like a frightened doe wanting very much to flee. A great ache cut through Jason.

The next instant there came a horrendous clap of thunder and the lights flickered, then went out altogether, plunging the house into utter darkness.

A wave of startled cries sounded, then died into near stillness. "It's all right, everyone. We'll have flashlights in a jiffy," a feminine voice cut jauntily into the piercing darkness. There came an answering male voice, scufflings, murmurings and laughter.

"Lauren?" Jason reached for her in the blackness, his eyes straining pointlessly. His hand closed around her upper arm, and he felt her shiver. "Are you all right?"

"Yes, of course" came her low tone. He pulled her close to him. "But, Ian, I'm worried for him. He'd gone—" She broke off, her voice a bare whisper.

The thunder rolled again, easily heard now above the low murmurings of voices. There was something about darkness that made people whisper. Lightning flashed, faintly illuminating people in the adjoining rooms, but leaving the front part of the hallway where Jason stood with Lauren in private darkness. The house creaked softly in the wind while rain pounded the windows. There came a crash, someone bumping into something, several curses, then laughter again.

Jason's eyes were becoming accustomed to the darkness, didn't strain so hard. He fancied he could see the outline of Lauren's dark head, but it was an illusion born of sweet memory.

His breath came rapid and hard, and he thought he could hear Lauren's, too. In that quiet, secluded moment he felt his heart beating in perfect rhythm with that of the woman whose shoulder brushed his chest. And he knew that he loved her. Certainly, profoundly. In his confusion he had doubted, but now, when he'd begun to know exactly who

Jason Kenyon was, he knew without a shadow of a doubt that he loved Lauren Howard, not just for a week's fling, not just for a month's distraction, but for as long as he lived.

He felt her breath touch his shirt; his heartbeat reverberated in his ears. Lord, how he ached inside. How he wanted her, to love her, to cherish her. There was no other woman like her. Slowly he lifted his other arm, allowing his hand to rest on the cool, silky fabric of her dress, to stroke upward, moving to her neck and on to her cheek. Her skin was warm velvet beneath his hand. And, thank heaven, she didn't pull away. He felt her answering response as if it were laden in the air; he felt her tremble and lean toward him.

He inhaled her scent—that of sweet jasmine on a hot August night. Her warmth radiated to him, enveloping him. Tilting her chin upward, he lowered his head, searching and finding her moist lips. Longing shot through him, and he kissed her fiercely, only half hearing cries of triumph and hilarity from the room beyond the hall, terribly aware of the quivering eagerness in Lauren's response.

Then suddenly she pulled her lips from his and pushed at his chest. He heard her breath coming as hard as his own, felt her arm trembling beneath the grip of his hand. There were flickers in the darkness. Candles. Then flashlight beams cutting across the blackness. Jason had the nearly overwhelming urge to pull Lauren back into a darkened corner, to hold on to this very private moment. And to feel again the pure touch of love. For he had an inkling that old barriers were crumbling, leaving the way wide for something new.

A waiter, holding high a candelabra in each hand, walked by and caught them in the flickering light. "Oh, here, sir, take one of these," the young man said.

"Thank you," Jason replied tersely, his gaze shooting quickly down at Lauren, searching her face in the glowing candlelight. Was she angry with him? Had he overstepped boundaries he himself had laid? Did she still care at all? Was it too damn late?

The candlelight etched Jason's face only inches from her own, accentuating the scar at his temple, the fine lines spreading from the outer corners of his eyes. His pupils were large and round and his gaze hard upon her own. For a brief moment all else but his face and his nearness faded from her mind. He was here, so close. He'd kissed her.

Then she saw the questions in his eyes. And she realized what she'd just done. For all their being right smack in the middle of public view, she felt stripped naked by what she'd just experienced. It was totally, utterly intimate and private, thank God hidden by the darkness. *Why?* What did Jason want? What did it mean?

Not now, Lauren thought, almost wildly. She couldn't deal with this now, here in full view of so many strangers. She wasn't certain what had just happened to her or if it meant anything at all. And she was terrified of it not meaning anything.

She turned from Jason. "I must find Ian," she said. Her voice came out hoarse and breathless.

"I'll help you," Jason said, following.

Catching a movement from the corner of her eye, Lauren glanced to the right and paused. Felice stood in the living room archway, her face a pale witch's mask in the faint candle's glow, her gaze pointedly glued on Lauren and Jason who stood so close. Lauren could almost taste the hate coming from the woman. She didn't know, or care, if Jason saw. She simply was not up to dealing with all this. Without a backward glance she continued on toward the back of the large hallway, in the direction Ian had taken earlier to find their hostess and bid a polite goodbye.

* * *

"Please, don't come up," Lauren said, laying a hand upon Ian's leg. "I can certainly find my own doorway. We have light here. There's no need for you to get soaked."

"All right," Ian agreed. He patted her hand, then instructed his driver to escort her with the umbrella.

Before they'd left the party Lauren had felt his close scrutiny, his curiosity at finding her with Jason close behind. But he'd kept quiet, and she was extremely grateful for his discretion as well as the dimness of the house and car. She wanted her expressions kept from other's view. She didn't have any answers, wasn't even certain of the questions.

Just before she stepped from the car, Ian held her hand. "I know I'm an old man, Lauren, but I'm here for you should you need an ear."

"Thank you," she managed in a hoarse whisper, tears blurring her vision.

"Thank you, my dear, for the pleasure you've brought into my life. Tonight . . . I was trying to help."

"I know." Quickly she dared to kiss his cheek, then slid from the car. Her feet slapped at the thin film of water on the sidewalk and stairs as she ran beneath the umbrella to the tiny porch of her building, the driver in dark uniform running beside her, inadequately, though thoughtfully, shielding them both with the umbrella. Lightning shot across the sky as she stepped through the door into the entry hall.

It was with a sense of peace at last that she opened the door to her apartment and fairly threw herself inside. For a moment she leaned against the closed door, looking around the darkened room, seeing the faint outlines of the furniture in the dim light cast from the streetlights. Thunder again crashed, and the next instant Leo had jumped into her arms, pushing his furry head into the crook of her elbow, seeking to hide.

Her mind filled with Jason and what had happened at the party, Lauren walked across the shadowy living room, unseeing, kicking off her shoes. Leaving the room in darkness, she curled into the cushions of one of the big chairs, crooning automatically to the kitten. And as she gave comfort to the animal, she herself sought it.

Why? Why had he kissed her tonight? Dare she believe what she'd sensed, what she thought she'd seen in his eyes? That he still wanted her? Still cared?

Blanketed and comforted by the darkness, even by the pattering of rain against the windows, Lauren waited. If there was any meaning at all to what she'd experienced with Jason tonight, he would come.

Jason had left the party soon after Ian and Lauren, arranging quickly for friends to escort Felice home. Everyone had been leaving, the party terminated due to lack of electricity. Lightning had hit a nearby transformer, taking it out for the better part of the night.

Now he struggled to see through the windshield as the wipers beat a rapid rhythm. The streetlights reflecting from the wet pavement gave distorted boundaries to the street before him, yet he didn't let off of the accelerator.

When he pulled to a stop at the curb in front of Lauren's apartment, the Mercedes's rear tires slid slightly. He looked up to her apartment windows and his heart pounded. The windows were dark.

Damn it! She had to be there!

That she may have gone home with Ian or to her mother's occurred to him, sinking his spirit. Clinging to hope, he dashed through the rain and up the stairs, hesitating only slightly at the door. He knew what he wanted now and intended to have it. Indeed wanted to shout it to the world.

Images of the evening flitted through his mind, the final one being the look on her face as he'd held the candles high and peered at her. Such longing had been written there. Longing that matched his own. Briefly. But it had been there. He was sure of that. Wasn't he? A scrap of horrible uncertainty nagged at him.

He opened the door and stepped quickly into the hallway, flinging drops of water to the carpet and walls as he did so.

Oh, please let her be there.

Bracing his arm against the doorjamb, struggling to catch his breath from his racing pace, he rapped on the door and called her name. Disappointment knotted within him as he listened and heard no sound from within.

Then suddenly the door opened wide and she stood there, a thin shadow in a darkened room.

The low light from the hall shone upon Jason's hair, sparkling on raindrops there, but left his face in shadow. His loosened black tie hung from either side of his opened collar; wet splotches darkened the fine sheen of his black coat. He didn't speak. And all Lauren could do was feel. The next instant she flung herself to him, reveling in the feel of the strong bands of his arms that closed around her. Dear Lord, he was here, she thought.

Then she was crying and laughing. Jason's large hands held her cheeks as he kissed her lips, her eyes, her nose. He, too, was crying. In wonder, she tasted his tears as she returned his kisses.

"I love you, Lauren," he whispered, his tone deep, raspy.

The words rang in her heart; she could hardly believe he'd said them. "Jason...Jason..." was all she could say. Then he took her breath away once more with his kisses.

He lifted her suddenly in his strong arms, stepped into the apartment and slammed the door shut behind them with his foot. Lauren clung to him, joy overwhelming her.

With unerring movements, Jason strode down the dark hall to the bedroom. Lauren's heart pounded with anticipation mixed with feminine apprehension. But when Jason stopped before the bed and eased her feet to the floor, once more finding her lips with his own, she forgot all else, except her need and desire of him.

He filled her senses. His thick hair was damp beneath her fingers, his pulse throbbing hard at the side of his neck. He smelled of summer night rain and masculine after-shave. He was so strong, so very strong against her, the muscles of his chest like iron beneath his shirt. It was comforting, stimulating, erotic.

She gazed up at him, seeing his face a bare silver shadow in the light that filtered through the window blinds from a near streetlamp. She saw his tight jaw, the throb of his pulse at the hollow of his neck.

"Jason..." she whispered. "I—" But he stopped her words when he covered her lips with his and kissed her fiercely. Passion overwhelmed her, shooting through her limbs and throbbing to an ache deep within her. Almost unaware of her actions, she fumbled impatiently with the buttons of his shirt and pulled it aside, allowing her hands to touch the hot sleekness of his skin stretched tight over muscular shoulders. Over and over she stroked the heated, smooth skin, savoring the feel of him. He whispered words of love into her ear.

"I love you, Jason," she spoke breathlessly as he buried his face in her hair and pressed her hard against him. "I love you."

"Lauren..." He pulled back, cupped her cheeks in his hands and gazed down into her eyes. "I love you. I'm sorry for hurting you." In the shadowy light Lauren saw pain tighten his eyes. She felt him inhale deeply as her hands stroked upward on his chest. "Thank God..." And then he was kissing her again, drawing her to him, into him.

They made beautiful, loving love. An urgency, born of a desire long held, swept Lauren. At last Jason held her. At last she tasted his lips. At last her fingers played upon his heated skin, his naked body pressed against hers. At last she knew his love.

She marveled that he'd grown even more muscular, harder, and that his body was as magnificent as she'd dreamed, even more so. And that even with his strength he was incredibly gentle with her. Tenderly, with a trembling urgency she could sense, but that Jason held back, he stroked and kissed seemingly every inch of her flesh, loving her far beyond words. His touch was magical, eliciting wondrous sensations she'd never before experienced. She moved against his hands, against his body, stroking him in return, pleading with her movements and small cries for him to soothe the demanding ache within her.

And they came together, with all the sensual passion written of through the ages. The magic known to man and woman since the beginning of life. Lauren gave to Jason, took from him, became one with him. Her body and mind totally swept away with throbbing, longing, and at long last, fulfillment. It came in a driving, pounding burst of incredibly sweet and pleasurable physical release.

In her woman's heart, Lauren knew the beautiful uniqueness of the moment—their first time, a time they'd so long denied, a time when they were both totally overcome and immersed in loving each other.

Chapter Twelve

Something softly tickling his leg was the first thing Jason became aware of as he awoke. The first thing he saw, taking his mind away from the mysterious tickling, was Lauren's brown and shining hair. She lay curled into him, her face soft and cherublike in sleep, with long, dark lashes brushing her pale cheeks. His hand rested on her hip, a hip covered with soft, velvety skin. Jason's whole position felt very, very good.

Gently, not wanting to wake her, he pressed his lips to the warm, fragrant skin of her shoulder. She'd lost a great deal of weight he saw now, had felt the night before. Remembering his hands upon her body, he grew warm. How magnificently loving and responsive she'd been. Everything he'd dreamed she'd be and more. So much more.

She'd given herself to him. The fact still had him reeling. He felt pure, unadulterated joy with all of life. No more did he feel his life passing before him, half over, with nothing left ahead. He felt strong and vibrant, with all the world, all of life just waiting for him to indulge in. And Lauren with him.

It wasn't a dreamy feeling, an illusion bigger than life, but one very real—very cognizant of realities. The age difference remained, and all that it carried with it. But he saw now the difference as something to consider, and even more to enjoy. A difference to enrich their lives. Somehow they'd found each other; they met each other's needs. And Jason was confident now in his ability to meet the changes that were bound to occur in his life ahead.

Again the soft, fuzzy thing brushed his leg, and he glanced down to see a cat patting a paw on his leg, as if testing a strange object. Leo, he realized, had grown quite a bit larger. The cat stared at Jason for a minute, as if to say: you're in my place.

Tough, Jason mentally told the cat. Because he was right where he intended to be, for the rest of his life. He glanced back to Lauren, finding her dark eyes open and staring at him. Very slowly a smile touched her lips.

"You are going to marry me?" Jason said then, knowing the answer and feeling absurdly uncertain at the same time.

"Yes," she answered simply, clearly. The wide smile that broke first in her eyes sent Jason's heart soaring.

They lingered in bed, touching, enjoying the nearness of each other. Leo was hilarious in his jealousy, going so far as to sit on Jason's chest in his disapproval. Lauren laughed, and for a fraction of a second the sweet memory of the day Jason had brought Leo to her passed through her thoughts. When Leo nuzzled her and she petted him, he seemed properly appeased and jumped from the bed.

"I need a cup of coffee," Jason mumbled gruffly, fluffing his pillow and scooting up into a half-sitting position. He gazed down at her, his usually stern expression softened with one of love. Lazily his hand traced her shoulder and the swell of her breast.

"Uhmm . . ." Lauren answered as she nestled more comfortably into the crook of his arm, her own hand stroking his strong chest. By his very size as well as the man he was, he made her feel secure, pampered.

Neither of them wanted to get up. The early morning dawning with dim, foggy rain closed them into a snug, private world. They lay very quiet. Lauren listened to the steady beating of Jason's heart and quietly held her joy. And pondered her questions.

"Can you tell me why, Jason?" she asked after a few moments, no longer afraid of the answers. "Can you explain what's happened, where we're going?"

He gave rather a wry smile. "I was lost. And I had to make some choices in order to find myself." His brow furrowed with thoughts. "I wasn't happy. I know that sounds rather childish and simplistic, but that was it in a nutshell. I had everything I wanted—and yet nothing." He raked at his hair and looked off, as if seeing for miles. "I don't even know how I got lost. But suddenly I was. And I felt trapped in a life that was going nowhere." Again he paused, as if trying to gather his thoughts as much for himself as for Lauren. She waited, wanting to know all this, but even more, knowing he needed to speak of it.

"I'd become involved with the bank because my parents wanted it," he continued. "It was expected. Don't get me wrong, it was a good thing. I enjoyed it. But I've done too many things in my life because it was expected—and I really had no strong objections. There didn't seem anything else I wanted to do. In fact, up until the past few years my life has fit me perfectly." He regarded her earnestly. "But now I want to do some other things. And to do those other things, I'm going to have to take some risks. I'm going to have to make some sacrifices. But I'm wanting things for the first time in my life.'' He spoke with enthusiasm and wonder. He stroked her cheek. ''It just took me some time, some deliberate changes to know who and what I was and what I really wanted from this life. I'm so damn glad I didn't lose you in all this craziness.''

''So am I,'' Lauren breathed, just before his lips closed over hers in a fierce kiss. He'd answered the why of it all. She was secure in his love.

Then Jason broke quickly away. ''The age difference is still between us,'' he said, his dark eyes growing seriously darker. ''We can't ignore things that could happen. I could get sick. The chances of me giving you children get more remote every day... if I can, I'll be old...''

''Shush...'' She traced his lips with her finger. ''No, we can't ignore all those things,'' she said. ''But neither can we give up what we have for fear of what might happen. I could get sick, too—my back will prevent me doing many things you may enjoy doing. One of those things could be having children.'' She looked at him, seeing the love in his eyes. Allowing her gaze to scan downward, she took in his magnificent chest that tapered to his loins now covered by the sheet. Her lips twitched with a deliberately teasing smile. ''I don't believe you need to think very much about infirmities, old man...''

With a swift movement, he pushed her to her back and towered above her on his elbows, laughing. ''That was a definite leer,'' he accused, then kissed her lips, taking her breath away.

They showered together, washing each other, playing, loving. Then with Lauren wrapped in a robe and Jason in his dress slacks only, they made breakfast together, much as they had that first evening Jason had come to her apartment. Leo came in and watched and even went so far as to take a piece of bacon from Jason. Lauren was surprised at her appetite, heaping eggs, bacon and toast upon her plate.

She and Jason talked nonstop, trying to make up for the time they'd been apart.

She learned of Jason's move to the ranch, of his love for it, of his plans for the ranch as well as for the senatorial seat in Washington. He even got rather impassioned when he spoke of the "fools" in Washington and what they'd been doing wrong, as he saw it, for the agriculture of the nation. Watching him, Lauren saw that the darkness that had shadowed his eyes when she first met him no longer existed. They were filled now with the light of strength and love.

It was all so much, so fast, all the talk of Jason's plans concerning the ranch and his political career, of how her own life would fit into his and his into hers. They laughed over the enormity of it all. Though it rained steadily outside, it was bursting sunshine within their world. There were absolutely no complications. They were in love. Nothing could be wrong.

When the telephone rang late in the morning, Lauren ignored it, reaching instead for Jason, pulling his lips to hers. Spurred by some odd sense of apprehension that the telephone call could in some way damage their wondrous world, she kissed Jason fiercely, sensuously, until the ringing of the telephone was eclipsed by her desire for him. She heard it only as from far away as he lay her back upon the couch and covered her body with his.

And then, laughing, they went rolling to the floor, Jason taking care to hold her in his strong arms, shielding her head from bumping. When his hands slipped inside her robe and caressed her skin, her passion rose. She felt tears of emotion too strong to hold inside slip from her tightly closed eyelids and skitter down her cheeks. He kissed them away, murmuring something teasingly about being too old, then huskily about love. Everything was a faint, rainbow-colored glow. His skin was hot beneath her touch, his muscles hard, his scent drugging. And again they made love, as if no one else but themselves existed in the world.

Squinting in the bright sunlight, Felice turned the Chrysler from the blacktopped county road and drove beneath the Kenyon Ranch sign. Too plain a sign, she'd always thought. The entry to such a ranch should have white stone pillars and rose bushes or other landscaping to mark the entry. But the Kenyon's preferred the understated—way understated, Felice thought scornfully.

Thinking of Jason, she pressed harder on the accelerator. She'd not telephoned, secretly fearing he would forbid her to come. She hoped he was in from his blasted godforsaken range or whatever they called all this grass. She still smarted a bit from the way he'd left her to be driven home by someone else after the party on Friday night. As if she were so much baggage—or his mother, or a sister. He'd been scrupulously polite, of course. Jason was always polite. But he'd ignored her question of where he was going. *Pointedly ignored her!* And in front of the many prying eyes, she'd been unwilling to question him like a poor relation begging for attention.

She strongly suspected he'd gone to Lauren Howard but argued this idea. He'd simply gone back to the ranch, his love of the moment. Still, her mind recalled with stark clarity the image of him and Lauren together as they'd stood in the darkened foyer. But she threw the memory away. It didn't matter, she told herself. It would be like it was before; he'd soon tire of her.

The drive continued on for a mile over rolling grass-covered hills and ended up in front of a sprawling four-stall garage. Nearby, with a front lawn that clearly needed mowing, sat the solid Kenyon ranch house, white, two stories with cupolas at the two front corners and wrapped on three sides by a wide veranda. The balusters and other trim were in the elaborate style of the late 1800s when the house had been built. It was grand, in its old-fashioned way, but not nearly so refined as the house in the city. She couldn't imagine what Jason saw to like out here. He had only a housekeeper, the foreman's wife, who fixed simple meals, and sometimes no meals since she had a family of her own.

Felice switched off the ignition and sat for several long seconds regarding Jason's truck parked outside one of the garage stalls. More than likely, with the truck here, so was Jason. He was foolishly fond of that ridiculous truck. Well, if the mountain wouldn't come, so the saying went, Felice thought then as she elegantly slipped her legs from the car. Her heart picked up tempo in anticipation of seeing Jason, and she fairly flew up the walk and across the cool shade of the porch.

The double doors stood open, air blowing through the screen doors. Felice frowned at the realization Jason had yet to turn on the air-conditioning, though it was late morning and over eighty degrees. But then her pique vanished as she picked up the sound of music. Jason was here, surely.

Opening the squeaking screen door, she stepped into the foyer. Voices sounded from the back of the house, and Felice walked down the hall toward them. The house was the same, she saw. It probably wouldn't change for another fifty years. Maybe before long, she thought, she could get Jason to let her redecorate. This could be a sort of retreat for him and others in his political circles. Her mind twirled with the possibilities.

And then she was at the entry to the breakfast room. What she saw made her stop in her tracks. Jason, dressed only in blue jeans, his wide chest bare, sitting across from Lauren Howard, who wore only what looked to be one of Jason's Western shirts. Sunlight fell to a pattern on the floor and illuminated the room in a bright glow. Everything seemed touched by this ethereal glow, Jason's silvery hair, his chest, Lauren Howard's pale face. Light music played from somewhere nearby. Jason leaned toward Lauren, laughing, taking a bite of cake from her fingers.

Felice's heart fairly stopped. Anger surged through her so hard it took her breath. And she surprised herself by stepping back behind the shelter of the wall, when a part of her imagined bursting into the room, screaming at the two figures within.

Her head spun and black dots, like pepper, whirled in front of her eyes. There was a bitter taste in her throat. *How dare Jason do this! How dare he do this to her!*

She struggled to think. So he was with that child. That bitch! It didn't mean anything. She wouldn't let it mean anything. She would still have him. But how? *How?* The question reverberated in her mind.

Hearing the scrape of a chair being pushed back and the sound of bare footsteps thudding against the floor, Felice's heart leaped to her throat. Turning, she stepped to the carpet that stretched the length of the hall and ran. She couldn't let Jason see her here. He would be angry. If she broke in on him, if she seemed in any way to censure him, he would be so angry, he may never come to her. *No, no,* even though the bitterness filled her throat to choking, she wouldn't let go now. She still had a chance. She had to think.

Jason pampered her. He wouldn't even let her go to the kitchen for the coffee, which he drank gallons of it seemed. Giving her a sensually teasing parting kiss, he went to the kitchen. Lauren stretched her arms high, then stood glancing happily around. It was a lovely room, done in whites and yellows and creams. Windows, the old-fashioned kind made of wood and with screens, formed one wall and part of another. They were thrown wide allowing a soft summer breeze to enter, bearing the scents of summer heat, honeysuckle and grass. She moved idly to the side windows and started when she saw a figure in a blue dress hurrying across the grass. It was Felice, Lauren realized, an icy tingling slipping down her spine.

Captivated, she watched Felice jerk open her car door and fairly jump inside. She could barely hear the smooth purr of the engine when it started, and then very quietly Felice drove away.

Some odd foreboding touched Lauren. Felice would not like the idea of her marrying Jason—that was an understatement by any means, she thought.

Had Felice spoken to Jason? There hadn't seemed to be time. Jason had been here with her until only moments ago—the thoughts ran on. Why had Felice been hurrying away?

Jason's lips touched her neck, and she jumped. So deep in thought, she'd not heard him come up behind her. Turning, she wrapped her arms about his neck and kissed him. They broke away, breathless, and Lauren looked into his eyes, touched his cheek.

"Jason, did you just speak to Felice?"

His brow furrowed. "No—why?"

"Because she was here." His eyes widened, and he glanced toward the window. "Yes," Lauren said, waving her hand in the direction of the drive. "I just saw her leaving."

"Here?"

"Yes, parrot," she teased. Then more seriously she said, "She seemed almost to be running."

Jason looked thoughtful and pulled away from her. Picking up a cup of coffee, he turned to the back windows. It was as if he were shutting her out, but Lauren wouldn't let him. She couldn't bear for him to. She moved to stand beside him.

"She must have seen us," she said.

Jason said nothing.

"Jason, I think Felice is in love with you."

He turned toward her then, his expression one of protest. "I've never done anything to make her think that." He shook his head and sighed. "I don't know—I guess what I thought of as a close friendship she took as more. And I've let her take over so much at the house. It was just easier and seemed to make her happy. She's Jeanne's sister." He raked a hand through his hair. "I should have done something a long time ago. Talked to her. Something." He paused. "I'm going to have to do it now."

"Just be gentle with her," Lauren said, giving a small smile and positioning herself within his arms. "You can seem so stern at times, Mr. Kenyon. And I know some of how she feels. I love you." The sensuous smile he gave her sent her heart to racing.

They'd come out to the ranch late Saturday evening, after spending most of the day simply enjoying being in each other's arms. Jason had talked much about his plans for the Senate and his campaign. Lauren had told of her work with Ian, of her volunteer work at the hospital and of her new little green car, which he teased her about. They spoke to no one else, except the ranch foreman and his wife when they arrived at the ranch. Those two were the first to know of the pending marriage. Jason told them immediately upon arriving. Actually seemed to burst forth with the news, Lauren thought, happily so. He couldn't very well let them think he was bringing her out here with the dishonorable intention of seducing her, he teased. What about his reputation? And since that meeting, they'd not seen anyone else. They'd kept their private world intact for a little longer.

Now, allowing further mention of Felice to drop, Jason insisted Lauren forget the breakfast dishes. It was too beautiful a day to remain indoors—he had a ranch to show her.

They spent most of the afternoon on horseback, Jason sharing with Lauren every inch of his found-again world. He chose for her an especially gentle mare; she was not a horsewoman, having ridden only about five times in her life. With instructions from Jason, she gamely rode with him, delighting in his delight, savoring the sun, sky and earth as he did, and stifling any complaints of pains from her back. It would be all right, she told herself. She was just a little stiff.

But when they finally rode back to the barn, her face was tightly drawn, and Jason noticed.

"Are you all right?" he asked, reaching up to help her from the saddle.

"Just a little stiff." She didn't want him to know how stiff. But, damn it! She couldn't quite straighten.

"I didn't think," Jason said. "We never should have ridden so long. Why didn't you say something?"

"I'm fine," Lauren snapped. "I'm just stiff. I'll get over it." She turned toward the house, still trying to straighten, to walk with dignity that denied her weakness, but knowing she was terribly crooked. Tears stung her eyes with the effort.

The next instant Jason had strode up behind her and scooped her up in his arms. She winced at the movement, then felt blessed relief with the pressure off her back.

"You're acting like a child," he said sternly.

"Don't say that," Lauren replied, hot anger flashing through her. Jason stopped in his tracks and looked at her. *"Don't ever say that,"* she told him.

Without answering, he carried her up to the bedroom and to its bath. There he set her down gently to a standing position while he ran the enormous tub with hot water.

"I'm so sorry, Jason," she said in a small voice. He turned to stare at her. "I want to ride with you. I want to be able to. I hate it that there are things I can't do." The tears rolled down her cheeks, and her back tightened even more painfully from the emotions. She wanted to turn so he could not see her face, but her muscles locked her where she stood.

"Come on and get into the bath."

"I can't move," she said after a moment, her voice a bare whisper.

Without a word, Jason stepped behind her and massaged at her lower back with his thumbs. She felt the muscles relaxing a fraction. With Jason's help, she shed her clothes and eased into the tub. Her sense of helplessness abated some as the pain eased and her energy returned.

"It's just that I hate being at the mercy of my back," she said, despair seeping into her heart. "That's what it feels like to me." She looked at him. "I will ride, Jason."

He smiled. "I believe you. But we'll just know you have to take it easy. It's a fact of life, kitten." He walked to the door.

Lauren stared at his back, the endearment he'd just used reverberating in her ears. "Jason?" she said. He stopped and turned back to her. "Do you think you often love me as a daughter?"

He looked at her a long moment. "I want to protect you and take care of you, if that's what you mean. I suppose it could be looked at in that way."

"I love you, Jason, in many ways. I think at times because you make me feel secure. I never knew before just how much I craved that."

"Like a father?" He smiled, cocked an eyebrow and bent near the tub.

"Uhmm . . . maybe." She watched his eyes dance just before he lowered his head and kissed her. It was a claiming kiss, a seductive kiss.

"That," she said when at last he broke away, "was no fatherly kiss."

"I know," he answered with a teasing leer.

He left her then, and she slipped even deeper into the relaxing water and pondered the many faces of love. She was so lucky, she thought. The luckiest woman in the world. And she would ride, she added to herself firmly.

Their private world was broken early that evening with the arrival of Adam Taylor, Jason's campaign manager. Lauren and Jason had been relaxing in the low-lighted living room, Lauren on the couch with Jason's head pillowed in her lap, when they heard the sound of a car pulling up outside. Jason, looking terribly young in his T-shirt, faded jeans and bare feet, cast her a curious and irritated glance as he fairly stomped across the room to the hall. She had to smile as she looked at him, though she felt irritation as well, and sadness, too. Their time, this time was so special. She resented any intrusion into it.

Jason's voice from the front door carried clearly through the quiet house. "Adam—I'd forgotten. Come in. Come in."

Adam Taylor stopped just inside the living room entry and stared in surprise at Lauren. It was an awkward moment, with the dim, truly romantic air of the room. There could be no doubt as to what had been occupying her and Jason only minutes before. Uncurling her legs, she straightened, resisting the temptation to smooth her off-the-shoulder cotton caftan up onto her shoulders. While definitely a lounging gown, it was quite presentable.

"I'm sorry for interrupting," Adam Taylor said. He didn't look sorry; he looked busy.

Lauren switched on a lamp, saying, "Please, come in and sit down."

"My fault," Jason added quickly, giving Lauren an apologetic look. "I clean forgot about our meeting." A slow grin, meant just for Lauren and saying exactly why he'd forgotten, slipped across his face. He touched Adam Taylor's shoulder. "Come on in. I want you to meet Lauren Howard, my fiancée."

Of course the man was shocked; he'd never met Lauren. She was sure it must look as if she'd appeared out of the blue—or out of hiding. But he seemed to recover well, and greeted Lauren graciously. He was a bit younger than Jason, though physically he looked older. He seemed all business and to hold little humor, already taking papers from his briefcase.

Lauren left the men and went to the kitchen to prepare fresh coffee. And to get her own poise in order. It wasn't fair to be irritated at the man for doing exactly what he was getting paid to do. And if she found this small intrusion irritating, what about the years ahead? Jason was entering politics, was going to be a senator, she reminded herself. This would not only be his life, but her own, as well.

When she went to lift the tray laden with cups, saucers and coffeepot, she stopped. She had to use both hands—had to rely on her right hand. She hesitated. Her right hand had probably healed as much as it ever was going to. It still lacked strength and reliability. If a person really thought about it, there were few times one actually needed both hands. There were other ways of doing things—except lifting a tray of dishes.

Massaging at her still-aching back, Lauren stared at the tray. Good grief, she thought, what a mess she was. Then she grasped one handle with her left hand and slipped her right hand through the other handle. She didn't have to grasp, just keep the handle shoved onto her palm. She fairly held her breath all the way to the living room, and hearing Jason's stern voice, she stopped just inside the entry.

"No, I won't wait," Jason said, his expression dark. "This is one thing I won't adjust in my life in the pursuit of a Senate seat."

Something, her breathing perhaps, must have alerted the men to her presence. They both turned to look at her. Then Jason moved swiftly to take the tray from her.

"What won't you adjust?" she asked. She spoke lightly as she picked up the coffeepot to pour coffee, but had a feeling whatever it was, Jason didn't take it lightly. And it was something to do with her. When neither man answered, she looked up.

"Adam thinks it may be best for us to hold off announcing our engagement for a while. He'd like to check around to be sure of the reaction we can expect."

"Oh." Lauren looked to Adam Taylor.

"If we're going to work together," Adam said then, "I want it straight. We're going to have to be able to talk about some things some of us don't want to hear. How Jason appears to the public is important, in many cases crucial. The public can't really know him—all their impressions come through what they read in the newspapers, see on the nightly news. And the impressions may be all wrong, but they're just as real to everybody out there."

"And Jason's marrying makes an impression," Lauren said.

"Exactly. And not only his marrying, but his marrying someone of . . . as young as yourself."

Lauren glanced immediately to Jason. That age thing again, she hated for anyone to point it out, feared Jason's reaction. Somewhat relieved, though a bit puzzled, she saw Jason simply smile at her.

"Now, this may be a good thing," Adam said, gesturing with his hand, very intense. "It may be great. People could see Jason as younger, very dynamic to be marrying a woman so much younger. Then again, they may see it as frivolous. But I want to check it out. It could go either way. We can never be sure about this . . ."

Lauren's eyes moved once again to Jason as Adam spoke. He regarded her calmly, as if patiently waiting for Adam to finish. And then suddenly Lauren wasn't thinking of Adam, or public responses, or age differences; she was thinking of cool sheets and summer breezes on hot skin and the way Jason's eyes were caressing her.

She started, suddenly realizing Adam had fallen silent. His gaze moved from Jason to herself and back again.

"I repeat," Jason said then, "I won't adjust this part of my life."

"Jason, if it would help, I don't mind," Lauren said.

He looked at her; she knew by his expression he would not give. "No," he said. "Because it doesn't matter which way public opinion would go. Checking won't change our plans. I'm telling everyone tomorrow. Everyone who should be told. And we're being married as soon as possible. If you want, Adam, I certainly don't need to announce it to the news media."

Adam sighed. "There won't be any formal announcement to the media—doesn't need to be at this stage of the game. But it will be mentioned anyway. You just better know it can affect things." He looked thoughtful. "Of course, maybe we should announce it. Play it up. The sooner the better before the election."

Jason sipped at his coffee. "Okay. We know. Let's get on to other things."

They got on with those other things, Jason and Adam discussing voting figures and questions that had been raised about Jason's views. Jason made a distinct effort to include Lauren in it all. More than once they smiled at each other, Lauren warming to the look in Jason's eyes.

When the clock chimed eleven, Jason threw the paper he was looking at to the table. Lauren knew he'd chanced to see her squirming uncomfortably in the chair, trying discreetly to ease her aching back and hips. She'd sat too long again.

And she was exhausted from their day. She desperately wanted to lie down, and cursed her weakness, for she wanted to be with Jason, too.

Adam glanced to the clock. It was evident there was more he'd like to discuss, but he began gathering up the papers. "Glad to have met you, Lauren," he said as they all walked to the door. "We'll need some information on you, too. A bio for publicity purposes. I'll get one of my publicity assistants to write it up. She'll give you a call." He shook hands with Jason and smiled at her. "Oh, congratulations, you two."

Lauren lay in the big cherry wood four-poster and waited while Jason locked up the house. She ached all over, not pain, just an energy-sapping ache. She was so tired, too tired. The thought sat heavily. She wanted so much to be lovely, feminine and seductive for Jason. And here she was, anything but.

She recalled things that had been said downstairs, the avid expression on Jason's face as he and Adam had discussed campaign plans and views on the issues. It was just beginning now.

In the months to come it would all pick up even a faster pace. There would be trips, dinners, luncheons, parties, speeches. A campaign trail could be grueling, she'd always heard. Hours of entertaining, standing, sitting, walking, always being on display. It definitely put a person in a glass house.

She wanted to be at Jason's side, to be a help, to be an asset. But would she physically be able to hold up under it all? If a bit of horseback riding today had put her in this condition, what about standing up for hours at a cocktail party or sitting in an uncomfortable chair? What about entertaining? She knew so little about the type of entertaining that went on for this type of society. And her right hand was bound to cause problems—and embarrassments. What if

Jason spent more time worrying about her, as he most surely would have done tonight, if he'd known the extent of her discomfort? What kind of an asset would she turn out to be?

Tears stung her eyes, but hearing Jason's heavy tread in the hallway, she held them back. She smiled to him when he entered.

She watched his muscles flex, his skin a gleaming brown in the soft lamplight as he undressed. Then he turned out the light and slipped into the bed, pulling her close to him.

He kissed her shoulder. "What is it?" he whispered.

"What?"

"Don't try that on me. I can tell something's wrong. I can feel it." He ran his hand up from her waist, over her ribs and softly covered her breast. "You don't have to tell me."

"You really wouldn't mind?"

"Hell, yes, I'd mind, but I'd try to understand. You don't ever have to tell me everything."

Lauren sucked in a ragged breath. "I get like this," she explained. "When my back bothers me. Very depressed, fearful." Speaking about it was like opening up the recesses of her soul. Opening up her pride and ego for the dearest person to her in the world to see. "It's not pain, just a damned, continual ache. It makes me very tired. I'm so sorry, Jason. I'm..."

He held her gently, crooning softly, then kissing her neck.

"You thought of your age," Lauren said. "But you don't know what you're letting yourself in for marrying me." She gave a hoarse laugh. "I don't even know. I know so little, Jason. I may not be a help to you in this campaign..."

"We'll handle it," Jason said quietly.

"But...there's so much..."

"We'll work it out. Now, roll over and I'll massage your back."

Lauren lay quietly, his strong words reverberating within her. After a moment, she rolled over. As Jason massaged away the tight ache in her back, she drifted into sleep. The last thought that played across her mind was the memory of Felice hurrying across the grass to her car. It was a shadowy thought.

Chapter Thirteen

Ian was the first person Lauren told. She hadn't meant to; your mother is the first person you're supposed to tell about marrying the man you love. But she was late to work—waking with Jason, breakfasting with him was still so novel and precious, she couldn't seem to get going. And there'd been the long drive.

Ian was in his office ahead of her. She ran in breathless, smiling, and though he didn't look one bit curious and asked no questions, she told him, the words happily flowing from her lips.

"I'm going to marry Jason." It was the first time she'd said it aloud. It sounded wonderful.

Ian, surprise sweeping his face, looked at her a long minute, and Lauren thought that she'd never seen him look so pleased in all the time she'd known him. But then some odd sense of caution came over his features.

"Congratulations," he said. And still he looked at her. She waited, sensing he had something more to say. But all it turned out to be was, "Now, can we get to work? You're late."

Giving a smart salute, she returned to her desk at the same moment a florist delivery girl arrived bearing a huge arrangement of bird-of-paradise flowers and the telephone began ringing. Reaching for the phone, Lauren beckoned the girl to set the vase on the desk. Her racing heart pulsed even faster when she heard Jason's voice. She grew both warm and cold at the same moment.

"It's been . . . ten minutes, and I miss you," he said. "I love you."

"Me, too."

"See you later. Lunch." And then he was gone.

She opened the card with the flowers. It said simply: To the woman in my life—Jason. She pressed the card to her heart with a sense of wonder. She'd thought that Saturday had been a most unforgettable day and that Sunday had been the best day of her life, but even today could be classified as that. Would they all be this way? Reason told her not to expect it, but her heart thought perhaps it could.

Several hours later, after she'd finally gotten herself to settle down to work, she heard a strange whispered whistle. Glancing up from her desk, she saw an arm sticking in the office doorway, waving a scarlet rose. A split second later Tony stepped into view. Smiling broadly, he whisked a vase from behind his back and plunked the rose into it.

"Come to give my congratulations and get a kiss from my future sister-in-law," he said.

"My . . . why, thank you, Tony." She stared at the exquisite vase Tony held toward her. Her gaze moved to the delicate rose and then flew up to meet his.

"I want to apologize again for the stuff I did before,"
Tony said, his eyes serious, apprehensive. "If I hadn't
butted in, you two might already be married."

Lauren shook her head and touched his arm. "You've
apologized before—that's sufficient. Never speak of it
again."

He nodded and smiled. Lauren placed the vase on the
desk and looked at it, thinking of Jason, his face so dear to
her. Her heart squeezed. Soon, very soon, they would be
married. So much had happened in the space of a few days,
so much precious to her beyond belief. How she loved that
man.

"Jason's sorry, but he has to cancel lunch today," Tony
was saying, drawing her attention from her thoughts.
"There's some things at the bank he needs to help with, and
then Dan Collins is in town today for a quick meeting with
him."

"Oh," Lauren said, disappointment sweeping her. But
she knew of his work, his drive, she reminded herself.

"Hey." Tony touched her chin. "He said to tell you he's
sorry and he loves you. Those were his exact words. And he
will be at your place at seven. How about letting me fill in
and take you to lunch? I'd be returning a favor." His handsome face looked hopeful.

"I'd like that, Tony. Thank you."

Tony looked at her a long moment across the small table
in the crowded restaurant, his usual luncheon place. "You
look great," he said. "And Jason—he's beaming from ear
to ear. He came straight to tell me the news first thing this
morning. You're good for him, Lauren. I can't remember
ever seeing him look this alive, this happy."

Lauren smiled. "He's good for me, too. I can't tell
you...well, you know," she ended, dropping her gaze. "I
guess you and Ian are the first to know. I'll call my mother
this afternoon. I just sort of had to catch my breath first."

"So when does it all take place? Have to get my tux ready, you know."

"Three weeks, I think," Lauren said. "That's about all the time Jason would agree to. He wanted to elope, but I told him we simply can't with his position, families, the campaign. And it would be such a disappointment to my mother as well as yours." She searched Tony's face. "Do you think your mother will be happy? Oh, heavens, Tony, I feel so silly, childish. But I do worry about her liking me. I mean—oh, I don't know what I mean."

Tony laughed. "You're nervous. It's to be expected, even for Lauren Howard. And don't worry about our mother. For one thing she's eighty-three years old. Nothing upsets her. And she will love you. She's that way, and so are you. She'll be pleased for Jason, to say the least."

"What about Felice?"

Tony blinked and returned her long look. "Felice will be fine. She always is," he said in a guarded tone. Lauren felt her heart contract.

"She's going to be terribly hurt," she said.

Tony nodded. "Yes."

"Jason promised to see her today, to tell her before it somehow got out and she heard it from someone else."

"I think that's a very good idea," he said, looking solemn for a moment. Then, giving a bright smile, he raised his glass of cognac and tapped Lauren's glass of wine. "To my brother and his lovely lady. May all their tomorrows be bright and sunny." Lauren returned the smile, finding her eyes misty. A waiter appeared at Tony's elbow saying there was a call for him. He looked hesitantly to Lauren, then told the waiter to tell whoever was on the telephone that he would return the call in one hour.

"I'm learning," he said with a crooked smile.

* * *

Jason sat alone with Dan Collins, having a last drink. His mind kept straying to Lauren, as it had all during the lunch, though he felt he'd done a good job of hiding it and paying attention to the business at hand. But now he looked at the senator and said, "I'm getting married." Somewhere inside him a light bulb burned brightly.

Dan didn't look surprised. "So Adam told me."

Boyishly, Jason felt the wind taken from his sails. He wanted to be the one to announce it to everyone.

Dan gazed down to his drink, his fingers wiping moisture from the glass. "The dark-haired, dark-eyed beauty," he said, and looked back up. Jason sensed a bit of disapproval. "She's lovely, Jason. But she's awfully young," he said bluntly.

"I know that," Jason replied slowly, his smile vanishing. He wanted to keep his temper. Dan was a friend, giving a friend's advice. It was bound to happen more than once when people found out about him and Lauren. "But I love her. I want to marry her."

Again Dan nodded. "I can understand that," he said slowly, "but you do need to think about what this will mean to your campaign." He paused, waiting for a comment.

Jason had nothing to say. He'd told his friend what he considered the best thing to happen to him in his life, and he'd been disappointed not to receive immediate congratulations.

"Don't look at me like that, Jason. Right now I'm trying to help you get elected. We have to think of everything that could possibly hurt your chances. It's true people are much more lenient these days, believing private lives are just that. There was that one governor who was living openly with his girlfriend a year or so ago. But he was already governor— not campaigning to be. And some people still feel it's their business to pry into how their elected officials live. These people are going to care about your marrying a woman young enough to be your daughter. And you'd better be prepared to face it." He gave the table three hard whacks with his index finger as he spoke the last. He looked imploringly to Jason. "Date her, sleep with her nights at her apartment, but keep it quiet. And let the marriage wait until well after the election. That's my advice."

Jason shook his head. "Lauren's not like that, and I won't do that to her. I love her. I haven't felt this way about a woman since Jeanne." His voice dropped a notch. "I don't even think I felt this strongly about Jeanne. There is something to be said for being older. I've learned a hell of a lot over the years about what it means to love someone, to give all of yourself to someone. I've wasted a lot of time already. I don't intend to ask Lauren to wait while I get elected. She means more to me than the election. Do you understand?"

"Yes," Dan said after staring at him a moment. "Are you having second thoughts about your decision to run?"

"Yes, I am," Jason said slowly. Dan waited. "I think I can do a lot of good. There's a lot I want to try. But I'm not sure it's the best thing for me, personally."

"There's no one else running that can touch you, Jace. You know I thought Garrett Baker would be good for the position, but what he knows about the needs of agriculture couldn't fill this damn glass. He's a city boy, born and bred. The state needs you."

Jason only nodded, slipping into thought.

"Well," Dan said, hoisting his heavy frame from the chair. "You think hard about it." He smiled. "And congratulations to you and your lady. I do wish you the best."

Jason stared into the bottom of his empty glass. Dan's parting words had helped some, but Jason wondered if Dan's reaction would be typical of others. No, he decided after a moment. There would be plenty of people, like his brother, who would be firstly and genuinely happy for him, thinking only of the love between him and Lauren. His mother, for one. She'd be very happy for him; Lauren's age wouldn't bother her in the least.

For a brief instant he anticipated the pleasure in her voice even over thousands of miles of telephone line. She was getting old, he thought in that sentimental moment. He would like to take Lauren to Mexico City to visit his mother and that part of the family. But where would he get the time between trying to wind things up at the bank and begin a campaign? He'd make it, he vowed.

He looked inwardly at himself. What other people said or thought about him or anything he did concerned him little these days. He knew himself, at least, and what he wanted from life. There was no wavering of his decision to marry Lauren, there never would be, no matter what the reaction from other people. For in his own mind, he knew it was right, for both him and Lauren.

He recalled his comment to Dan Collins earlier: *Lauren means more to me than any election.* Was he being fair to her by getting into politics, at least in such a big way? It would be a drain on her.

And what about for himself? Was it really and truly what he wanted? Yes, there was a duty here. The thought of accomplishment, of what he could do as a senator lured him, but was it right for him at this point in time? Maybe he needed to think of the duty to himself, too.

He glanced to his watch, and seeing the lateness of the hour, his thoughts turned to Felice. He'd better get telling her over with.

He couldn't imagine what to expect here, hoped his apprehension was all overblown. He intended to assure Felice that the city house would always be home to her, could remain her domain. Hopefully that would make her feel secure and wanted, he thought as he pushed heavily from his chair.

He found her in the living room arranging flowers in a large vase on the table at the front window. The light filtering through the sheer curtains lit her features with a pale glow. Surprise at seeing him in the middle of the day flitted across her face, and she said as much.

He told her then, while carefully watching her expression. There came a smile at the news, but it didn't reach her green eyes. Her pale face seemed to freeze. The cool poise he knew so well came to the front. As if knowing he could read her, she averted her gaze to the flowers. He noted her elegant hands shook. She gave polite, cool congratulations. Still watching her, Jason went on to tell of his and Lauren's plans to live at the ranch, assuring Felice that their marriage in no way disrupted her own presence in the city house; it was her home. He wanted her to know that. She thanked him, pressed his hand, then murmured something about cleaning up the unused flowers and glided gracefully from the room.

He watched the hallway even after she'd left. There was an odd, unsettled feeling within him, as if he'd just seen storm clouds gathering. What, he asked himself, had he expected? Why should he have expected Felice to act anything other than the way she had? He wasn't certain. But he didn't like the feeling that settled over him. It was one he often experienced when a business deal was about to go sour.

Crumbling the cut stems within the newspaper, Felice smashed it again and again on the kitchen counter, then furiously stuffed the wad into the garbage compactor. With swift, feverish movements she pulled a glass from the cabinet, found a bottle of brandy in another cabinet, and splashed the amber liquid liberally into the glass. Grace entered the kitchen and stopped, staring at her.

"We don't pay you to stand idle, Grace," Felice said. "If you can find nothing to do, I'm sure you can be replaced." Whirling, she hurried out the back door.

She stalked out on the stone terrace, then down the walkway toward the back of the yard. She didn't realize where she was walking, until she found herself near the back fence of the large lawn.

Anger boiled within her. She swallowed the brandy in several gulps, then clutched the glass in her hand. She damned Jason over and over in her mind.

He thought he could appease her with the house. Damn right she would stay. *It was hers, hers!* She'd done more for this house than Jason or her sister had ever thought of doing. They didn't care about it. Even Jason's own mother hadn't cared enough for her husband's home. As soon as she could, Ardis had raced back to Mexico. But Felice wouldn't leave. She wouldn't!

She trembled with hot thoughts tumbling helter-skelter through her mind. Catching a movement, she saw a squirrel stop at the base of a nearby tree. Suddenly, hating the sight of the very lively creature, she lifted the empty glass and flung it at the small animal. Missing the squirrel by inches as the animal scampered away, the glass shattered against the tree trunk.

She cried then, calling Jason and his little "bitch" every obscenity she could think of. How could he do it, after all these years! And he would not marry that little conniving upstart! He wouldn't! He wouldn't!

Gradually the tears ceased, and she fought for calm. Nothing would be gained by losing control of herself. She had to think.

Jason would not marry Lauren Howard, Felice vowed again to herself. She'd see to it. She wasn't finished yet.

She'd known this could happen, had been prepared. It was all still okay. She'd handled it extremely well, she congratulated herself, recalling the earlier scene in the house when Jason had told her of his plans to marry. She'd remained perfectly controlled and cordial.

She was quite aware of the fact Jason had the extraordinary ability to read beneath her exterior, but she'd still done well. He couldn't tell for certain that she was other than happy for him. She would remain the loving, doting sister-in-law. The one who was always there for him.

And she would speak to Lauren Howard about what she knew. That investigation she'd had done on her would come in handy, just as she'd suspected. No one was as pure as that child seemed. She would point out a few things to Miss Howard. *And before she was through, Miss Howard would back out of the picture.*

It was five after seven when Jason rang the doorbell. Silly, but she'd been worried, some shadow lurking in her heart. Perhaps he wouldn't come, she'd thought, watching the hands on the clock move ever so slowly. Perhaps Felice... what? She didn't know. It was stupid. He loved her. She loved him. They were to be married. She'd even told her mother, had been discussing wedding dresses.

Opening the door, Lauren threw herself upon him, and he kissed her, scooped her into his arms, just the same way he'd done that wonderful Friday night, and closed the door behind them.

He set her on her feet and looked down at her for long seconds. She was aware of rough male palms cradling her cheeks, of his firm waist muscles beneath his heat-dampened shirt where her hands rested and of his strong features through vision blurred by tears. Slowly his face lowered, his lips parted to take hers.

His demanding, probing kiss took her breath. Her fingers curled into his shirt. It was as if he, too, needed to be reassured. That it wasn't a dream, a mirage destined to disintegrate into stardust. That what they shared was indeed real, tangible, lasting.

Forgotten was the wine chilling in the ice bucket, the fresh shrimp she'd stopped and purchased because she'd discovered Jason's fondness for it, the crisp, cool salad, the candles, the pillows waiting for another romantic indoor picnic. Lauren knew only desire and longing for this man she loved.

It was she who broke the kiss and took his hand, leading him into the bedroom. Pulling the cord to the blinds she shut out the summer evening glow. She looked at Jason, his image a silver shadow. He looked at her. Love surrounded them.

He reached for her, pulled her across the bed and slowly began removing her clothes. With feminine anticipation, she'd not worn many. He chuckled; she did, too.

"I love you," he murmured, his lips caressing the tender skin of her neck.

"I love you," she answered, seemingly saying the words with every cell of her body.

His hands moved to knead her back. She sighed in contentment and enjoyment. "Better now?" he asked.

"I've been fine all day. And I've been a very good girl, too." He huskily murmured something about how very good she was as he threaded kisses down her neck.

She reveled in having his large, so very male chest against her own, and in his powerful thighs that covered hers and in the feel of his hands that caressed her body, expertly, tenderly, longingly.

She thought of how she loved him, of the magic taking place in her body and her heart, and then of nothing more because all she could do was feel. His skin. Her pounding heart echoing in her ears. His hot breath against her neck.

His body covering hers, merging with hers. So sweetly, so roughly, so completely. For one indefinable space in time everything stood still. There was no thought save desire and fulfillment with this man she loved.

Tears of pleasure and joy overflowed and slipped through her tightly closed eyelids as Lauren experienced a feeling of love beyond any spoken description. It flooded her being. She loved Jason so much, wanted to tell him, hoped she just had, because there simply were no words.

He kissed her hair, her temple, her eyes, and cradled her to him with his incredibly strong and tender arms. There didn't need to be any words between them, she realized then. They lay together for a long while, savoring the contentment.

"I'm hungry," Jason said at last.

"Me, too," Lauren murmured. Then giggling, she rolled from his embrace, eluding him when he grabbed for her. Reaching into the closet, she pulled out a blue satin robe and slipped it on, saying as she did so, "I've got fresh boiled shrimp waiting."

"I'm coming," Jason called after her as she scurried playfully from the room.

They sat on a blanket spread on the living room floor and illuminated by five candles on various nearby shelves and tables. A bottle of wine in its bucket of ice caught and sparkled in the yellow candlelight, as did the china bowls containing the shrimp salad and the silver forks, and even the edge of the wicker bread basket. Leo, disdain and curiosity mixed upon his cat face, sat two feet away, but refused to come closer.

"He's angry with me for leaving him for two days," Lauren said. "I never left him before."

"We could have taken him."

"Too much upset for him. Cats aren't like dogs. They don't generally travel well."

"You should bring him to the ranch now." Jason's eyes twinkled. "To stay."

They'd discussed it before. Jason wanted Lauren to go ahead and move to the ranch with him. Lauren refused, saying he must think of his campaign, of his position. To which Jason replied that he didn't give a damn—and to what position, reminding her he'd quit the bank. But he couldn't quit his family and society, Lauren told him.

She looked at him now and smiled, thinking to herself that perhaps he was right. Perhaps all of her arguments were simply because she wasn't ready to move there. Good grief, everything was moving too fast. But wonderfully so, she thought then.

Sliding a tiny plate of shrimp in Leo's direction, she called to the kitten. Leo looked haughty.

"He's mad at you and plain doesn't like me," Jason said.

Lauren looked to him with reluctant agreement. "Jealousy." She handed him the plate. "Here—you try."

Leo sat, ears twitching disapprovingly, because he lacked a tail. He remained just beyond their reach, but his gaze fell on the dish, and with proper coaxing from them delicately nibbled at the shrimp.

"I loved the flowers," Lauren said, digging her fork into her salad. Jason's eyes smiled at her. "Tony brought me a rose and a beautiful vase along with your message. He took me to lunch. He's very happy for us." She knew her joy showed in her voice.

Jason nodded. "My brother's something special." He sipped his wine, then grinned at her. "What did your mother say? Hope she wasn't upset at the short notice or that I'm having so much of the details handled by someone else."

"She's ecstatic." Lauren laughed. "She's relieved not to have to do anything but pick her dress and mine and set up the church. You are a saint in her eyes. She rushed over here, was waiting when I got home, already bearing an armload of bride's magazines." She gestured to the pile on the coffee table. "I began to wonder if she would ever leave."

She gazed at him, forgetting what she was saying, losing herself in simply looking at him. His silver hair caught the light in places. Several loose strands fell across his forehead. His gray eyes seemed to glow with happiness—a happiness mirroring her own. It seemed wonderful, miraculous.

"What about your mother?" she asked then, uncertainty touching her.

Jason laughed aloud. "My mother is grateful to the woman who has consented to marry me, to put up with me as she says it. She can't wait to meet this 'paragon'—her words. I think you're up there somewhere with the angels of mercy," he added when she stared at him. "She'll arrive in a week."

Lauren sat digesting that information. Where, she wondered, did the magic end and the reality of this time begin?

"And Felice?" she said softly after a moment.

Jason looked at her. "She took it fine. Very well in fact, complete with congratulations."

"Oh." It didn't fit. It seemed . . . threatening somehow.

Jason took her glass and refilled it with the golden wine. His hand touched hers as he handed it to her. His eyes regarded her warmly, sending heat like small charges of lightning shooting through her veins. It was good between them, intimate, promising a richness for years ahead, and very quietly Lauren savored the moment, storing it in her heart.

Jason left her in the early hours of the morning, grumbling at her refusal to move to the ranch. She pushed him out, after clutching him to her, savoring the feel and taste of his mouth on hers. Closing the door behind him, listening for the sound of his truck, Lauren debated her decision, wavering toward his way.

The pending wedding was for others, not themselves. She and Jason were already committed to each other, married, welded by God, by their acts and whispered words of love. It seemed not only foolish but also wrong to deny him and herself the joy of living together now simply for the sake of what could be said about them. Hypocritical, she thought, frowning, disappointed at herself. Good grief! They should elope, should speak the vows to one another, make the commitment solid on paper, now, and forget all the rest.

Then she gave a soft sigh. There were others to think of: her mother and stepfather, Ardis, Tony, friends. It was all terribly frustrating.

Leo purred and rubbed Lauren's leg. She picked him up and cuddled him to her. "Life's a puzzle," she murmured into his fur. Then she added, "I hope you like ranch life. We're moving very soon."

Jason called late the following morning to say he had to go to Topeka. He wouldn't be home until late the following afternoon. Disappointment struck hard, though Lauren struggled to hide it.

"I'd ask you to come with me," Jason said, apology touching his voice, "but I'll be in meetings most of the time. It's all come up so fast. Dan's rearranged his schedule so he can be available for a couple of days. It'll be political strategy stuff—arguing a lot. I think you'd find it pretty boring."

"I understand, Jason. I'll be fine," she said. "I'll miss you, but we have days ahead of us. And this will give me more time for dress hunting."

"I love you." His voice came huskily across the line. "I'll call."

"I love you, too." Gently she replaced the receiver. She stared at it. Hours stretched before her, it would be so long until she could hold him, have him hold her. Quit being silly, she scolded herself. It was only a day and a half. Hardly a desperate separation. And she'd done well. She hadn't said one thing that could be construed as a selfish woman not wanting her lover out of her sight. Even if she did feel that way. She never wanted to be a drag on Jason, she thought, squaring her shoulders. She wanted to be a help. So she might as well face and adjust right now to the fact he would be taking a lot of trips away, spur of the moment trips, longer trips than a day and a half. And he would spend much time working on this campaign. This was only the beginning.

Besides, she had tons of work with the manuscript typing she'd probably need to take home with her, and she hadn't visited the children at the hospital since last Thursday. Certainly, she'd be too busy to even think of Jason, she thought, then added: fat chance.

Ian poked his head from his office; he still rarely used the telephone between them. Hated it, he said.

"Was that Jason?" he asked.

"Yes." Lauren nodded.

"Where is he? I need to see him about something."

Lauren blinked. "In Topeka for the night. Do you want me to give him a message when I speak to him next?"

"No," Ian barked. "I'll see him soon."

The telephone rang just as she was about to lock up and leave for the day. For a moment, her arms full of manuscript, purse and notes, Lauren considered not answering it. But she rarely could leave a ringing telephone, so juggling everything, she walked back to the desk and answered. When she heard Felice Rischard identify herself, she wished very much she'd left well enough alone.

"I thought we should get together and talk," Felice said, her voice coming softly over the line.

"Oh?" What in the world would Felice want to talk to her about? She experienced a second of guilt. Perhaps the woman wanted to extend a friendly hand.

"Yes. I think it would be better all around if we settle a few differences."

Lauren couldn't read Felice's voice, but she had to agree with her words. "Yes. I believe you're right. When?"

"Tonight," Felice said.

Lauren wanted to protest the short notice, but it could look to Felice like a slap at her friendly hand. She didn't want to risk that. And she didn't want the older woman to think she was in the least intimidated by her. And actually, Felice had done first what Lauren herself had considered doing.

"All right," she said. "I can stop by. . ." She glanced to her watch. "about six-thirty."

Hastily, drinking a blended fruit drink for her dinner as she moved around the apartment, Lauren chose and discarded four outfits before finally settling on a cotton sundress of a well-made designer label. And though running a bit late, she took time to put on fresh makeup and to take a final uncertain look in the mirror. Why did she feel this way? This childish uncertainty and ineptness? Why did she feel she had to appear perfect.

Because she needed all her strength and poise with Felice. The woman threatened her simply by her dislike. *The woman threatened her.* The thought sat there.

And when she pulled into the wide curved drive in front of the white-columned house, she felt the threat even more. She reminded herself that this was Jason's home. Somehow it didn't help. It didn't seem like him, didn't echo with any part of him.

Her gaze resting on the house, she thought of Felice and she found it hard to believe the woman would be willing to extend the hand of peace. She wanted to believe it, always tried to believe the best of others, but she had to admit to being highly skeptical.

Perspiration trickled between her breasts as she stepped lightly to the wide porch and pressed the doorbell. She brushed at imaginary wrinkles in her dress. The door flew open and she started. Felice, not a maid, stood there.

"Come in," the older woman said cordially.

She stepped inside. Felice had already begun walking toward the living room, leaving Lauren to shut the door and follow. Like a subordinate, she thought in that instant.

Chapter Fourteen

"Please, sit down." Felice made the comment over her shoulder as she herself sunk smoothly to a chair. Lauren took a seat on the couch opposite.

Lauren sat easily, but it was a forced relaxation, perfected in the months of recovery. Several back muscles twitched, tightened, from nerves, she knew. Feelings of timidity, defensiveness sought to take over, and irritated with herself, she forced them away, with more than a little struggle. She suspected that Felice, by her attitude, by her delicate expression of disdain, wanted her to feel exactly this way—and found it was an unpleasant suspicion. But she had enough confidence in her own instincts to know she was very close to the mark.

Watching Felice survey her closely, she kept a quiet look of unconcern upon her face. She thought of what she could say, of words that could bring peace and harmony between them, but felt it would be much better to allow Felice to speak first—even if she had to sit there and stare at the woman for forty-five minutes.

Felice raised a carefully arched eyebrow. "Let's be honest here—there's no one to hear. I don't like your marrying Jason, and you know it."

Lauren couldn't have been more surprised if Felice had up and kissed her.

"Oh," she said. Good grief, why couldn't she think of something more quick-witted? Finally she said, "That you don't like it isn't going to change it. I'd hoped we could settle this . . . this rivalry between us."

"Darling . . ." Felice said, giving a caustic laugh. "Jason *is* the rivalry."

They sized up one another. Lauren, looking at the beautiful, confident woman, felt more disadvantaged than ever, but held her poise. She'd be damned if Felice ever knew how threatened she felt.

Felice waved a long-fingered hand. "In any case, that's not the point I'm trying to make." Again her delicate eyebrow raised. "I thought it best we got this all out in the open. Yes, I don't want you to marry Jason. One reason you're already fully aware of: I love him. I want to marry him." She paused, and it took all Lauren's strength to remain looking calm and unruffled. The boldness of the woman flabbergasted her. "And because I love him, I want what's best for him. Regardless of how much I have to give up."

"Do you think I don't?" Lauren asked after a long moment, seconds in which Felice regarded her questioningly.

"Darling, I'm not sure. Can any woman ever be sure if another woman loves her man the way she does?" She said it as if it were a fact of life that every person in the universe knew. "But if you do, I wonder if you've completely thought out what marriage to you will mean to Jason."

"In what ways?" Lauren's guard rose.

Felice's gaze ran pointedly up and down Lauren's body. "Your physical health for one thing." Her voice softened. "Your stamina is limited. There's no getting around it. And Jason will need you to host endless parties, to be at his side for heaven knows how many trips, hours on the plane, hours in airports, in hotels, in restaurants. Hours that you are bound to have to stand. Do you think you can always, with your condition, be at his side? What if you can't be?" She paused and raised that annoying eyebrow. "What if sometime he needs you and you can't be there because you've broken down?"

Again Felice paused. Lauren simply looked at her, aware of what the woman was saying, hearing a ring of truth, but unwilling for Felice to know any of her feelings.

"You know why Jason's attracted to you, don't you?" Felice said, though not waiting for an answer. "He wants to take care of you. Like a child. And he would be terribly torn if you were to get ill, wanting to be at your side instead of out there doing his duty as Senator. What kind of support in this area will you be to him?" Her voice grew harsh. "Do you know how to arrange and host dinner parties? Luncheons? How to decide whom to invite? How to deal with publicity?"

"I don't think any of this is your business," Lauren said sharply.

"Well I think it is. I love him, I care for his happiness. I've cared for the past ten years."

Anger swept Lauren. She was damn tired of hearing how Felice loved Jason. "I'm sorry," she said. "But I came here hoping we could make peace between us. Since that is far from your intention, I think it best to end this discussion right now." She rose and took a step, but Felice's voice stopped her.

"There's one more thing you haven't thought of," Felice said, her voice cutting the air with authority. Lauren, her heart oddly racing, looked at her. Felice's face seemed to hold a threatening secret. "What effect do you think your being Scott Howard's sister will have on Jason's bid for senator?"

"Scott?" Lauren managed after a moment, her mind racing ahead, perplexed and wary. "What do you mean?"

"I'm referring to the fact that your brother was legal representative for some very questionable people. Organized crime, I believe is the term." Felice's eyes narrowed in close regard.

While she tried to process Felice's words, to make some sense of them, Lauren stopped the expression of pure amazement she felt brimming from inside.

"I had you investigated, and your brother simply fell out of the woodwork, so to speak," Felice said. "You don't need to look so shocked. It was simply precautionary thinking on my part. That's the difference between you and me. I know to think of these things. You don't. That's why I will be a better help to Jason."

"You disgust me. Prying into a person's private life." Rage boiled within Lauren. No more timidity toward this woman remained.

"I don't particularly care what you think," Felice said. "That I found out about your brother means others will, also. You can't hide something like that. It's almost common knowledge in some circles. It's even rumored that his accident—the one that crippled you—was no accident at all. He'd done some dirty dealing with his friends. Have you mentioned to Jason any of this?" She gave a cold smile, while Lauren simply looked at her, not knowing what to say, not trusting herself to say anything. It was all so fantastic.

"I think not," Felice said, still smiling. "How can you say to Jason, knowing the man he is, that your brother was rather a black sheep? And, of course, that most of the money you're living off of was his—and who knows how he came about it?"

Something cold and hard pricked Lauren. How could this woman be saying these things? These lies. *But were they?* And, Lord, she simply couldn't let on that she knew nothing. Scott. *Oh, Scott.* The horrible memory of his battered and bleeding face filled her mind.

"This is all supposition on your part," Lauren said, feeling colder than she'd ever felt in her life. "I don't know who told you all this." She stopped. "I don't even know *if* anyone told you all this." She let the point stand. "Good evening, Miss Rischard." Pivoting, she walked quickly to the hall.

Felice came behind her. It was gratifying to Lauren to notice that the older woman had to practically run to keep up with her own longer strides.

"My dear," Felice said, "in a political campaign gossip and innuendo are flung all over the place and do as much damage as truth." Lauren turned to her. Felice looked as if speaking to an inept child. "And all this will come out. Believe me, if you so much as got sent to the principal's office in grade school, it will come out."

"And you'll make sure these . . . lies . . . will come out?" Lauren looked straight into Felice's glittering green eyes. That the woman was blackmailing her was nearly impossible to comprehend.

"Yes," Felice said. There was no doubt the woman would do what she said.

"You'd spread these lies, knowing Jason would be hurt as well as myself."

"I won't have to spread them. This knowledge will spread itself." Felice's green eyes glittered with triumph.

It wasn't until Lauren was blocks away from the house that she realized Felice had not said one word about the age difference between herself and Jason. She laughed aloud. Trust Felice to be smart enough to figure out that had been something she and Jason already worked beyond.

Forgetting her intended visit to the hospital, she drove home. Not even quite certain of how she got there, she found herself sitting in the wide chair, looking out the window toward Ward Parkway. Two teenage boys played catch there, young lovers lay on a blanket on the grass, a mother chased her runaway toddler.

What a fantastic accusation, Lauren thought. Again and again Scott's battered face flashed through her mind, interspersed with images of his laughter the day he graduated college. The whole family had flown out east to be there. Then his look of delighted triumph in taking her to the swankiest restaurant in San Francisco to show off that he could afford it. She hadn't seen him often. He'd never kept close ties with either her or their parents. It had simply been his way, and they'd all accepted it.

Could it possibly be true? Surely not. Surely it was just something Felice had made up in her determined effort to have Jason. In her twisted, determined effort.

But what could she do about this? Lauren thought, trying to see it all clearly. She knew absolutely none of Scott's friends. No one. She didn't even know if he'd had a girl. How strange it seemed now when she really thought about it.

She reached for the telephone to call Jason but remembered then that he wasn't at the ranch. And he hadn't told her the name of the hotel where he was staying.

She remembered Scott's face when he'd met her in Kansas City over eighteen months ago. He'd seemed nervous. She'd thought maybe he'd been working too hard, and that was why he'd come home to visit. It was wonderful to be home with him, though they'd been strangers after so many years apart. She'd had a terribly hard time, but finding out that Scott was home, she managed a few days off from the musical she was working in and had flown in to join them all. It had been Scott's first visit home in years.

She recalled the accident, and it sent pain driving deep into her. Oh, Lord, how she'd wished over and over it had been her killed instead of Scott. She'd been the one to lose control of the car when the enormous tractor-trailer truck had come up so close beside them. She'd never been certain, never would be—was it the truck that had bumped her off the road and right smack into a concrete abutment?

Neither the truck nor its driver had ever been discovered. The police had questioned and requestioned her. She'd been able to tell them so little. A big truck, white, with black lettering, that was all she could recall. It was just assumed that the truck had kept on its way across the state, across the country.

And all Lauren had wanted to do since was forget. Was it so wrong to want to forget such a horrible thing as being responsible for her brother's death?

But she couldn't now. She had to face this thing, these memories of Scott and figure out what to do. First, she thought, trying to straighten her mind, she had to find out if there was any truth in Felice's accusations. Only how to begin?

In her purse she found Ian's home number. Ian would know what to do.

It was with frustration close to tears that Lauren heard Ian was out for the evening. Wasn't expected until very late.

She thought of her mother, but she simply couldn't mention this to her mother. If it were all nonsense, which it probably was, Sybil would be upset. She'd demand to know where Lauren dreamed all this up. And if it were all true—and Sybil never knew—Lauren surely wasn't going to tell her.

She sat, with Leo in her lap, as the room grew darker. She thought of what she knew of Scott, which wasn't much. He'd always loved the expensive and the best. He was quiet, yet driven in achieving his goals, which Lauren admitted seemed to revolve around money. He'd been a junior lawyer with a firm in San Francisco for a while, years ago. She couldn't even remember the name of the firm; maybe she'd never known. And then he was with a partner, she thought. Then it seemed he worked on his own. There'd been no partner to come forward at his death; at least she didn't remember one.

But she really wouldn't know. She'd been clinging to life those first weeks after the accident. Ian, mostly, had taken care of everything, by long distance, seeing to the closing of Scott's house in Los Angeles, of getting the business straight. Thinking of it, she realized all she was left with of her brother were impressions. She knew few facts.

What would all this mean? How would this affect Jason—and his campaign? She recalled the tense, ugly conversation with Felice. Though Lauren knew the reasons that lay behind all the older woman had said, she also knew there was a ring of truth to it all. Aside from all the speculations about Scott, Lauren's health could be a factor. She could very well turn out to be a liability, a dragging stone around Jason's neck. And she would never be able to stand that.

Her heart cried out for Jason. She longed for him to hold her and soothe her with his gentle strength. It was as if she were grasping for the happiness she had with him, feeling it slip steadily beyond her.

Jason was surprised to say the least at Ian coming to Topeka to see him, and in the old man's sharp command that they meet alone. So he knew it had to be important and more than likely about Lauren. He was extremely curious and not a little apprehensive. He stood now in his small, low-lighted suite, splashing some whiskey into two glasses. He handed a glass to Ian and then lowered himself to the couch directly across. Ian regarded him quietly.

"So, it's about Lauren?" Jason said, briefly wondering if Ian was taking it upon himself to be the giver of a bit of fatherly warning.

"Yes—in a way," Ian said. "It's about her brother Scott. And I'll tell you right from the start, Lauren knows nothing about it."

"That's why this quiet nighttime meeting," Jason said, regarding the older man.

"That's why."

Jason listened while Ian explained about Scott Howard. A quiet and extremely ambitious young man, he'd become involved with underworld figures shortly out of college. Ian didn't know how, but speculated that Scott had met someone in college with connections. Ian also didn't know the extent of the involvement; he did know Scott had represented several small fish in court, keeping them clear of naming names. He'd also handled getting money out of the country. And right before Scott was killed he'd come to Kansas City. He'd come to see Ian.

"To tell you the truth, I don't know exactly what Scott wanted," Ian said. "He was nervous. He wanted to know if I knew certain people and how well. I, of course didn't like the questions he was asking. I never like snooping. I never liked Scott much, but he was Sybil's son. I'd always done what I could for him. But I'd heard the rumors.'' Ian gestured with his already empty glass. ''I know a lot of people.'' He leveled a knowing look at Jason. ''Questionable people, you might say. I just know 'em. Don't do business with them. I've just always been a man with open ears and a closed mouth.''

He looked thoughtful. ''I closed Scott's place in Los Angeles. Sybil wasn't up to it, her husband didn't know how. And I thought I'd be the best person to do the job and keep things quiet. Didn't find any incriminating evidence—except a very nice bank account. Anyway there was a lot of speculation about the crash, that it could have been deliberate. There was no proof. I don't see how there ever will be. But there was talk. Nothing that could be printed, nothing that reached Lauren's or Sybil's ears. And nothing that didn't die pretty quickly—can't flame a dead fire. But talk could start again if it's to someone's advantage to bring it up.''

Jason got Ian's drift. He sat there looking at the dab of amber liquid in the bottom of his glass. He rose and poured two more. And he pictured Lauren's face. This would hurt her if it came out.

''Know what this could do to your campaign?'' Ian said.

''What?'' Jason had only half heard. ''Oh, yeah. I was thinking of Lauren. It will hurt her if she hears all this.''

''And Sybil.''

''Yes.'' Jason sighed. ''There's probably not a lot of chance to keep it perfectly quiet. Well, maybe a bit of a chance.'' He raised an eyebrow to Ian. ''But it could come out. Some eager reporter remembering, chancing upon something.''

Ian grunted, swallowed his drink, then rose and stiffly stomped over to pour himself another.

"You driving, Ian?" Jason said as a mild reminder.

"That's the reason I have a driver," Ian said. "So I can drink all I want whenever I want."

"It shouldn't make all that much difference in the campaign," Jason commented, rising to look out at the city lights. "Lauren hadn't anything to do with her brother. It's pretty far removed."

"You can't tell about these things. Rumors could fly," Ian said. "And there's Lauren. And Sybil."

Jason caught a tone in Ian's voice. He could tell Ian was thinking most of all of Sybil. It surprised him, and yet didn't.

"Well," Ian said, swallowing another whiskey with several gulps. "I just wanted to tell you. Forewarned, forearmed." His expression softened. "Take care of her, Jace. She thinks she's so damn strong, but, well, she isn't always."

Jason nodded. "I know—and thanks, Ian." He walked with the older man toward the door. "You know, none of this would come out at all, Sybil would never know, if I simply didn't run."

"You thinking about that, Jace?" Ian asked, raising a bushy white eyebrow.

"Yes," he admitted with a heavy breath. "I keep asking myself why I'm doing it. The answer is that because someone needs to get in there and make some changes. Changes our farmers and ranchers desperately need." He gave a hoarse laugh. "But you know, forty-eight never looked so young to me. I have years ahead. I'd really like to take some of those years, now, and play some. With Lauren. See things. Do things. I want some time for me."

"Nothing wrong with that, Jason." Ian replied. "I was in that arena, you know. Here's something you may think about. Sometimes a man can do more for his country, other people, outside of politics. Sort of like a man of God. Oftentimes he can do a lot more for people not hemmed in by the laws and preconceptions of the church.'' Ian raised that eyebrow again. ''Get my drift?''

Jason laid a hand on the older man's shoulder. ''I get it. And thanks.'' Reluctant to let Ian go, Jason walked with him down to the parking lot, where Ian's car and driver sat waiting.

''Take care of Lauren,'' Ian said again as he got stiffly into the limo.

''I will,'' Jason vowed.

Up in the suite again, he put in a call to Tony, asking him to hire someone to find out everything possible on Scott Howard. He could need the information. Then he called Lauren. Just to hear her voice, he told her. He'd made a mistake, he thought instantly, as a tightening started in his loins. He'd have to take a cold shower. She sounded wonderful to him, yet he picked up a sense of weariness. What in the world was she doing up so late? He commanded her to go to bed.

He lay in the darkness and thought of her. And of himself.

Suddenly he realized he'd been too busy to think about getting a ring for Lauren. What in the hell kind of thing was that, too busy? Quickly he put in another call to Tony. After his brother said some terse things about being awakened, Jason told him what he wanted.

Then again he lay in the darkness, thinking of years behind and years ahead.

''What in the hell am I going to do when you run off and marry Jason?'' Ian grumbled when Lauren greeted him with his morning coffee. ''No one else knows what you do about this damn book—and other secretaries won't get coffee.''

"I get coffee because I'm so poor at other secretarial duties."

Lauren managed a smile, though her mind lay heavily on thoughts of Scott. She set Ian's cup in front of him along with a Danish on a napkin. "Ian...how can I go about finding out about Scott? I mean what he did?" At his look, she fumbled to be more clear. "Can you tell me about him?"

Ian tossed his pencil to the desk. "What is it you want to know?"

Lauren took a deep breath. "What kind of man he was. I've heard something. I need to know if it's the truth. I think maybe I need an investigator." She knew she sounded silly; she definitely felt silly.

But a second study of Ian's face sent suspicion spiraling through her. Perhaps not so silly after all, she thought. Ian knew something. "You know what I mean, don't you?" Her voice came softly; her heart pounded.

Ian told her then. Directly and extremely gently. She marveled at this, and at the realization that he'd tried to shield both herself and Sybil, for all these months, all these years. Ian told her what he knew of Scott's activities, which he said was little, but sounded like so much to Lauren.

When he spoke of the accident and the suspicions that it had been a deliberate attempt to silence Scott, Lauren just couldn't quite comprehend. That seemed something that happened only in the movies or at least to other people. But she knew it did happen. She recalled now the repeated questioning from the police and even an FBI agent. They'd told her then that it was routine.

As she sat very still, Ian went on to tell her why he'd never mentioned his knowledge: it would have done everyone more harm than good. And it didn't matter, was all behind now. Over and done.

Lauren really didn't know what to say. She just sat there. "Where did you hear this?" Ian asked her after a moment.

Lauren shook her head. "It's not important." She wasn't about to tell him of Felice's threats. What was between herself and Felice was too private for anyone to know of. Not Ian, not Sybil, not even Jason.

The horrible sensation of feeling the car jar off the road, feeling the steering wheel rip to the right in her hands flashed through her thoughts. "All this time, I thought it was my mistake, my carelessness that caused the accident. I should have been more alert so that I could have...done something." She looked at Ian. "And all along it could have happened on purpose. There might not have been anything I could've done."

Pain touched Ian's eyes. "We'll never know for sure about the driver of that truck, Lauren. But one thing is certain. There was nothing you could have done, nothing that you didn't do. It was an accident caused by someone else. Not you."

Lauren sat with her heartache, whispering softly in her heart: *I'm sorry, Scott.*

"How much do you think this will affect Jason in the campaign?" Lauren asked then.

Ian shook his head. "Not all that much."

"But it could. Through me, this could rub off on Jason."

"I really don't believe it would be damaging. And it may never even come up."

"Oh, it will come up all right," Lauren said as she rose and walked to the door. "It will come up."

A Kitty Blanchard called about midmorning and said she was one of the publicists working for Jason's campaign. She wanted to meet with Lauren over lunch and get the information they would need. Lauren hesitated, but Ms. Blanchard insisted, saying that it had come rather as an order from Adam Taylor. They'd need this information on Lauren if she and Jason were getting married as quickly as planned. She mentioned something about Adam aiming at forestalling any adverse reaction by playing this like the romance of the century. Seeing no way out, Lauren gave in.

As she replaced the receiver, she felt as if she'd been carried along against her will. Reluctance sat heavily upon her shoulders. She'd have to speak of her family. Perhaps, she thought, she could simply step around Scott for now. There'd be no reason to mention his name. Though there was no doubt in her mind that Felice would see that it came up eventually.

Kitty Blanchard was in her mid-thirties, obviously knew her business and was exceedingly cordial. She immediately sought to put Lauren at ease. And Lauren sought to comply; Kitty was awfully nice and trying so hard. What the woman couldn't know was that there was no way to put Lauren at ease. She'd just had too much thrown at her at once without time to sort it all out and come to terms with it. And she'd never cared much for speaking about herself; she was inherently a very private person. So much like Scott, she thought oddly.

"Thank you, Miss Howard," Kitty said as they emerged from the restaurant. Summer heat radiated up from the concrete. Kitty squinted behind her eyeglasses. She stuck out her hand to Lauren, and Lauren took it in a firm shake.

"I should think you could call me Lauren," she said. From the outset of their conversation she'd used Kitty's first name.

"Lauren." Kitty smiled. "I'll be in touch. And congratulations to you and Jason."

"Thank you," Lauren said. Kitty turned and walked swiftly away, her legs giving swift kicks to the small slit in the back of her tailored skirt.

More slowly, Lauren began walking toward her office building. She was aware of heat, of birds twittering in the near scaffolding of a building under construction and of exhaust fumes.

She'd just seen a beginning, she told herself. A bare insight into this game of politics. And she knew more of what to expect.

Grave doubts trickled one by one into her mind. All centering on Jason.

He wanted this senatorial seat. He'd talked so enthusiastically about what he could accomplish. He was brimming with vitality and purpose, as if he'd taken a hold on the big balloon for a once-in-a-lifetime ride around the world. He'd found something he'd been looking for.

Oh, Lord, I don't want to hold him back, Lauren thought. Not in any way. *I want to be an asset, a strong support to this man I love. Not a hindrance.*

She loved Jason. More than anything. More than her own life. She wanted him to have everything in this world that he wanted and deserved. But the more she looked at what she could offer him, the more she saw herself as one big liability.

Chapter Fifteen

Jason entered the cool hotel lobby, leaving behind the dry and windy heat. Garrett Baker, Adam Taylor and two other men came behind him. Jason broke away from them and headed for the front desk just as the two men whom he recognized as reporters, approached.

"Catch you down here in about thirty minutes," Garrett called after him.

Jason gave a wave that he'd heard. He spent two minutes arranging for express checkout, then hurried up to his room. He wanted to head on home. He thought it amusing the way he felt, the way even his blood coursed in a rushing fashion. But he missed that damn beautiful woman with the dark hair. He couldn't wait to hold her—and had decided he'd try one more time to convince her to elope with him.

The red message light on the telephone was blinking. There were two messages, the operator told him. A Mr. Ian

Walsh had telephoned twice and wanted a return call. And a Mr. Tony Kenyon waited for him in the bar.

Puzzled, Jason dialed the hotel bar and asked for Tony.

"Mission accomplished," Tony said when he came on the line. "I've got eight samples for you to choose from."

"And you drove all the way here to give them to me?" Jason couldn't believe it.

"Well, I figured if you were going to call me in the middle of the night with the order, you wanted them pretty badly. The sooner the better, right?" Tony laughed. "Anyway, it was a slow day at the office."

"What happened? Stock market holiday?"

"No, just trying to ease up and live longer," Tony replied. "And Garrett called. Thought maybe you could use both me and the samples."

Jason's heart swelled. He was one lucky man; Tony was a good brother.

"Come on down to the bar and get these things," Tony said then. "I'm getting tired of being responsible. I'd like to get them locked up for a while."

"Ten minutes," Jason said, then hung up.

He'd call Ian later, from the ranch, he decided quickly. Now he wanted to hear only Lauren's voice.

Since it was well after five, he called Lauren's apartment. His heartbeat picked up tempo when he heard her soft voice come across the line. He wondered if she could tell his reaction in his own voice.

"I'm later than I thought, sweetheart," he said. "But I'll be in tonight. Shouldn't be any later than nine. I'll come by your place."

"No, Jason. I'll go out to the ranch and wait for you," Lauren said, a familiar breathless quality to her voice.

The idea pleased him immensely. "You do that. I'll be home soon." His thoughts raced ahead. He'd give Garrett and the others as much as thirty minutes, and then that truck of his would have him home in an hour and a half. Less, he vowed.

Lauren gently replaced the receiver. Leo jumped into her lap, and she stroked his fur. Then abruptly setting him to the floor, she went to the bedroom closet. Repeatedly, she studied, then discarded clothes. She had to wear just the right thing.

Was she really going to do this? She asked herself. Her hand holding a hanger shook. It would hurt him so. *Oh, Lord, she couldn't think about how it would hurt him, couldn't bear it.*

There just seemed nothing else to do.

It was a case of hurting him now, quickly, or causing him hurts and frustrations day by day in the months and years to come.

She thought of Felice, picturing her, seeing her polish, her elegant ability. Next to Felice, Lauren saw herself as quite an amateur. Oh, she could definitely learn all the things Felice knew, things like handling travel plans, hosting elegant dinner parties, conversing with people, soothing people when necessary. If she had to, she could even hire someone to do most of those things. It was a hindrance, but not one that couldn't be overcome.

It was her past, Lauren knew, thinking of Scott and of what her being the sister of Scott Howard could mean to Jason. If the election got sticky, how could she look at him, knowing it was because of her? And it would be a thousand times worse if he lost. She'd never be able to face him then. And what would she do, how would she feel if she simply couldn't stand up to the rigorous campaign trail? She pictured herself lying alone, at home, and being like a rock around Jason's neck. She imagined how he would feel.

What was best? Hurting him now or ruining his entire life later?

Forget what you want, she told herself vehemently, tossing the summer jumpsuit to the bed. Think of Jason. Of what's best for him.

Stripping her clothes, she donned the long-panted jumpsuit. With flat-heeled sandals, she looked terribly young. She brushed her hair with a vengeance and thought heatedly of Felice.

That woman was in for a shock, she thought, the fact coming as small but at least some consolation. Felice may think she's gotten what she wants, but she still won't. Jason was no fool. He knew exactly the true measure of Felice Rischard. She wasn't for him. He'd never cared for Felice; he never would.

Lauren drove through the hot, late-day sunshine to the ranch. The small car's air-conditioning cooled her body, but her hands grew damp on the steering wheel. When she pulled beneath the Kenyon Ranch sign, she drove slower. She wanted to turn around, but clutching at her courage, she kept going.

When she stepped from the car, her legs moved with stiff reluctance. Her back twitched and tightened. She'd become only too aware of how much her emotions affected the muscles of her back and hips. And she hated it.

The door was locked; no sounds came from within. Apparently the housekeeper wasn't around. Using the key Jason had given her, Lauren unlocked the door, stepped inside and then laid the key on a nearby table. It seemed a somewhat final act.

She walked through the shadowy, quiet house, first into the back breakfast room, hearing in memory Jason's deep voice, their loving laughter. In the living room she stood and looked at the couch, remembering sitting there with Jason's head in her lap. Then she went up the stairs to "their" bedroom.

Shaded by an enormous old elm, the room was surprisingly cool, even without air-conditioning. Lauren gazed out the window, seeing the miles of grassland that Jason loved so much. She sat on the bed and ran her hands over the nubby chenille spread. She lay down and, closing her eyes, remembered how it felt when Jason lay beside her.

How hard it all was. But, she told herself, it was for the best. Jason would find someone else. He would find a lovely woman, a whole woman. A woman who'd be perfectly suited for him, would be an asset as his wife, as the wife of a senator.

How would she do it? she asked herself, imagining and discarding ideas of how to tell Jason. She even, in a moment of extreme panic, thought of leaving him a note. Oh, so cowardly, she told herself. And it wouldn't work.

She had to tell him in a way he would accept. Some way that he would believe her, that would tear his love from her so completely he would be free to love again.

And because she loved him more than she loved her own life, she had to do what was best for him. She had to love him enough to let him go.

After looking around the dimly lit bar for several long seconds, Jason finally spied a hand waving at him from far in the back corner. On closer inspection he saw Tony's smiling face. And beside Tony sat a very beautiful, statuesque blonde.

Jason couldn't repress a full grin of admiration. If there was one beautiful woman in the hotel, trust Tony to locate her like a man equipped with special radar.

The young woman smiled shyly at Jason as Tony made the introductions.

"They're having a honey producers convention here," Tony informed him. "Pamela is the honey queen from

Colorado.'' His brother smiled seductively at the young woman.

Jason reached for the somewhat battered cigar box in front of Tony, casting his brother a disparaging look.

''Well, how would you carry around a hundred thousand dollars of jewelry?'' Tony asked defensively. ''Jewelry that wasn't even yours yet and that you'd promised to guard with your life?''

''Did you take care of that other matter?'' Jason asked as he opened the box.

''Yes. It's going on now.''

''Then keep whatever you find out in a safe place.'' Tony nodded and Jason looked into the box. Inside were ten small, velvet ring boxes containing wedding sets that he'd asked Tony to gather for him to choose from. Leaning forward, Jason held each set beneath the lone light above the table, studying it closely, trying to decide on the perfect one for Lauren.

Tony had chosen well. It was as if he knew Lauren, too.

''This one,'' Jason said at last, holding the rings up for Tony's opinion. His eyes met and rested on those of his younger brother. He saw then what he hadn't seen before. Tony cared very much for Lauren, understood her far more than Jason had thought. And, Jason knew in that split second, Tony would be there to care for her should she ever need him. It was oddly comforting.

''That's the one,'' Tony agreed quietly.

Immediately Jason rose to go. He knew a rather foolish grin split his face, but he couldn't seem to help it. He was thinking of Lauren and couldn't seem to help that, either. It was as if she were thinking of him, calling him.

''Good luck, brother,'' Tony said. His arm slipped around the shoulders of the woman at his side.

''You mean you're not coming out with me into the circus that's gathering...'' Jason nodded toward the lobby and conference area. "Thought that's why you drove all the way over here," he teased.

"Well, it was. But you seem to be doing just fine, and I promised Pam here to show her some of the city."

Jason gave a mock salute. "You bet I'm fine. Thanks, little brother. Nice to have met you, Pamela." Pocketing the ring box, Jason strode swiftly and purposefully from the lounge.

The conference room was alive with voices, questions, answers, laughter. Jason was late. Making his way to the front beside Adam and Garrett, he stood quietly as Adam Taylor spoke into a microphone. The room quieted, and everyone listened as Adam announced that Garrett Baker would be seeking the seat of U.S. senator. Jason Kenyon would not, has decided to withdraw from the race at this time.

Senator Dan Collins gave Garrett his complete support, as did several other state senators and representatives gathered in the room. Then Jason, in a few short words and with no regrets, added his wholehearted support.

"What are your plans now, Mr. Kenyon?" a young male reporter asked. "Will you rejoin the bank? And do you plan to enter public service in the future?"

"Yes, some time in the future I will again consider politics," Jason said shortly. "Now I'm marrying the most beautiful woman in the world. I'm going to enjoy myself." A ripple of laughter swept the room, and he gave a very satisfied smile.

When Lauren heard the vehicle pull up to the house and stop, an icy tremor shot down her spine. She went to the window and watched Jason hop from the seat of his pickup.

Moving from the window to the living room entry, she rehearsed in her mind what she was about to say. She reminded herself of why she was doing it.

Then the front door burst inward and Jason stood there. He seemed to tower in the doorway, his hair gleaming in the hall light. He stared at her, and she stared back. Love and longing were written plainly on his face.

How could she say... she had to. *She had to.*

"Jason—"

But he cut her off. In four swift and long strides he reached her and scooped her into his arms. His lips bore down on hers, warm and seductive. Lauren struggled to think. Her heart twisted and cracked. How could she give this up? How could she give him up?

Then Jason drew back and looked at her. "What is it? What's the matter?"

Taking advantage of the moment, she pushed from his arms and tried to straighten her muddled thoughts. She looked at him. She saw his strength, his honesty, his dedication. He would be a good senator. He could help many people. If she weren't a nuisance, a handicap to him.

"I... we need to talk." She sensed his guard come up, recognized his close scrutiny. "I've done some thinking," she said, lifting her chin. "You were right when you said there were many differences between us. I couldn't see it. Until I spent time out here with you."

She turned away from him. Dear Lord, she couldn't stand to look into his face. But she had to, she reminded herself, and again turned back to look straight at him.

"I'm much too young for you, Jason. For your world. The differences are too great. You're too old for me." She took a breath. "I don't want to marry you."

Silence hung thick, so thick and heavy Lauren felt it taking her breath. She continued to meet Jason's gaze. And she wondered what now. And if she could ever bring herself to walk away from him.

Then seeing the anger flick into his eyes, she felt he might hit her, might throw her from the house. In that moment, a part of her heart withered, dying.

He stepped from between herself and the door. Lauren walked toward it, her heart pounding in her ears, every step an effort.

Then suddenly Jason's hand closed around her arm, and she was jerked to his chest. His arms closed around her like steel bands. His mouth pressed hers, forcing her lips to part, to accept his probing tongue, and to kiss him in return. She melted inside, her blood turning hot and pumping furiously throughout her body as she inhaled deeply the familiar scent of him. She clutched at his chest and pressed herself against the hard length of him.

She knew she was casting away all she'd just tried to do, ruining it, burying it. But it was right to be in his arms. She could no more resist than she could stop breathing.

Jason dragged his mouth from hers. His hot, confused anger had slipped away, burnt away by a fierce desire. Her words had hurt, had cut him wide. But he couldn't let her go. And deep inside there was a questioning. He couldn't quite believe what he'd heard. Maybe he was a fool, he thought raggedly. Maybe he simply couldn't face it.

But she was warm and pliable in his arms. She was pressing against his groin. Her breath came soft upon his neck. He felt her tremble.

Taking her cheeks in his hands, he forced her face upward where he could look at her. Tears streamed from beneath her tightly closed lids.

A sob escaped her. Lauren condemned herself. *She was selfish, foolish; it would come to no good.* She would end up hurting him even more than her words had tonight. *But she couldn't help herself.* And a flicker of joy strove to rise in her heart.

"I can't..." she sobbed. He kissed her cheeks, her eyes, her mouth. "I know I should, but I can't. I love you, Jason." Opening her eyes she looked into his face. She reached up and touched his dear, dear cheeks. They were scratchy from the stubble of his beard. How she loved every inch of that rough and handsome face.

Slowly, almost muscle by muscle, the pain on his face faded. He looked at her with love. And desire.

"Not now," Jason said. "Not now..." He murmured as his lips came again to claim hers.

She struggled against him, finally freeing her mouth. "I have to tell you, Jason." He buried his lips at the base of her neck, kissing, tasting, sending tingling sensations of desire to the pit of her stomach. "I have to..." She tried again, but couldn't finish. She was lost in a whirl of hot and mounting desire.

Forgive me, Jason, she thought. *I love you. I do.*

With strong arms he lifted her and strode up the stairs. Lauren felt the power of him, the determination. She clung to him, tasting the saltiness of the skin at his neck. Pulling at his shirt, she parted it to run her hands over his sleek and hard shoulder muscles.

Gently he lay her on the bed. Silver moonlight lit his features and her skin as he deftly removed her clothes, his hands stroking her body with every movement. She was aware of it all, and yet not. His lips, his hands were working such magic on her body that she felt drugged, wonderfully so.

She delighted in his hard and muscled body and in the fragrant night air that wafted through the open window and caressed her heated skin. Wondrous sensations claimed her body. She wanted it all, all the sweet desire and passion that could be theirs. She wanted to please Jason, to give herself to him, which was the most she had to offer.

Jason shed his clothes quickly, an odd fear edging in that something would happen to keep her from him. And then, as if drawn by that very fear, the telephone beside the bed rang, cutting the silvery darkness with its shrill summons. Ice cut through the heat that possessed his body. He saw Lauren still. The moonlight bathed her face. She looked at him with sweet longing.

The telephone rang again as he stretched beside her. His love, he thought. How he loved her. He kissed her and told her so, his heart soaring at the response she gave with her body. The telephone rang a third time, and with one stroke, he sent it flying from the table, and a pillow to land right on top of it.

Then he made love to his woman, received love from her. Their bodies throbbed and touched and rubbed. Enjoying. Sharing. Recommitting.

Later, much later, after they'd made love, cooled down and made love again, Lauren lay satiated in Jason's arms. His thumb rubbed circles at the side of her breasts. She breathed in his scent and savored the warmth that signaled his very comforting male strength. Never in all her life had she experienced such a feeling.

"I'm going to keep it a secret," she whispered.

"What's that?" he whispered in return.

"I'm never going to tell a soul about how wonderful it is to make love to you. Every woman would be after you. And I pray those women that do know keep their mouths shut." She felt his smile in the darkness.

"How many do you think that is?" He chuckled quietly.

"Hundreds," she teased. "You are a man of experience."

"Years," he whispered, stroking her skin and nibbling at her neck.

Lauren felt the tingle of desire, unbelievably, begin again. "Oh, Jason," she said, her voice coming breathless. "You are the most...I can't imagine another man like you."

"You won't have to."

He massaged her, then pulled her close and held her to him as if gathering her into his love. Lauren tried to keep all thoughts at bay. She wanted to enjoy this time, savor it, store it up. For soon, very soon, she must tell him about Scott. They must discuss what to do. Minutes later Jason gently released her and rose up to turn on the bedside lamp.

Lauren blinked and looked around, knowing mostly that she couldn't look at Jason. But she felt he was about to call for an accounting. With a palm to her cheek, he turned her face to the light. His eyebrows were knitted in consternation, rippling the scar on his temple. The planes of his face were shadowed with beard, and his eyes probed hers.

"Now tell me," he said firmly, "what all that stuff downstairs was about."

"I found out something—something I didn't know before, or I would have told you," she said. Jason waited. "It's about my brother, Scott."

She told him what she knew about Scott and her worries over what this would mean to his campaign. He looked at her a long moment before speaking.

"I know about Scott, Lauren."

Lauren stared at him in shock. "You know? But how..."

"Ian told me. Last night." His voice was clipped, and he continued to regard her speculatively.

"But Ian didn't say anything today when I talked to him, when he admitted to me that he knew." She thought about it and knew Ian wouldn't want her to know he'd gone behind her back again, interfering, to help her, of course. And still, Jason's gaze probed her.

"How did you find out?" Jason asked, his voice hard.

Lauren didn't want to mention Felice. She didn't want to start a brew of trouble. But Jason simply pinned her with his gaze, and she knew they had to discuss it. She told him then of her meeting with Felice. She told him of her own impressions and the inadequacies she felt. His expression grew darker, and she saw him fighting to control his temper.

He pushed from the bed, anger tracing his movements as he pulled on his pants and spoke. "And so Felice would get exactly what she wanted. Damn it, Lauren! What in the hell could you have been thinking?"

"You can get angry, Jason," she said, "but it won't help anything. It's done and over. And I was trying to do what I thought was right."

"Ian and I had hoped to keep it from you. From Sybil," Jason said. "There was no need for you to know."

"Once the campaign gets fully under way," Lauren said, "Scott's activities are bound to come out. I would have found out anyway."

"And Felice was making sure," he quipped. He raked a hand through his hair.

"Yes, she was making sure. But Jason, I'm perfectly capable of seeing what Felice was doing, what she wanted. She's not to blame for my actions. I saw the truth of the situation." She tensed as she watched his face. "I'm not physically strong at times—we both know that. I'm worried about being a terrible liability to you, Jason. But I love you so much. I want to be yours, I want to be with you, to love you." Tears stung her eyes, and she fought to hold them back.

Jason cradled her to him. "Ah, Lauren, you could never be anything but a help to me. I love you, woman." He fairly shook her. "Just to know you love me gives me strength. Think about how you feel and then take a look at me. It's the same. Your love enriches my life. And don't you know you can tell me these things? We can work them out together. You don't have to go off and do it all alone. Not anymore." He looked at her. "We're together. We're one now."

She smiled through her tears. "I just wanted the best for you."

"I know..." He kissed her. Then he pulled back and moved away. "I'm not running for senator. I've withdrawn."

Lauren was amazed, wondered if she'd understood.

"You've what?"

"I've decided I don't want to run for senator. Not now."

"But..." Pain touched her heart. "You were so set on it, so certain. All you talked about was..." Her heart sank. "Is it because of me, Jason? Are you doing this because of me—Scott—because if you are—"

"No." Jason's voice rang hard. "We could have worked around that. I didn't want you to know about Scott—you, nor your mother. But that's not the reason. I simply decided at this time it's not what I want. If I do this now, I'll be hemmed in again, by responsibilities and duties that I just don't want now. Right now I want to live out some of my dreams. I want to live them with you.

"It doesn't mean I never want to run for senator. The idea is exciting—and it's still there. And definitely with you at my side. But later on. There's time. And if it turns out that there isn't time, I'd rather first do the things that are calling me so strongly."

She looked at him. Raising an eyebrow, she said, "Who was telling me that we're in this together? You made this decision all on your own, without talking to me."

"Okay, you got me there. I'll try to do better." He came and kissed her, again, and again. "I have something for you," he said then.

He went to his suit coat and rifled in the pocket, pulling out a small box. A ring box, Lauren saw immediately. She let out an audible, and embarrassing, gasp when she opened the box and beheld the delicate beauty of the rings that sat nestled in a slit of velvet.

"Do you think Sybil would consent to us eloping if we let her come to the ceremony?" Jason asked.

From back in the family room, Felice heard Jason's voice in the hall. She didn't want to face him but knew there was no escape. She thought bitterly of Lauren. The damn child had more to her than she'd thought. She thought bitterly of Jason, too, condemning him silently for a fool. Only a fool would've stepped down from the senatorial campaign. He could've had so much. And yet he'd flung it all away. And for a little snip of a girl.

She stayed where she was, forcing Jason to come to her. When he called her name, she turned from where she stood at the window. As she looked at him, the small sound she'd heard over the telephone line the previous evening came to mind. She'd called Jason at the ranch. She never expected Lauren to be there; she'd expected Lauren to be long gone. And she'd been desperate to try talking some sense into Jason after she'd heard he'd withdrawn from the campaign.

But that one tiny, almost imperceptible sound—and the fact she tried to call back only to receive a busy signal—told her that Jason and Lauren were together. And that the telephone would not be answered.

Jason looked at her. She could stand the anger, but despised the pity she read in his face. He pulled an envelope from his breast pocket, waved it slightly, then laid it on the nearby table.

"I've gotten an apartment for you," he said. "In New York. Here's a one-way ticket. A six-o'clock flight this evening. Be on it." He turned and walked from the room. She heard his boots echoing as he walked through the hall to the front door.

Holding herself stiff, Felice reached for the envelope and looked inside. Along with the plane ticket, there was a scrap of white paper with an address written on it. She recognized the address; it was quite nice. She'd take it, she thought, bitterly. No reason why she shouldn't. He owed her that. And he was a fool.

For five days Lauren had been Mrs. Jason Kenyon. They were at the beach house on St. Thomas in the Caribbean; secluded, the area was all their own. In two days they would fly to Mexico City to visit Jason's mother, Ardis, who'd said they showed good sense in eloping. They'd stay in Mexico for a week and then return to the beach house for three more weeks—or less, Lauren thought. Because she didn't think Jason would be happy here much longer than that. All he needed was enough time to get the sailing and diving out of his system. He wanted to sail to Trinidad. After that, he'd probably be content.

They'd enjoyed sight-seeing, dancing, swimming and lying on the beach. Jason had spoken to Garrett Baker twice already, keeping his promise to be available to help with the campaign and advise on matters pertaining to agriculture. Lauren had teased him that he just should've run for the office himself. There'd also been several calls to the ranch, checking on things, giving instructions on ideas that had popped into his mind as he'd lain beneath the Caribbean sun.

But she knew he was supremely happy. For the first time in a long time. He was rather having his cake and eating it too, she thought, amused. And she herself was happier and more content than she could ever remember. And at times she wondered if it were all some beautiful dream that would burst suddenly and be gone.

She'd told Jason of this, and he'd nodded, not laughed, saying that he sometimes felt the same. ''But it will cement tight as the days pass," he said. "I love you, Lauren. I'll make you secure in that."

"I am secure in that," she answered, taking his hand in hers. "It's just that I'm all too aware of the swift and sometimes unpleasant turns life can take."

Jason nodded and held her close. There was nothing he could say to this, and she knew it.

"Tony told me Felice left quite suddenly for New York the evening before our wedding." Lauren studied him closely. He looked back. She knew he'd had something to do with it.

"Yes, she did," Jason said. "She has a new apartment there."

"I feel sorry for her."

"Don't waste your time." He kissed her shoulder. "It's for the best," he said, meaning Felice's move.

Lauren nodded, knowing he was right. She didn't know how she would've reacted to seeing Felice in the city house. For there'd certainly be times she and Jason would want to go there. She wouldn't have wanted to go there, but she would've tried, for Jason.

They were lying on chaise longues on the wide veranda. The sun was just setting; a light, cooling breeze blew. Jason gave her a lazy smile. He looked terribly funny and sexy with a battered fishing hat on his head.

"I gave the town house to Tony," he said then. "He's given me his share of the ranch. Given us his share. It's going in your name, too."

"That's fine," Lauren said, her gaze moving to Jason's strong and tanned chest, darkened even more by shadows of the evening.

"You should know these things," Jason said, moving to sit on the edge of her lounger. He bent close and murmured, "I'll educate you in all your vast holdings, Mrs. Kenyon."

She welcomed his kiss, savored his lips and the sensations they caused. He pulled back and looked at her for long seconds.

"How about a walk before bed?"

"That sounds wonderful."

With her hand neatly in his, she walked beside him, her feet sinking in the soft, cool sand to the water's edge. And he began to talk to her about getting a computer for the ranch and the way he'd like to set it up. The fragrant night breeze caressed her skin, and she delighted in listening to Jason's deep voice. Ocean waves rippled in gentle rhythm upon the sandy shore. Jason pressed her to him; she heard his heartbeat. And in that crystal moment, Lauren knew the uniqueness of their love. A love above and beyond anything she could have imagined. They'd found it and dared to reach out and call it their own.

* * * * *